Skylark Three

E. E. Smith

Alpha Editions

This edition published in 2023

ISBN : 9789357950817

Design and Setting By
Alpha Editions
www.alphaedis.com
Email - info@alphaedis.com

Contents

Author's Note:

To all profound thinkers in the realms of Science who may chance to read SKYLARK THREE, greetings:

I have taken certain liberties with several more or less commonly accepted theories, but I assure you that those theories have not been violated altogether in ignorance. Some of them I myself believe sound, others I consider unsound, still others are out of my line, so that I am not well enough informed upon their basic mathematical foundations to have come to any definite conclusion, one way or the other. Whether or not I consider any theory sound, I did not hesitate to disregard it, if its literal application would have interfered with the logical development of the story. In "The Skylark of Space" Mrs. Garby and I decided, after some discussion, to allow two mathematical impossibilities to stand. One of these immediately became the target of critics from Maine to California and, while no astronomer has as yet called attention to the other, I would not be surprised to hear about it, even at this late date.

While I do not wish it understood that I regard any of the major features of this story as likely to become facts in the near future—indeed, it has been my aim to portray the highly improbable—it is my belief that there is no mathematical or scientific impossibility to be found in "Skylark Three."

In fact, even though I have repeatedly violated theories in which I myself believe, I have in every case taken great pains to make certain that the most rigid mathematical analysis of which I am capable has failed to show that I have violated any known and proven scientific fact. By "fact" I do not mean the kind of reasoning, based upon assumptions later shown to be fallacious, by which it was "proved" that the transatlantic cable and the airplane were scientifically impossible. I refer to definitely known phenomena which no possible future development can change—I refer to mathematical proofs whose fundamental equations and operations involve no assumptions and contain no second-degree uncertainties.

Please bear in mind that we KNOW very little. It has been widely believed that the velocity of light is the limiting velocity, and many of our leading authorities hold this view—but it cannot be proved, and is by no means universally held. In this connection, it would appear that J. J. Thompson, in "Beyond the Electron" shows, to his own satisfaction at least, that velocities vastly greater than that of light are not only possible, but necessary to any comprehensive investigation into the nature of the electron.

We do not know the nature of light. Neither the undulatory theory nor the quantum theory are adequate to explain all observed phenomena, and they seem to be mutually exclusive, since it would seem clear by definition that no one thing can be at the same time continuous and discontinuous. We know nothing of the ether—we do not even know whether or not it exists, save as a concept of our own extremely limited intelligence. We are in total ignorance of the ultimate structure of matter, and of the arrangement and significance of those larger aggregations of matter, the galaxies. We do not know nor understand, nor can we define, even such fundamental necessities as time and space.

Why prate of "the impossible"?

Edward Elmer Smith, Ph.D.

CHAPTER I

DuQuesne Goes Traveling

In the innermost private office of Steel, Brookings and DuQuesne stared at each other across the massive desk. DuQuesne's voice was cold, his black brows were drawn together.

"Get this, Brookings, and get it straight. I'm shoving off at twelve o'clock tonight. My advice to you is to lay off Richard Seaton, absolutely. Don't do a thing. *Nothing, hold everything.* Keep on holding it until I get back, no matter how long that may be," DuQuesne shot out in an icy tone.

"I am very much surprised at your change of front, Doctor. You are the last man I would have expected to be scared off after one engagement."

"Don't be any more of a fool than you have to, Brookings. There's a lot of difference between scared and knowing when you are simply wasting effort. As you remember, I tried to abduct Mrs. Seaton by picking her off with an attractor from a space-ship. I would have bet that nothing could have stopped me. Well, when they located me—probably with an automatic Osnomian ray-detector—and heated me red-hot while I was still better than two hundred miles up, I knew then and there that they had us stopped; that there was nothing we could do except go back to my plan, abandon the abduction idea, and eventually kill them all. Since my plan would take time, you objected to it, and sent an airplane to drop a five-hundred-pound bomb on them. Airplane, bomb, and all simply vanished. It didn't explode, you remember, just flashed into light and disappeared, with scarcely any noise. Then you pulled several more of your fool ideas, such as long-range bombardment, and so on. None of them worked. Still you've got the nerve to think that you can get them with ordinary gunmen! I've drawn you diagrams and shown you figures—I've told you in great detail and in one-syllable words exactly what we're up against. Now I tell you again that they've *got something.* If you had the brains of a pinhead, you would know that anything I can't do with a space-ship can't be done by a mob of ordinary gangsters. I'm telling you, Brookings, that you can't do it. My way is absolutely the only way that will work."

"But five years, Doctor!"

"I may be back in six months. But on a trip of this kind anything can happen, so I am planning on being gone five years. Even that may not be enough—I am carrying supplies for ten years, and that box of mine in the vault is not to be opened until ten years from today."

"But surely we shall be able to remove the obstructions ourselves in a few weeks. We always have."

"Oh, quit kidding yourself, Brookings! This is no time for idiocy! You stand just as much chance of killing Seaton——"

"Please, Doctor, please don't talk like that!"

"Still squeamish, eh? Your pussyfooting always did give me an acute pain. I'm for direct action, word and deed, first, last, and all the time. I repeat, you have exactly as much chance of killing Richard Seaton as a blind kitten has."

"How do you arrive at that conclusion, Doctor? You seem very fond of belittling our abilities. Personally, I think that we shall be able to attain our objectives within a few weeks—certainly long before you can possibly return from such an extended trip as you have in mind. And since you are so fond of frankness, I will say that I think that Seaton has you buffaloed, as you call it. Nine-tenths of these wonderful Osnomian things, I am assured by competent authorities, are scientifically impossible, and I think that the other one-tenth exists only in your own imagination. Seaton was lucky in that the airplane bomb was defective and exploded prematurely; and your space-ship got hot because of your injudicious speed through the atmosphere. We shall have everything settled by the time you get back."

"If you have, I'll make you a present of the controlling interest in Steel and buy myself a chair in some home for feeble-minded old women. Your ignorance and unwillingness to believe any new idea do not change the facts in any particular. Even before they went to Osnome, Seaton was hard to get, as you found out. On that trip he learned so much new stuff that it is now impossible to kill him by any ordinary means. You should realize that fact when he kills every gangster you send against him. At all events be very, *very* careful not to kill his wife in any of your attacks, even by accident, until after you have killed him."

"Such an event would be regrettable, certainly, in that it would remove all possibility of the abduction."

"It would remove more than that. Remember the explosion in our laboratory, that blew an entire mountain into impalpable dust? Draw in your mind a nice, vivid picture of one ten times the size in each of our plants and in this building. I know that you are fool enough to go ahead with your own ideas, in spite of everything I've said; and, since I do not yet actually control Steel, I can't forbid you to, officially. But you should know that I know what I'm talking about, and I say again that you're going to make an utter fool of yourself; just because you won't believe anything possible, that hasn't been done every day for a hundred years. I wish that I could make you understand that Seaton and Crane have got something that we haven't—but for the good of our plants, and incidentally for your own, please remember one thing, anyway; for if you forget it, we won't have a plant left and you personally will be blown into a fine red mist. Whatever you start, kill Seaton first, and be absolutely certain that he is definitely, completely, finally and totally dead before you touch one of Dorothy Seaton's red hairs. As long as you only attack him personally he won't do anything but kill every man you send against him. If you kill her while he's still alive, though—Blooie!" and the saturnine scientist waved both hands in an expressive pantomime of wholesale destruction.

"Probably you are right in that," Brookings paled slightly. "Yes, Seaton would do just that. We shall be very careful, until after we succeed in removing him."

"Don't worry—you won't succeed. I shall attend to that detail myself, as soon as I get back. Seaton and Crane and their families, the directors and employees of their plants, the banks that by any possibility may harbor their notes or solutions—in short, every person and everything standing between me and a monopoly of 'X'—all shall disappear."

"That is a terrible program, Doctor. Wouldn't the late Perkins' plan of an abduction, such as I have in mind, be better, safer and quicker?"

"Yes—except for the fact that it will not work. I've talked until I'm blue in the face—I've proved to you over and over that you can't abduct her now without first killing him, and that you can't even touch him. My plan is the only one that will work. Seaton isn't the only one who learned anything—I learned a lot myself. I learned one thing in particular. Only four other inhabitants of either Earth or Osnome ever had even an inkling of it, and they died, with their brains disintegrated beyond reading. That thing is my ace in the hole. I'm going after it. When I get it, and not until then, will I be ready to take the offensive."

"You intend starting open war upon your return?"

"The war started when I tried to pick off the women with my attractor. That is why I am leaving at midnight. He always goes to bed at eleven-thirty, and I will be out of range of his object-compass before he wakes up. Seaton and I understand each other perfectly. We both know that the next time we meet one of us is going to be resolved into his component atoms, perhaps into electrons. He doesn't know that he's going to be the one, but I do. My final word to you is to lay off—if you don't, you and your 'competent authorities' are going to learn a lot."

"You do not care to inform me more fully as to your destination or your plans?"

"I do not. Goodbye."

CHAPTER II

Dunark Visits Earth

Martin Crane reclined in a massive chair, the fingers of his right hand lightly touching those of his left, listening attentively. Richard Seaton strode up and down the room before his friend, his unruly brown hair on end, speaking savagely between teeth clenched upon the stem of his reeking, battered briar, brandishing a sheaf of papers.

"Mart, we're stuck—stopped dead. If my head wasn't made of solid blue mush I'd have had a way figured out of this thing before now, but I can't. With that zone of force the Skylark would have everything imaginable—without it, we're exactly where we were before. That zone is immense, man—terrific—its possibilities are unthinkable—and I'm so cussed dumb that I can't find out how to use it intelligently—can't use it at all, for that matter. By its very nature it is impenetrable to any form of matter, however applied; and this calc here," slapping viciously the sheaf of papers containing his calculations, "shows that it must also be opaque to any wave whatever, propagated through air or through ether, clear down to cosmic rays. Behind it, we would be blind and helpless, so we can't use it at all. It drives me frantic! Think of a barrier of pure force, impalpable, immaterial, and exerted along a geometrical surface of no thickness whatever—and yet actual enough to stop even a Millikan ray that travels a hundred thousand light-years and then goes through twenty-seven feet of solid lead just like it was so much vacuum! That's what we're up against! However, I'm going to try out that model, Mart, right now. Come on, guy, snap into it! Let's get busy!"

"You are getting idiotic again, Dick," Crane rejoined calmly, without moving. "You know, even better than I do, that you are playing with the most concentrated essence of energy that the world has ever seen. That zone of force probably can be generated——"

"Probably, nothing!" barked Seaton. "It's just as evident a fact as that stool," kicking the unoffending bit of furniture half-way across the room as he spoke. "If you'd've let me, I'd've shown it to you yesterday!"

"Undoubtedly, then. Grant that it is impenetrable to all matter and to all known waves. Suppose that it should prove impenetrable also to gravitation and to magnetism? Those phenomena probably depend upon the ether, but we know nothing fundamental of their nature, nor of that of the ether. Therefore your calculations, comprehensive though they are, cannot predict the effect upon them of your zone of force. Suppose that that zone actually does set up a barrier in the ether, so that it nullifies gravitation, magnetism, and all allied phenomena; so that the power-bars, the attractors and repellers, cannot work through it? Then what? As well as showing me the zone of force, you might well have shown me yourself flying off into space, unable to use your power and helpless if you released the zone. No, we must know more of the fundamentals before you try even a small-scale experiment."

"Oh, bugs! You're carrying caution to extremes, Mart. What can happen? Even if gravitation should be nullified, I would rise only slowly, heading south the angle of our latitude—that's thirty-nine degrees—away from the perpendicular. I couldn't shoot off on a tangent, as some of these hot-heads have been claiming. Inertia would make me keep pace, approximately, with the earth in its rotation. I would rise slowly—only as fast as the tangent departs from the curvature of the earth's surface. I haven't figured out how fast that is, but it must be pretty slow."

"Pretty slow?" Crane smiled. "Figure it out."

"All right—but I'll bet it's slower than the rise of a toy balloon." Seaton threw down the papers and picked up his slide-rule, a twenty-inch trigonometrical duplex. "You'll concede that it is allowable to neglect the radial component of the orbital velocity of the earth for a first approximation, won't you—or shall I figure that in too?"

"You may ignore that factor."

"All right—let's see. Radius of rotation here in Washington would be cosine latitude times equatorial radius, approximately—call it thirty-two hundred miles. Angular velocity, fifteen degrees an hour. I want secant fifteen less one times thirty-two hundred. Right? Secant equals one over cosine—um-m-m-m—one point oh three five. Then point oh three five times thirty-two hundred. Hundred and twelve miles first hour. Velocity constant with respect to sun, accelerated respecting point of departure. Ouch! You win, Mart—I'd kinda step out! Well, how about this, then? I'll put on a vacuum suit and carry rations. Harness outside, with the same equipment I used in the test flights before we built *Skylark I—plus* the new stuff and a coil. Then throw on the zone, and see what happens. There can't be any jar in taking off, and with that outfit I can get back O. K. if I go clear to Jupiter!"

Crane sat in silence, his keen mind considering every aspect of the motions possible, of velocity, of acceleration, of inertia. He already knew well Seaton's resourcefulness in crises and his physical and mental strength.

"As far as I can see, that might be safe," he admitted finally, "and we really should know something about it besides the theory."

"Fine, Mart—let's get busy! I'll be ready in five minutes. Yell for the girls, will you? They'd break us off at the ankles if we pull anything new without letting them in on it."

A few minutes later the "girls" strolled out into Crane Field, arms around each other—Dorothy Seaton, her gorgeous auburn hair framing violet eyes and vivid coloring; black-haired, dark-eyed Margaret Crane.

"Br-r-r, it's cold!" Dorothy shivered, wrapping her coat more closely about her. "This must be the coldest day Washington has seen for years!"

"It is cold," Margaret agreed. "I wonder what they are going to do out here, this kind of weather?"

As she spoke, the two men stepped out of the "testing shed"—the huge structure that housed their Osnomian-built space-cruiser, "Skylark II." Seaton waddled clumsily, wearing as he did a Crane vacuum-suit which, built of fur, canvas, metal and transparent silica, braced by steel netting and equipped with air-tanks and heaters, rendered its wearer independent of outside conditions of temperature and pressure. Outside this suit he wore a heavy harness of leather, buckled about his body, shoulders, and legs, attached to which were numerous knobs, switches, dials, bakelite cases, and other pieces of apparatus. Carried by a strong aluminum framework in turn supported by the harness, the universal bearing of a small power-bar rose directly above his grotesque-looking helmet.

"What do you think you're going to do in that thing, Dickie?" Dorothy called. Then, knowing that he could not hear her voice, she turned to Crane. "What are you letting that precious husband of mine do now, Martin? He looks as though he were up to something."

While she was speaking, Seaton had snapped the release of his face plate.

"Nothing much, Dottie. Just going to show you-all the zone of force. Mart wouldn't let me turn it on, unless I got all cocked and primed for a year's journey into space."

"Dot, what is that zone of force, anyway?" asked Margaret.

"Oh, it's something Dick got into his head during that awful fight they had on Osnome. He hasn't thought of anything else since we got back. You know how the attractors and repellers work? Well, he found out something funny about the way everything acted while the Mardonalians were bombarding them with a certain kind of a wave-length. He finally figured out the exact ray that did it, and found out that if it is made strongly enough, it acts as if a repeller and attractor were working together—only so much stronger that nothing can get through the boundary, either way—in fact, it's so strong that it cuts anything in two that's in the way. And the funny thing is that there's nothing there at all, really; but Dick says that the forces meeting there, or something, make it act as though something really important were there. See?"

"Uh-huh," assented Margaret, doubtfully, just as Crane finished the final adjustments and moved toward them. A safe distance away from Seaton, he turned and waved his hand.

Instantly Seaton disappeared from view, and around the place where he had stood there appeared a shimmering globe some twenty feet in diameter—a globe apparently a perfect spherical mirror, which darted upward and toward the south. After a moment the globe disappeared and Seaton was again seen. He was now standing upon a hemispherical mass of earth. He darted back toward the group upon the ground, while the mass of earth fell with a crash a quarter of a mile away. High above their heads the mirror again encompassed Seaton, and again shot upward and southward. Five times this maneuver was repeated before Seaton came down, landing easily in front of them and opening his helmet.

"It's just what we thought it was, only worse," he reported tersely. "Can't do a thing with it. Gravitation won't work through it—bars won't—nothing will. And dark? *Dark!* Folks, you ain't never seen no darkness, nor heard no silence. It scared me stiff!"

"Poor little boy—afraid of the dark!" exclaimed Dorothy. "We saw absolute blackness in space."

"Not like this, you didn't. I just saw absolute darkness and heard absolute silence for the first time in my life. I never imagined anything like it—come on up with me and I'll show it to you."

"No you won't!" his wife shrieked as she retreated toward Crane. "Some other time, perhaps."

Seaton removed the harness and glanced at the spot from which he had taken off, where now appeared a hemispherical hole in the ground.

"Let's see what kind of tracks I left, Mart," and the two men bent over the depression. They saw with astonishment that the cut surface was perfectly smooth, with not even the slightest roughness or irregularity visible. Even the smallest loose grains of sand had been sheared in two along a mathematically exact hemispherical surface by the inconceivable force of the disintegrating copper bar.

"Well, that sure wins the——"

An alarm bell sounded. Without a glance around, Seaton seized Dorothy and leaped into the testing shed. Dropping her unceremoniously to the floor he stared through the telescope sight of an enormous ray-generator which had automatically aligned itself upon the distant point of liberation of intra-atomic energy which had caused the alarm to sound. One hand upon the switch, his face was hard and merciless as he waited to make sure of the identity of the approaching space-ship, before he released the frightful power of his generator upon it.

"I've been expecting DuQuesne to try it again," he gritted, striving to make out the visitor, yet more than two hundred miles distant. "He's out to get you, Dot—and this time I'm not just going to warm him up and scare him away, as I did last time. This time that misguided mutt's going to get frizzled right.... I can't locate him with this small telescope, Mart. Line him up in the big one and give me the word, will you?"

"I see him, Dick, but it is not DuQuesne's ship. It is built of transparent arenak, like the 'Kondal.' Even though it seems impossible, I believe it is the 'Kondal'."

"Maybe so, and again maybe DuQuesne built it—or stole it. On second thought, though, I don't believe that DuQuesne would be fool enough to tackle us again in the same way—but I'm taking no chances.... O. K., it is the 'Kondal,' I can see Dunark and Sitar myself, now."

The transparent vessel soon neared the field and the four Terrestrials walked out to greet their Osnomian friends. Through the arenak walls they recognized Dunark, Kofedix of Kondal, at the controls, and saw Sitar, his beautiful young queen, lying in one of the seats near the wall. She attempted a friendly greeting, but her face was strained as though she were laboring under a burden too great for her to bear.

Trying to help her, half kneeling over her, Dunark struggled, his green skin paling to a yellowish tinge at the touch of the bitter and unexpected cold.

As they watched, Dunark slipped a helmet over his head and one over Sitar's, pressed a button to open one of the doors, and supported her toward the opening.

"They mustn't come out, Dick!" exclaimed Dorothy in dismay. "They'll freeze to death in five minutes without any clothes on!"

"Yes, and Sitar can't stand up under our gravitation, either—I doubt if Dunark can, for long," and Seaton dashed toward the vessel, motioning the visitor back.

But misunderstanding the signal, Dunark came on. As he clambered heavily through the door he staggered as though under an enormous weight, and Sitar collapsed upon the frozen ground. Trying to help her, half-kneeling over her, Dunark struggled, his green skin paling to a yellowish tinge at the touch of the bitter and unexpected cold. Seaton leaped forward and gathered Sitar up in his mighty arms as though she were a child.

"Help Dunark back in, Mart," he directed crisply. "Hop in, girls—we've got to take these folks back up where they can live."

Seaton shut the door, and as everyone lay flat in the seats Crane, who had taken the controls, applied one notch of power and the huge vessel leaped upward. Miles of altitude were gained before Crane brought the cruiser to a stop and locked her in place with an anchoring attractor.

"There," he remarked calmly, "gravitation here is approximately the same as it is upon Osnome."

"Yes," put in Seaton, standing up and shedding clothing in all directions, "and I rise to remark that we'd better undress as far as the law allows—perhaps farther. I never did like Osnomian ideas of comfortable warmth, but we can endure it by peeling down to bedrock——"

Sitar jumped up happily, completely restored, and the three women threw their arms around each other.

"What a horrible, terrible, frightful world!" exclaimed Sitar, her eyes widening as she thought of her first experience with our earth. "Much as I love you, I shall never dare try to visit you again. I have never been able to understand why you Terrestrials wear what you call 'clothes,' nor why you are so terribly, brutally strong. Now I really know—I will feel the utterly cold and savage embrace of that awful earth of yours as long as I live!"

"Oh, it's not so bad, Sitar." Seaton, who was shaking both of Dunark's hands vigorously, assured her over his shoulder. "All depends on where you were raised. We like it that way, and Osnome gives us the pip. But you poor fish," turning again to Dunark, "with all my brains inside your skull, you should have known what you were letting yourself in for."

"That's true, after a fashion," Dunark admitted, "but your brain told me that Washington was *hot.* If I'd have thought to recalculate your actual Fahrenheit degrees into our loro ... but that figures only forty-seven and, while very cold, we could have endured it—wait a minute, I'm getting it. You have what you call 'seasons.' This, then, must be your 'winter.' Right?"

"Right the first time. That's the way your brain works behind my pan, too. I could figure anything out all right after it happened, but hardly ever beforehand—so I guess I can't blame you much, at that. But what I want to know is, how'd you get here? It would take more than my brains—you can't see our sun from anywhere near Osnome, even if you knew exactly where to look for it."

"Easy. Remember those wrecked instruments you threw out of *Skylark I* when we built *Skylark II*?" Having every minute detail of the configuration of Seaton's brain engraved upon his own, Dunark spoke English in Seaton's own characteristic careless fashion. Only when thinking deeply or discussing abstruse matter did Seaton employ the carefully selected and precise phrasing, which he knew so well how to use. "Well, none of them was beyond repair and the juice was still on most of them. One was an object-compass bearing on the Earth. We simply fixed the bearings, put on some minor improvements, and here we are."

"Let us all sit down and be comfortable," he continued, changing into the Kondalian tongue without a break, "and I will explain why we have come. We are in most desperate need of two things which you alone can supply—salt, and that strange metal, 'X'. Salt I know you have in great abundance, but I know that you have very little of the metal. You have only the one compass upon that planet?"

"That's all—one is all we set on it. However, we've got close to half a ton of the metal on hand—you can have all you want."

"Even if I took it all, which I would not like to do, that would be less than half enough. We must have at least one of your tons, and two tons would be better."

"Two tons! Holy cat! Are you going to plate a fleet of battle cruisers?"

"More than that. We must plate an area of copper of some ten thousand square miles—in fact, the very life of our entire race depends upon it."

"It's this way," he continued, as the four earth-beings stared at him in wonder. "Shortly after you left Osnome we were invaded by the inhabitants of the third planet of our fourteenth sun. Luckily for us they landed upon Mardonale, and in less than two days there was not a single Osnomian left alive upon that half of the planet. They wiped out our grand fleet in one brief engagement, and it was only the *Kondal* and a few more like her that enabled us to keep them from crossing the ocean. Even with our full force of these vessels, we cannot defeat them. Our regular Kondalian weapons were useless. We shot explosive copper charges against them of such size as to cause earthquakes all over Osnome, without seriously crippling their defenses. Their offensive weapons are almost irresistible—they have generators that burn arenak as though it were so much paper, and a series of deadly frequencies against which only a copper-driven ray screen is effective, and even that does not stand up long."

"How come you lasted till now, then?" asked Seaton.

"They have nothing like the *Skylark*, and no knowledge of intra-atomic energy. Therefore their space-ships are of the rocket type, and for that reason they can cross only at the exact time of conjunction, or whatever you call it—no, not conjunction, exactly, either, since the two planets do not revolve around the same sun: but when they are closest together. Our solar system is so complex, you know, that unless the trips are timed exactly, to the hour, the vessels will not be able to land upon Osnome, but will be drawn aside and be lost, if not actually drawn into the vast central sun. Although it may not have occurred to you, a little reflection will show that the inhabitants of all the central planets, such as Osnome, must perforce be absolutely ignorant of astronomy, and of all the wonders of outer space. Before your coming we knew nothing beyond our own solar system, and very little of that. We knew of the existence of only such of the closest planets as were brilliant enough to be seen in our continuous sunlight, and they were few. Immediately after your coming I gave your knowledge of astronomy to a group of our foremost physicists and mathematicians, and they have been working ceaselessly from space-ships—close enough so that observations could be recalculated to Osnome, and yet far enough away to afford perfect 'seeing,' as you call it."

"But I don't know any more about astronomy than a pig does about Sunday," protested Seaton.

"Your knowledge of details is, of course, incomplete," conceded Dunark, "but the detailed knowledge of the best of your Earthly astronomers would not help us a great deal, since we are so far removed from you in space. You, however, have a very clear and solid knowledge of the fundamentals of the science, and that is what we need, above all things."

"Well, maybe you're right, at that. I do know the general theory of the motions, and I studied some Celestial Mechanics. I'm awfully weak on advanced theory, though, as you'll find out when you get that far."

"Perhaps—but since our enemies have no knowledge of astronomy whatever, it is not surprising that their rocket-ships can be launched only at one particularly favorable time; for there are many planets and satellites, of which they can know nothing, to throw their vessels off the course.

"Some material essential to the operation of their war machinery apparently must come from their own planet, for they have ceased attacking, have dug in, and are simply holding their ground. It may be that they had not anticipated as much resistance as we could offer with space-ships and intra-atomic energy. At any rate, they have apparently saved enough of that material to enable them to hold out until the next conjunction—I cannot think of a better word for it—shall occur. Our forces are attacking constantly, with all the armament at our command, but it is certain that if the next conjunction is allowed to occur, it means the end of the entire Kondalian nation.'"

"What d'you mean 'if the next conjunction is *allowed* to occur?'" interjected Seaton. "Nobody can stop it."

"I am stopping it," Dunark stated quietly, grim purpose in every lineament. "That conjunction shall never occur. That is why I must have the vast quantities of salt and 'X'. We are building abutments of arenak upon the first satellite of our seventh planet, and upon our sixth planet itself. We shall cover them with plated active copper, and install chronometers to throw the switches at precisely the right moment. We have calculated the exact times, places, and magnitudes of the forces to be used. We shall throw the sixth planet some distance out of its orbit, and force the first satellite of the seventh planet clear out of that planet's influence. The two bodies whose motions we have thus changed will collide in such a way that the resultant body will meet the planet of our enemies in head-on collision, long before the next conjunction. The two bodies will be of almost equal masses, and will have opposite and approximately equal velocities; hence the resultant fused or gaseous mass will be practically without velocity and will fall directly into the fourteenth sun."

"Wouldn't it be easier to destroy it with an explosive copper bomb?"

"Easier, yes, but much more dangerous to the rest of our solar system. We cannot calculate exactly the effect of the collisions we are planning—but it is almost certain that an explosion of sufficient violence to destroy all life upon the planet would disturb its motion sufficiently to endanger the entire system. The way we have in mind will simply allow the planet and one satellite to drop out quietly—the other planets of the same sun will soon adjust themselves to the new conditions, and the system at large will be practically unaffected—at least, so we believe."

Seaton's eyes narrowed as his thoughts turned to the quantities of copper and "X" required and to the engineering features of the project; Crane's first thought was of the mathematics involved in a computation of that magnitude and character; Dorothy's quick reaction was one of pure horror.

"He can't, Dick! He mustn't! It would be too ghastly! It's outrageous—it's unthinkable—it's—it's—it's simply too horrible!" Her violet eyes flamed, and Margaret joined in:

"That would be awful, Martin. Think of the destruction of a whole planet—of an entire world—with all its inhabitants! It makes me shudder, even to think of it."

Dunark leaped to his feet, ablaze. But before he could say a word, Seaton silenced him.

"Shut up, Dunark! Pipe down! Don't say anything you'll be sorry for—let *me* tell 'em! Close your mouth, I tell you!" as Dunark still tried to get a word in, "I tell you I'll tell 'em, and when I tell 'em they stay told! Now listen, you two girls—you're going off half-cocked and you're both full of little red ants. What do you think Dunark is up against? Sherman chirped it when he described war—and this is a real he-war; a brand totally unknown on our Earth. It isn't a question of whether or not to destroy a population—the only question is which population is to be destroyed. One of them's got to go. Remember those folks go into a war thoroughly, and there isn't a thought, even remotely resembling our conception of mercy in any of their minds on either side. If Dunark's plans go through the enemy nation will be wiped out. That is horrible, of course. But on the other hand, if we block him off from salt and 'X,' the entire Kondalian nation will be destroyed just as thoroughly and efficiently, and even more horribly—not one man, woman, or child would be spared. Which nation do you want saved? Play that over a couple of times on your adding machine, Dot, and let me know what you get."

Dorothy, taken aback, opened and closed her mouth twice before she found her voice.

"But, Dick, they couldn't possibly. Would they kill them all, Dick? Surely they wouldn't—they *couldn't*."

"Surely they would—and could. They do—it's good technique in those parts of the Galaxy. Dunark has just told us of how they killed every member of the entire race of Mardonalians, in forty hours. Kondal would go the same way. Don't kid yourself, Dimples—don't be a child. War up there is *no* species of pink tea, believe me—half of my brain has been through thirty years of Osnomian warfare, and I know precisely what I'm talking about. Let's take a vote. Personally, I'm in favor of Osnome. Mart?"

"Osnome."

"Dottie? Peggy?" Both remained silent for some time, then Dorothy turned to Margaret.

"You tell him, Peggy—we both feel the same way."

"Dick, you know that we wouldn't want the Kondalians destroyed—but the other is so—such a—well, such an utter *shrecklichkeit*—isn't there some other way out?"

"I'm afraid not—but if there is any other possible way out, I'll do my da—to help find it," he promised. "The ayes have it. Dunark, we'll skip over to that 'X' planet and load you up."

Dunark grasped Seaton's hand. "Thanks, Dick," he said, simply. "But before you help me farther, and lest I might be in some degree sailing under false colors, I must tell you that, wearer of the seven disks though you are, Overlord of Osnome though you are, my brain brother though you are; had you decided against me, nothing but my death could have kept me away from that salt and your 'X' compass."

"Why sure," assented Seaton, in surprise. "Why not? Fair enough! Anybody would do the same—don't let that bother you."

"How is your supply of platinum?" asked Dunark.

"Mighty low. We had about decided to hop over there after some. I want some of your textbooks on electricity and so on, too. I see you brought a load of platinum with you."

"Yes, a few hundred tons. We also brought along an assortment of books I knew you would be interested in, a box of radium, a few small bags of gems of various kinds, and some of our fabrics, Sitar thought your Karfediro would like to have. While we are here, I would like to get some books on chemistry and some other things."

"We'll get you the Congressional Library, if you want it, and anything else you think you'd like. Well, gang, let's go places and do things! What to do, Mart?"

"We had better drop back to Earth, have the laborers unload the platinum, and load on the salt, books, and other things. Then both ships will go to the 'X' planet, as we will each want compasses on it, for future use. While we are loading, I should like to begin remodeling our instruments; to make them something like these; with Dunark's permission. These instruments are wonders, Dick—vastly ahead of anything I have ever seen. Come and look at them, if you want to see something really beautiful."

"Coming up. But say, Mart, while I think of it, we mustn't forget to install a zone-of-force apparatus on this boat, too. Even though we can't use it intelligently, it certainly would be a winner as a defense. We couldn't hurt anybody through it, of course, but if we should happen to be getting licked anywhere, all we'd have to do would be to wrap ourselves up in it. They couldn't touch us. Nothing in the ether spectrum is corkscrewy enough to get through it."

"That's the second idea you've had since I've known you, Dicky," Dorothy smiled at Crane. "Do you think he should be allowed to run at large, Martin?"

"That is a real idea. We may need it—you never can tell. Even if we never find any other use for the zone of force, that one is amply sufficient to justify its installation."

"Yes, it would be, for you—and I'm getting to be a regular Safety-First Simon myself, since they opened up on us. What about those instruments?"

The three men gathered around the instrument-board and Dunark explained the changes he had made—and to such men as Seaton and Crane it was soon evident that they were examining an installation embodying sheer perfection of instrumental control—a system which only those wonder instrument-makers, the Osnomians, could have devised. The new object-compasses were housed in arenak cases after setting, and the housings were then exhausted to the highest attainable vacuum. Oscillation was set up by means of one carefully standardized electrical impulse, instead of by the clumsy finger-touch Seaton had used. The bearings, built of arenak and Osnomian jewels, were as strong as the axles of a truck and yet were almost perfectly frictionless.

"I like them myself," admitted Dunark. "Without a load the needles will rotate freely more than a thousand hours on the primary impulse, as against a few minutes in the old type; and under load they are many thousands of times as sensitive."

"You're a blinding flash and a deafening report, ace!" declared Seaton, enthusiastically. "That compass is as far ahead of my model as the *Skylark* is ahead of Wright's first glider."

The other instruments were no less noteworthy. Dunark had adopted the Perkins telephone system, but had improved it until it was scarcely recognized and had made it capable of almost unlimited range. Even the guns—heavy rapid-firers, mounted in spherical bearings in the walls—were aimed and fired by remote control, from the board. He had devised full automatic steering controls; and meters and recorders for acceleration, velocity, distance, and flight-angle. He had perfected a system of periscopic vision, which enabled the pilot to see the entire outside surfaces of the shell, and to look toward any point of the heavens without interference.

"This kind of takes my eye, too, prince," Seaton said, as he seated himself, swung a large, concave disk in front of him, and experimented with levers and dials. "You certainly can't call this thing a periscope—it's no more a periscope than I am a polyp. When you look through this plate, it's better than looking out of a window—it subtends more than the angle of vision, so that you can't see anything but out-of-doors—I thought for a second I was going to fall out. What do you call 'em, Dunark?"

"Kraloto. That would be in English ... Seeing-plate? Or rather, call it 'visiplate'."

"That's a good word. Mart, take a look if you want to see a set of perfect lenses and prisms."

Crane looked into the visiplate and gasped. The vessel had disappeared—he was looking directly down upon the Earth below him!

"No trace of chromatic, spherical, or astigmatic aberration," he reported in surprise. "The refracting system is invisible—it seems as though nothing intervenes between the eye and the object. You perfected all these things since we left Osnome, Dunark? You are in a class by yourself. I could not even copy them in less than a month, and I never could have invented them."

"I did not do it alone, by any means. The Society of Instrument-Makers, of which I am only one member, installed and tested more than a hundred systems. This one represents the best features of all the systems tried. It will not be necessary for you to copy them. I brought along two complete duplicate sets for the *Skylark*, as well as a dozen or so of the compasses. I thought that perhaps these particular improvements might not have occurred to you, since you Terrestrials are not as familiar as we are with complex instrumental work."

Crane and Seaton spoke together.

"That was thoughtful of you, Dunark, and we appreciated it fully."

"That puts four more palms on your *Croix de Guerre*, ace. Thanks a lot."

"Say, Dick," called Dorothy, from her seat near the wall. "If we're going down to the ground, how about Sitar?"

"By lying down and not doing anything, and by staying in the vessel, where it is warm, she will be all right for the short time we must stay here," Dunark answered for his wife. "I will help all I can, but I do not know how much that will be."

"It isn't so bad lying down." Sitar agreed. "I don't like your Earth a bit, but I can stand it a little while. Anyway, I *must* stand it, so why worry about it?"

"'At-a-girl!" cheered Seaton. "And as for you, Dunark, you'll pass the time just like Sitar does—lying down. If you do much chasing around down there where we live, you're apt to get your lights and liver twisted all out of shape—so you'll stay put, horizontal. We've got men enough around the shop to eat this cargo in three hours, let alone unload it. While they unload and load you up, we'll install the zone apparatus, put a compass on you, put one of yours on us, and then you can hop back up here where you're comfortable. Then as soon as we can get the 'Lark' ready for the trip, we'll jump up here and be on our way. Everything clear? Cut the rope, Mart—let the old bucket drop!"

CHAPTER III

Skylark Two Sets Out

"Say, Mart, I just got conscious! It never occurred to me until just now, as Dunark left, that I'm as good an instrument-maker as Dunark is—the same one, in fact—and I've got a hunch. You know that needle on DuQuesne hasn't been working for quite a while? Well, I don't believe it's out of commission at all. I think he's gone somewhere, so far away that it can't read on him. I'm going to house it in, re-jewel it, and find out where he is."

"An excellent idea. He has even you worrying, and as for myself——"

"Worrying! That bird is simply pulling my cork! I'm so scared he'll get Dottie, that I'm running around in circles and biting myself in the small of the back. He's got a hen on, you can bet your shirt on that—what gravels me is he's aiming at the girls, not at us or the job."

"I should say that someone had aimed at you fairly accurately, judging by the number of bullets stopped lately by that arenak armor of yours. I wish that I could take some of the strain, but they are centering all their attacks upon you."

"Yes—I can't stick my nose outside our yard without somebody throwing lead at it. It's funny, too. You're more important to the power-plant than I am."

"You should know why. They are not afraid of me. While my spirit is willing enough, it was your skill and rapidity with a pistol that frustrated four attempts at abduction in as many days. It is positively uncanny, the way you explode into action. With all my practice, I didn't even have my pistol out yesterday until it was all over. And besides Prescott's guards, we had four policemen with us—detailed to 'guard' us—because of the number of gunmen you had to kill before that!"

"It ain't practice so much, Mart—it's a gift. I've always been fast, and I react automatically. You think first, that's why you're slow. Those cops were funny. They didn't know what it was all about until it was all over—all but calling the wagon. That was the worst yet. One of their slugs struck directly in front of my left eye—it was kinda funny, at that, seeing it splash—and I thought I was inside a boiler in a riveting shop when those machine-guns cut loose. It was hectic, all right, while it lasted. But one thing I'll tell the attentive world—we're not doing all the worrying. Very few, if any, of the gangsters they send after us are getting back. Wonder what they think when they shoot at us and we don't drop?

"But I'm afraid I'm beginning to crack, Mart," Seaton went on, his voice becoming grimly earnest. "I don't like anything about this whole mess. I don't like all four of us wearing armor all the time. I don't like living constantly under guard. I don't like all this killing. And this constant menace of losing Dorothy, if I let her out of my sight for five seconds, is driving me mad. To tell you the real truth, I'm devilishly afraid that they'll figure out something that'll work. I could grab off two women, or kill two men, if they had armor and guns enough to stock a war. I believe that DuQuesne could, too—and the rest of that bunch aren't imbeciles, either, by any means. I won't feel safe until all four of us are in the *Skylark* and a long ways from here. I'm sure glad we're pulling out; and I don't intend to come back until I get a good line on DuQuesne. He's the bird I'm going to get, and get right—and when I get him I'll tell the cock-eyed world he'll stay got. There won't be any two atoms of his entire carcass left in the same township. I meant that promise when I gave it to him!"

"He realizes that fully. He knows that it is now definitely either his life or our own, and he is really dangerous. When he took Steel over and opened war upon us, he did it with his eyes wide open. With his ideas, he must have a monopoly of 'X' or nothing; and he knows the only possible way of getting it. However, you and I both know that he would not let either one of us live, even though we surrendered."

"You chirped it! But that guy's going to find he's started something, unless I get paralysis of the intentions. Well, how about turning up a few R. P. M.? We don't want to keep Dunark waiting too long."

"There is very little to do beyond installing the new instruments; and that is nearly done. We can finish pumping out the compass *en route*. You have already installed every weapon of offense and defense known to either Earthly or Osnomian warfare, including those ray-generators and screens you moaned so about not having during the battle over Kondal. I believe that we have on board every article for which either of us has been able to imagine even the slightest use."

"Yes, we've got her so full of plunder that there's hardly room left for quarters. You ain't figuring on taking anybody but Shiro along, are you?"

"No. I suppose there is no real necessity for taking even him, but he wants very much to go, and may prove himself useful."

"I'll say he'll be useful. None of us really enjoys polishing brass or washing dishes—and besides, he's one star cook and an A-1 housekeeper."

The installation of the new instruments was soon completed, and while Dorothy and Margaret made last-minute preparations for departure, the men called a meeting of the managing directors and department heads of the "Seaton-Crane Co., Engineers." The chiefs gave brief reports in turn. Units Number One and Number Two of the immense new central super-power plant were in continuous operation. Number Three was almost ready to cut in. Number Four was being rushed to completion. Number Five was well under way. The research laboratory was keeping well up on its problems. Troubles were less than had been anticipated. Financially, it was a gold mine. With no expense for boilers or fuel, and thus with a relatively small investment in plant and a very small operating cost, they were selling power at one-sixth of prevailing rates, and still profits were almost paying for all new construction. With the completion of Number Five, rates would be reduced still further.

"In short, Dad, everything's slick," remarked Seaton to Mr. Vaneman, after the others had gone.

"Yes; your plan of getting the best men possible, paying them well, and giving them complete authority and sole responsibility, has worked to perfection. I have never seen an undertaking of such size go forward so smoothly and with such fine co-operation."

"That's the way we wanted it. We hand-picked the directors, and put it up to you, strictly. You did the same to the managers. Everybody knows that his end is up to him, and him alone—so he digs in."

"However, Dick, while everything at the works is so fine, when is this other thing going to break?"

"We've won all the way so far, but I'm afraid something's about due. That's the big reason I want to get Dot away for a while. You know what they're up to?"

"Too well," the older man answered. "Dottie or Mrs. Crane, or both. Her mother—she is telling her goodbye now—and I agree that the danger here is greater than out there."

"Danger out there? With the old can fixed the way she is now, Dot's a lot safer there than you are in bed. Your house might fall down, you know."

"You're probably right, son—I know you, and I know Martin Crane. Together, and in the *Skylark*, I believe you invincible."

"All set, Dick?" asked Dorothy, appearing in the doorway.

"All set. You've got the dope for Prescott and everybody Dad. We may be back in six months, or we may see something to investigate, and be gone a year or so. Don't begin to lose any sleep until after we've been out—oh, say three years. We'll make it a point to be back by then."

Farewells were said; the party embarked, and *Skylark Two* shot upward. Seaton flipped a phone set over his head and spoke.

"Dunark!... Coming out, heading directly for 'X'.... No, better stay quite a ways off to one side when we get going good.... Yes, I'm accelerating twenty six point oh oh oh.... Yes. I'll call you now and then, until the radio waves get lost, to check the course with you. After that, keep on the last course, reverse at the calculated distance, and by the time we're pretty well slowed down, we'll feel around for each other with the compasses and go in together.... Right.... Uh-huh.... Fine! So long!"

In order that the two vessels should keep reasonably close together, it had been agreed that each should be held at an acceleration of exactly twenty-six feet per second, positive and negative. This figure represented a compromise between the gravitational forces of the two worlds upon which the different parties lived. While considerably less than the acceleration of gravitation at the surface of the Earth, the Terrestrials could readily accustom themselves to it; and it was not enough greater than that of Osnome to hamper seriously the activities of the green people.

Well clear of the Earth's influence, Seaton assured himself that everything was functioning properly, then stretched to his full height, wreathed his arms over his head, and heaved a deep sigh of relief.

"Folks," he declared, "This is the first time I've felt right since we got out of this old bottle. Why, I feel so good a cat could walk up to me and scratch me right in the eye, and I wouldn't even scratch back. Yowp! I'm a wild Siberian catamount, and this is my night to howl. Whee-ee-yerow!"

Dorothy laughed, a gay, lilting carol.

"Haven't I always told you he had cat blood in him, Peggy? Just like all tomcats, every once in a while he has to stretch his claws and yowl. But go ahead, Dickie, I like it—this is the first uproar you've made in weeks. I believe I'll join you!"

"It most certainly is a relief to get this load off our minds: I could do a little ladylike yowling myself," Margaret said; and Crane, lying completely at ease, a thin spiral of smoke curling upward from his cigarette, nodded agreement.

"Dick's yowling is quite expressive at times. All of us feel the same way, but some of us are unable to express ourselves quite so vividly. However, it is past bedtime, and we should organize our crew. Shall we do it as we did before?"

"No, it isn't necessary. Everything is automatic. The bar is held parallel to the guiding compass, and signal bells ring whenever any of the instruments show a trace of abnormal behavior. Don't forget that there is at least one meter registering and recording every factor of our flight. With this control system we can't get into any such jam as we did last trip."

"Surely you are not suggesting that we run all night with no one at the controls?"

"Exactly that. A man camping at this board is painting the lily and gilding fine gold. Awake or asleep nobody need be closer to it than is necessary to hear a bell if one should ring, and you can hear them all over the ship. Furthermore, I'll bet a hat we won't hear a signal a week. Simply as added precaution, though, I've run lines so that any time one of these signals lets go, it sounds a buzzer on the head of our bed, so I'm automatically taking the night shift. Remember, Mart, these instruments are thousands of times as sensitive as the keenest human senses—they'll spot trouble long before we could, even if we were looking right at it."

"Of course, you understand these instruments much better than I do, as yet. If you trust them, I am perfectly willing to do the same. Goodnight."

Seaton sat down and Dorothy nestled beside him, her head snuggled into the curve of his shoulder.

"Sleepy, cuddle-pup?"

"Heavens, no! I couldn't sleep now, lover—could you?"

"Not any. What's the use?"

His arm tightened around her. Apparently motionless to its passengers, the cruiser bored serenely on into space, with ever-mounting velocity. There was not the faintest sound, not the slightest vibration—only the peculiar violet glow surrounding the shining copper cylinder in its massive universal bearing gave any indication of the thousands of kilowatts being generated in the mighty intra-atomic power-plant. Seaton studied it thoughtfully.

"You know, if that violet aura and copper bar were a little different in shade and tone of color, they'd be just like your eyes and hair," he remarked finally.

"You burn me up, Dick!" she retorted, her entrancing low chuckle bubbling through her words. "You do say the weirdest things at times! Possibly they would—and if the moon were made of different stuff than it is and had a different color, it might be green cheese, too! What say we go over and look at the stars?"

"As you were, Rufus!" he commanded sternly. "Don't move a millimeter—you're a drive fit, right where you are. I'll get you any stars you want, and bring them right in here to you. What constellation would you like? I'll get you the Southern Cross—we never see it in Washington."

"No, I want something familiar; the Pleiades or the Big Dipper—no, get me Canis Major—'where Sirius, brightest jewel in the diadem of the firmament, holds sway'," she quoted. "There! Thought I'd forgotten all the astronomy you ever taught me, didn't you? Think you can find it?"

"Sure. Declination about minus twenty, as I remember it, and right ascension between six and seven hours. Let's see—where would that be from our course?"

He thought for a moment, manipulated several levers and dials, snapped off the lights, and swung number one exterior visiplate around, directly before their eyes.

"Oh.... Oh ... this is magnificent, Dick!" she exclaimed. "It's stupendous. It seems as though we were right out there in space itself, and not in here at all. It's ... it's just too perfectly darn wonderful!"

Although neither of them was unacquainted with interstellar space, it presents a spectacle that never fails to awe even the most seasoned observer: and no human being had ever before viewed the wonders of space from such a coign of vantage. Thus the two fell silent and awed as they gazed out into the abysmal depths of the interstellar void. The darkness of Earthly night is ameliorated by light-rays scattered by the atmosphere: the stars twinkle and scintillate and their light is diffused, because of the same medium. But here, what a contrast! They saw the utter, absolute darkness of the complete absence of all light: and upon that indescribable blackness they beheld superimposed the almost unbearable brilliance of enormous suns concentrated into mathematical points, dimensionless. Sirius blazed in blue-white splendor, dominating the lesser members of his constellation, a minute but intensely brilliant diamond upon a field of black velvet—his refulgence unmarred by any trace of scintillation or distortion.

As Seaton slowly shifted the field of vision, angling toward and across the celestial equator and the ecliptic, they beheld in turn mighty Rigel; The Belt, headed by dazzlingly brilliant-white Delta-Orionis; red Betelguese; storied Aldebaran, the friend of mariners; and the astronomically constant Pleiades.

Seaton's arm contracted, swinging Dorothy into his embrace; their lips met and held.

"Isn't it wonderful, lover," she murmured, "to be out here in space this way, together, away from all our troubles and worries? I am so happy."

"It's all of that, sweetheart mine!"

"I almost died, every time they shot at you. Suppose your armor cracked or something? I wouldn't want to go on living—I'd just naturally die!"

"I'm glad it didn't—and I'm twice as glad that they didn't succeed in grabbing you away from me...." His jaw set rigidly, his gray eyes became hard as tempered drills. "Blackie DuQuesne has something coming to him. So far, I have always paid my debts.... I shall settle with him ... IN FULL."

"That was an awfully quick change of subject," he continued, his voice changing instantly into a lighter vein, "but that's one penalty of being human. We can't live in high altitudes all our lives—if we could there would be no thrill in ascending them so often.

"Yes, we love each other just the same—more than anybody else I ever heard of." After a moment she eyed him shrewdly and continued:

"You've got something on your mind besides that tangled mop of hair, big boy. Tell it to Red-Top."

"Nothing much...."

"Come on, 'fess up—it's good for the soul. You can't fool your own wife, guy; I know your little winning ways too well."

"Let me finish, woman; I was about to bare my very soul. To resume—nothing much to go on but a hunch, but I think DuQuesne's somewhere out here in the great open spaces, where men are sometimes schemers as well as men; and if so, I'm after him—foot, horse, and marines."

"That object compass?"

"Yes. You see, I built that thing myself, and I know darn well it isn't out of order. It's still on him, but doesn't indicate. Ergo, he is too far away to reach—and with his weight, I could find him anywhere up to about one and a half light-years. If he wants to go that far away from home, where is his logical destination? It can't be anywhere but Osnome, since that is the only place we stopped at for any length of time—the only place where he could have learned anything. He's learned something, or found something useful to him there, just as we did. That is certain, since he is not the type of man to do anything without a purpose. Uncle Dudley is on his trail—and will be able to locate him pretty soon."

"When will you get that new compass-case exhausted to a skillionth of a whillimeter or something, whatever it is? I thought Dunark said it took five hundred hours of pumping to get it where he wanted it?"

"It did him—but while the Osnomians are wonders at some things, they're not so hot at others. You see, I've got three pumps on that job, in series. First, a Rodebush-Michalek super-pump[A] then, backing that, an ordinary mercury-vapor pump, and last, backing both the others, a Cenco-Hyvac motor-driven oil pump. In less than fifty hours that case will be as empty as a flapper's skull. Just to make sure of cleaning up the last infinitesimal traces, though, I'm going to flash a getter charge of tantalum in it. After that, the atmosphere in that case will be tenuous—take my word for it."

"I'll have to; most of that contribution to science being over my head like a circus tent. What say we let *Skylark Two* drift by herself for a while, and catch us some of Nature's sweet restorer?"

[A] J. Am. Chem. Soc. 51: 3, 750.

CHAPTER IV

The Zone of Force Is Tested

Seaton strode into the control room with a small oblong box in his hand. Crane was seated at the desk, poring over an abstruse mathematical treatise in *Science*. Margaret was working upon a bit of embroidery. Dorothy, seated upon a cushion on the floor with one foot tucked under her, was reading, her hand straying from time to time to a box of chocolates conveniently near.

"Well, this is a peaceful, home-like scene—too bad to bust it up. Just finished sealing off and flashing out this case, Mart. Going to see if she'll read. Want to take a look?"

He placed the compass upon the plane table, so that its final bearing could be read upon the master circles controlled by the gyroscopes; then simultaneously started his stop-watch and pressed the button which caused a minute couple to be applied to the needle. Instantly the needle began to revolve, and for many minutes there was no apparent change in its motion in either the primary or secondary bearings.

"Do you suppose it is out of order, after all?" asked Crane, regretfully.

"I don't think so," Seaton pondered. "You see, they weren't designed to indicate such distances on such small objects as men, so I threw a million ohms in series with the impulse. That cuts down the free rotation to less than half an hour, and increases the sensitivity to the limit. There, isn't she trying to quit it?"

"Yes, it is settling down. It must be on him still." Finally the ultra-sensitive needle came to rest. When it had done so, Seaton calculated the distance, read the direction, and made a reading upon Osnome.

"He's there, all right. Bearings agree, and distances check to within a light-year, which is as close as we can hope to check on as small a mass as a man. Well, that's that—nothing to do about it until after we get there. One sure thing, Mart—we're not coming straight back home from 'X'."

"No, an investigation is indicated."

"Well, that puts me out of a job. What to do? Don't want to study, like you. Can't crochet, like Peg. Darned if I'll sit cross-legged on a pillow and eat candy, like that Titian blonde over there on the floor. I know what—I'll build me a mechanical educator and teach Shiro to talk English instead of that mess of language he indulges in. How'd that be, Mart?"

"Don't do it," put in Dorothy, positively. "He's just too perfect the way he is. Especially don't do it if he'd talk the way you do—or could you teach him to talk the way you write?"

"Ouch! That's a dirty dig. However, Mrs. Seaton, I am able and willing to defend my customary mode of speech. You realize that the spoken word is ephemeral, whereas the thought, whose nuances have once been expressed in imperishable print is not subject to revision—its crudities can never be remodeled into more subtle, more gracious shading. It is my contention that, due to these inescapable conditions, the mental effort necessitated by the employment of nice distinctions in sense and meaning of words and a slavish adherence to the dictates of the more precise grammarians should be reserved for the print...."

He broke off as Dorothy, in one lithe motion, rose and hurled her pillow at his head.

"Choke him, somebody! Perhaps you had better build it, Dick, after all."

"I believe that he would like it, Dick. He is trying hard to learn, and the continuous use of a dictionary is undoubtedly a nuisance to him."

"I'll ask him. Shiro!"

"You have call, sir?" Shiro entered the room from his galley, with his unfailing bow.

"Yes. How'd you like to learn to talk English like Crane there does—without taking lessons?"

Shiro smiled doubtfully, unable to take such a thought seriously.

"Yes, it can be done," Crane assured him. "Doctor Seaton can build a machine which will teach you all at once, if you like."

"I like, sir, enormously, yes, sir. I years study and pore, but honorable English extraordinary difference from Nipponese—no can do. Dictionary useful but ..." he flipped pages dexterously, "extremely cumbrous. If honorable Seaton can do, shall be extreme ... gratification."

He bowed again, smiled, and went out.

"I'll do just that little thing. So long, folks, I'm going up to the shop."

Day after day the *Skylark* plunged through the vast emptiness of the interstellar reaches. At the end of each second she was traveling exactly twenty-six feet per second faster than she had been at its beginning; and as day after day passed, her velocity mounted into figures which became meaningless, even when expressed in thousands of miles per second. Still she seemed stationary to her occupants, and only different from a vessel motionless upon the surface of the Earth in that objects within her hull had lost three-sixteenths of their normal weight. Acceleration, too, had its effect. Only the rapidity with which the closer suns and their planets were passed gave any indication of the frightful speed at which they were being hurtled along by the inconceivable power of that disintegrating copper bar.

When the vessel was nearly half-way to "X," the bar was reversed in order to change the sign of their acceleration, and the hollow sphere spun through an angle of one hundred and eighty degrees around the motionless cage which housed the enormous gyroscopes. Still apparently motionless and exactly as she had been before, the *Skylark* was now actually traveling in a direction which seemed "down" and with a velocity which was being constantly decreased by the amount of their negative acceleration.

A few days after the bar had been reversed Seaton announced that the mechanical educator was complete, and brought it into the control room.

In appearance it was not unlike a large radio set, but it was infinitely more complex. It possessed numerous tubes, kino-lamps, and photo-electric cells, as well as many coils of peculiar design—there were dozens of dials and knobs, and a multiple set of head-harnesses.

"How can a thing like that possibly work as it does?" asked Crane. "I know that it does work, but I could scarcely believe it, even after it had educated me."

"That is nothing like the one Dunark used, Dick," objected Dorothy. "How come?"

"I'll answer you first, Dot. This is an improved model—it has quite a few gadgets of my own in it. Now, Mart, as to how it works—it isn't so funny after you understand it—it's a lot like radio in that respect. It operates on a band of frequencies lying between the longest light and heat waves and the shortest radio waves. This thing here is the generator of those waves and a very heavy power amplifier. The headsets are stereoscopic transmitters, taking or receiving a three-dimensional view. Nearly all matter is transparent to those waves; for instance bones, hair, and so on. However, cerebin, a cerebroside peculiar to the thinking structure of the brain, is opaque to them. Dunark, not knowing chemistry, didn't know why the educator worked or what it worked on—he found out by experiment that it did work; just as we found out about electricity. This three-dimensional model, or view, or whatever you want to call it, is converted into electricity in the headsets, and the resulting modulated wave goes back to the educator. There it is heterodyned with another wave—this second frequency was found after thousands of trials and is, I believe, the exact frequency existing in the optic nerves themselves—and sent to the receiving headset. Modulated as it is, and producing a three-dimensional picture, after rectification in the receiver, it reproduces exactly what has been 'viewed,' if due allowance has been made for the size and configuration of the different brains involved in the transfer. You remember a sort of flash—a sensation of seeing something—when the educator worked on you? Well, you did see it, just as though it had been transmitted to the brain by the optic nerve, but everything came at once, so the impression of sight was confused. The result in the brain, however, was clear and permanent. The only drawback is that you haven't the visual memory of what you have learned, and that sometimes makes it hard to use your knowledge. You don't know whether you know anything about a certain subject or not until after you go digging around in your brain looking for it."

"All set," he reported crisply, and barked a series of explosive syllables at Shiro, ending upon a rising note.

"I see," said Crane, and Dorothy, the irrepressible, put in:

"Just as clear as so much mud. What are the improvements you added to the original design?"

"Well, you see, I had a big advantage in knowing that cerebrin was the substance involved, and with that knowledge I could carry matters considerably farther than Dunark could in his original model. I can transfer the thoughts of somebody else to a third party or to a record. Dunark's machine couldn't work against resistance—if the subject wasn't willing to give up his thoughts he couldn't get them. This one can take them away by force. In fact, by increasing plate and grid voltages in the amplifier, I can pretty nearly burn out a man's brain. Yesterday, I was playing with it, transferring a section of my own brain to a magnetized tape—for a permanent record, you know—and found out that above certain rather low voltages it becomes a form of torture that would make the best efforts of the old Inquisition seem like a petting party."

"Did you succeed in the transfer?" Crane was intensely interested.

"Sure. Push the button for Shiro, and we'll start something."

"Put your head against this screen," he directed when Shiro had come in, smiling and bowing as usual. "I've got to caliper your brains to do a good job."

The calipering done, he adjusted various dials and clamped the electrodes over his own head and over the heads of Crane and Shiro.

"Want to learn Japanese while we're at it, Mart? I'm going to."

"Yes, please. I tried to learn it while I was in Japan, but it was altogether too difficult to be worth while."

Seaton threw in a switch, opened it, depressed two more, opened them, and threw off the power.

"All set," he reported crisply, and barked a series of explosive syllables at Shiro, ending upon a rising note.

"Yes, sir," answered the Japanese. "You speak Nipponese as though you had never spoken any other tongue. I am very grateful to you, sir, that I may now discard my dictionary."

"How about you two girls—anything you want to learn in a hurry?"

"Not me!" declared Dorothy emphatically. "That machine is too darn weird to suit me. Besides, if I knew as much about science as you do, we'd probably fight about it."

"I do not believe I care to...." began Margaret.

She was interrupted by the penetrating sound of an alarm bell.

"That's a new note!" exclaimed Seaton, "I never heard that note before."

He stood in surprise at the board, where a brilliant purple light was flashing slowly. "Great Cat! That's a purely Osnomian war-gadget—kind of a battleship detector—shows that there's a boatload of bad news around here somewhere. Grab the visiplates quick, folks," as he rang Shiro's bell. "I'll take visiplate area one, dead ahead. Mart, take number two. Dot, three; Peg, four; Shiro, five. Look sharp!... Nothing in front. See anything, any of you?"

None of them could discover anything amiss, but the purple light continued to flash, and the bell to ring. Seaton cut off the bell.

"We're almost to 'X'," he thought aloud. "Can't be more than a million miles or so, and we're almost stopped. Wonder if somebody's there ahead of us? Maybe Dunark is doing this, though. I'll call him and see." He threw in a switch and said one word—"Dunark!"

"Here!" came the voice of the Kofedix from the speaker. "Are you generating?"

"No—just called to see if you were. What do you make of it?"

"Nothing as yet. Better close up?"

"Yes, edge over this way and I'll come over to meet you. Leave your negative as it is—we'll be stopped directly. Whatever it is, it's dead ahead. It's a long ways off yet, but we'd better get organized. Wouldn't talk much, either—they may intercept our wave, narrow as it is."

"Better yet, shut off your radio entirely. When we get close enough together, we'll use the hand-language. You may not know that you know it, but you do. Turn your heaviest searchlight toward me—I'll do the same."

There was a click as Dunark's power was shut off abruptly, and Seaton grinned as he cut his own.

"That's right, too, folks. In Osnomian battles we always used a sign-language when we couldn't hear anything—and that was most of the time. I know it as well as I know English, now that I am reminded of the fact."

He shifted his course to intercept that of the Osnomian vessel. After a time the watchers picked out a minute point of light, moving comparatively rapidly against the stars, and knew it to be the searchlight of the *Kondal*. Soon the two vessels were almost side by side, moving cautiously forward, and Seaton set up a sixty-inch parabolic reflector, focused upon a coil. As they went on, the purple light continued to flash more and more rapidly, but still nothing was to be seen.

"Take number six visiplate, will you, Mart? It's telescopic, equivalent to a twenty-inch refractor. I'll tell you where to look in a minute—this reflector increases the power of the regular indicator." He studied meters and adjusted dials. "Set on nineteen hours forty-three minutes, and two hundred seventy-one degrees. He's too far away yet to read exactly, but that'll put him in the field of vision."

"Is this radiation harmful?" asked Margaret.

"Not yet—it's too weak. Pretty soon we may be able to feel it; then I'll throw out a screen against it. When it's strong enough, it's pretty deadly stuff. See anything, Mart?"

"I see something, but it is very indistinct. It is moving in sharper now. Yes, it is a space-ship, shaped like a dirigible airship."

"See it yet, Dunark?" Seaton signaled.

"Just sighted it. Ready to attack?"

"I am not. I'm going to run. Let's go, and go fast!"

Dunark signaled violently, and Seaton shook his head time after time, stubbornly.

"A difficulty?" asked Crane.

"Yes. He wants to go jump on it, but I'm not looking for trouble with any such craft as that—it must be a thousand feet long and is certainly neither Terrestrial nor Osnomian. I say beat it while we're all in one piece. How about it?"

"Absolutely," concurred Crane and both women.

The bar was reversed and the *Skylark* leaped away. The *Kondal* followed, although the observers could see that Dunark was raging. Seaton swung number six visiplate around, looked once, and switched on the radio.

"Well, Dunark," he said grimly. "You get your wish. That bird is coming out, with at least twice the acceleration we could get with both motors full on. He saw us all the time, and was waiting for us."

"Go on—get away if you can. You can stand a higher acceleration than we can. We'll hold him as long as possible."

"I would, if it would do any good, but it won't. He's so much faster than we are that he could catch us anyway, if he wanted to, no matter how much of a start we had—and it looks now as though he wanted us. Two of us stand a lot better chance than one of licking him if he's looking for trouble. Spread out a mile or two, and pretend this is all the speed we've got. What'll we give him first?"

"Give him everything at once. Rays six, seven, eight, nine, and ten...." Crane, with Seaton, began making contacts, rapidly but with precision.

"Heat wave two-seven. Induction, five-eight. Oscillation, everything under point oh six three. All the explosive copper we can get in. Right?"

"Right—and if worse comes to worst, remember the zone of force. Let him shoot first, because he may be peaceable—but it doesn't look like olive branches to me."

"Got both your screens out?"

"Yes. Mart, you might take number two visiplate and work the guns—I'll handle the rest of this stuff. Better strap yourselves in solid, folks—this may develop into a kind of rough party, by the looks of things right now."

As he spoke, a pyrotechnic display enveloped the entire ship as a radiation from the foreign vessel struck the other neutralizing screen and dissipated its force harmlessly in the ether. Instantly Seaton threw on the full power of his refrigerating system and shot in the master switch that actuated the complex offensive armament of his dreadnought of the skies. An intense, livid violet glow hid completely main and auxiliary power bars, and long flashes leaped between metallic objects in all parts of the vessel. The passengers felt each hair striving to stand on end as the very air became more and more highly charged—and this was but the slight corona-loss of the frightful stream of destruction being hurled at the other space-cruiser, now scarcely a mile away!

Seaton stared into number one visiplate, manipulating levers and dials as he drove the *Skylark* hither and yon, dodging frantically, the while the automatic focusing devices remained centered upon the enemy and the enormous generators continued to pour forth their deadly frequencies. The bars glowed more fiercely as they were advanced to full working load—the stranger was one blaze of incandescent ionization, but she still fought on; and Seaton noticed that the pyrometers recording the temperature of the shell were mounting rapidly, in spite of the refrigerators.

"Dunark, put everything you've got upon one spot—right on the end of his nose!"

As the first shell struck the mark, Seaton concentrated every force at his command upon the designated point. The air in the *Skylark* crackled and hissed and intense violet flames leaped from the bars as they were driven almost to the point of disruption. From the forward end of the strange craft there erupted prominence after prominence of searing, unbearable flame as the terrific charges of explosive copper struck the mark and exploded, liberating instantaneously their millions upon millions of kilowatt-hours of intra-atomic energy. Each prominence enveloped all three of the fighting vessels and extended for hundreds of miles out into space—but still the enemy warship continued to hurl forth solid and vibratory destruction.

A brilliant orange light flared upon the panel, and Seaton gasped as he swung his visiplate upon his defenses, which he had supposed impregnable. His outer screen was already down, although its mighty copper generator was exerting its utmost power. Black areas had already appeared and were spreading rapidly, where there should have been only incandescent radiance; and the inner screen was even now radiating far into the ultra-violet and was certainly doomed. Knowing as he did the stupendous power driving those screens, he knew that there were superhuman and inconceivable forces being directed against them, and his right hand flashed to the switch controlling the zone of force. Fast as he was, much happened in the mere moment that passed before his flying hand could close the switch. In the last infinitesimal instant of time before the zone closed in, a gaping black hole appeared in the incandescence of the inner screen, and a small portion of a ray of energy so stupendous as to be palpable, struck, like a tangible projectile, the exposed flank of the *Skylark*. Instantly the refractory arenak turned an intense, dazzling white and more than a foot of the forty-eight-inch skin of the vessel melted away, like snow before an oxy-acetylene flame: melting and flying away in molten globes and sparkling gases—the refrigerating coils lining the hull were of no avail against the concentrated energy of that titanic thrust. As Seaton shut off his power, intense darkness and utter silence closed in, and he snapped on the lights.

"They take one trick!" he blazed, his eyes almost emitting sparks, and leaped for the generators. He had forgotten the efforts of the zone of force, however, and only sprawled grotesquely in the air until he floated within reach of a line.

"Hold everything, Dick!" Crane snapped, as Seaton bent over one of the bars. "What are you going to do?"

"I'm going to put as heavy bars in these ray-generators as they'll stand and go out and get that bird. We can't lick him with Osnomian rays or with our explosive copper, but I can carve that sausage into slices with a zone of force, and I'm going to do it."

"Steady, old man—take it easy. I see your point, but remember that you must release the zone of force before you can use it as a weapon. Furthermore, you must discover his exact location, and must get close enough to him to use the zone as a weapon, all without its protection. Can those ray-screens be made sufficiently powerful to withstand the beam they employed last, even for a second?"

"Hm ... m ... m. Never thought of that, Mart," Seaton replied, the fire dying out of his eyes. "Wonder how long the battle lasted?"

"Eight and two-tenths seconds, from first to last, but they had had that heavy ray in action only a fraction of one second when you cut in the zone of force. Either they underestimated our strength at first, or else it required about eight seconds to tune in their heavy generators—probably the former."

"But we've *got* to do something, man! We can't just sit here and twiddle our thumbs!"

"Why, and why not? That course seems eminently wise and proper. In fact, at the present time, thumb-twiddling is distinctly indicated."

"Oh, you're full of little red ants! We can't do a thing with that zone on—and you say just sit here. Suppose they know all about that zone of force? Suppose they can crack it? Suppose they ram us?"

"I shall take up your objections in order," Crane had lighted a cigarette and was smoking meditatively. "First, they may or may not know about it. At present, that point is immaterial. Second, whether or not they know about it, it is almost a certainty that they cannot crack it. It had been up for more than three minutes, and they have undoubtedly concentrated everything possible upon us during that time. It is still standing. I really expected it to go down in the first few seconds, but now that it has held this long it will, in all probability, continue to hold indefinitely. Third, they most certainly will not ram us, for several reasons. They probably have encountered few, if any, foreign vessels able to stand against them for a minute, and will act accordingly. Then, too, it is probably safe to assume that their vessel is damaged, to some slight extent at least; for I do not believe that any possible armament could withstand the forces you directed against them and escape entirely unscathed. Finally, if they did ram us, what would happen? Would we feel the shock? That barrier in the ether seems impervious, and if so, it could not transmit a blow. I do not see exactly how it would affect the ship dealing the blow. You are the one who works out the new problems in unexplored mathematics—some time you must take a few months off and work it out."

"Yes, it would take that long, too, I guess—but you're right, he can't hurt us. That's using the old bean, Mart! I was going off half-cocked again, darn it! I'll pipe down, and we'll go into a huddle."

Seaton noticed that Dorothy's face was white and that she was fighting for self-control. Drawing himself over to her, he picked her up in a tight embrace.

"Cheer up, Red-Top! This man's war ain't started yet!"

"Not started? What do you mean? Haven't you and Martin just been admitting to each other that you can't do anything? Doesn't that mean that we are beaten?"

"Beaten! Us? How do you get that way? Not on your sweet young life!" he ejaculated, and the surprise on his face was so manifest that she recovered instantly. "We've just dug a hole and pulled the hole in after us, that's all! When we get everything doped out to suit us, we'll snap out of it and that bird'll think he's been petting a wildcat!"

"Mart, you're the thinking end of this partnership," he continued, thoughtfully. "You've got the analytical mind and the judicial disposition, and can think circles around me. From what little you've seen of those folks, tell me who, what, and where they are. I'm getting the germ of an idea, and maybe we can make it work."

"I will try it." Crane paused. "They are, of course, neither from the Earth nor from Osnome. It is also evident that they have solved the secret of intra-atomic energy. Their vessels are not propelled as ours are—they have so perfected that force that it acts upon every particle of the structure and its contents...."

"How do you figure that?" blurted Seaton.

"Because of the acceleration they can stand. Nothing even semi-human, and probably nothing living, could endure it otherwise. Right?"

"Yes—I never thought of that."

"Furthermore, they are far from home, for if they were from anywhere nearby, the Osnomians would have known of them—particularly since it is evident from the size of the vessel that it is not a recent development with them, as it is with us. Since the green system is close to the center of the Galaxy, it seems reasonable, as a working hypothesis, to assume that they are from some system far from the center, perhaps close to the outer edge. They are very evidently of a high degree of intelligence. They are also highly treacherous and merciless...."

"Why?" asked Dorothy, who was listening eagerly.

"I deduce those characteristics from their unprovoked attack upon peaceful ships, vastly smaller and supposedly of inferior armament; and also from the nature of that attack. This vessel is probably a scout or an exploring ship, since it seems to be alone. It is not altogether beyond the bounds of reason to imagine it upon a voyage of discovery, in search of new planets to be subjugated and colonized...."

"That's a sweet picture of our future neighbors—but I guess you're hitting the old nail on the head, at that."

"If these deductions are anywhere nearly correct, they are terrible neighbors. For my next point, are we justified in assuming that they do or do not know about the zone of force?"

"That's a hard one. Knowing what they evidently do know, it's hard to see how they could have missed it. And yet, if they had known about it for a long time, wouldn't they be able to get through it? Of course it may be a real and total barrier in the ether—in that case they'd know that they couldn't do a thing as long as we keep it on. Take your choice, but I believe that they know about it, and know more than we do—that it is a total barrier set up in the ether."

"I agree with you, and we shall proceed upon that assumption. They know, then, that neither they nor we can do anything as long as we maintain the zone—that it is a stalemate. They also know that it takes an enormous amount of power to keep the zone in place. Now we have gone as far as we can go upon the meager data we have—considerably farther than we really are justified in going. We must now try to come to some conclusion concerning their present activities. If our ideas as to their natures are even approximately correct, they are waiting, probably fairly close at hand, until we shall be compelled to release the zone, no matter how long that period of waiting shall be. They know, of course, from our small size, that we cannot carry enough copper to maintain it indefinitely, as they could. Does that sound reasonable?"

"I check you to nineteen decimal places, Mart, and from your ideas I'm getting surer and surer that we can pull their corks. I can get into action in a hurry when I have to, and my idea now is to wait until they relax a trifle, and then slip a fast one over on them. One more bubble out of the old think-tank and I'll let you off for the day. At what time will their vigilance be at lowest ebb? That's a poser, I'll admit, but the answer to it may answer everything—the first shot will, of course, be the best chance we'll ever have."

"Yes, we should succeed in the first attempt. We have very little information to guide us in answering that question." He studied the problem for many minutes before he resumed, "I should say that for a time they would keep all their rays and other weapons in action against the zone of force, expecting us to release it immediately. Then, knowing that they were wasting power uselessly, they would cease attacking, but would be very watchful, with every eye fastened upon us and with every weapon ready for instant use. After this period of vigilance, regular ship's routine would be resumed. Half the force, probably, would go off duty—for, if they are even remotely like any organic beings with which we are familiar, they require sleep or its equivalent at intervals. The men on duty—the normal force, that is—would be doubly careful for a time. Then habit will assert itself, if we have done nothing to create suspicion, and their watchfulness will relax to the point of ordinary careful observation. Toward the end of their watch, because of the strain of the battle and because of the unusually long period of duty, they will become careless, and their vigilance will be considerably below normal. But the exact time of all these things depends entirely upon their conception of time, concerning which we have no information whatever. Though it is purely a speculation, based upon Earthly and Osnomian experience, I should say that after twelve or thirteen hours would come the time for us to make the attack."

"That's good enough for me. Fine, Mart, and thanks. You've probably saved the lives of the party. We will now sleep for eleven or twelve hours."

"Sleep, Dick! How could you?" Dorothy exclaimed.

CHAPTER V

First Blood

The next twelve hours dragged with terrible slowness. Sleep was impossible and eating was difficult, even though all knew that they would have need of the full measure of their strength. Seaton set up various combinations of switching devices connected to electrical timers, and spent hours trying, with all his marvelous quickness of muscular control, to cut shorter and ever shorter the time between the opening and the closing of the switch. At last he arranged a powerful electro-magnetic device so that one impulse would both open and close the switch, with an open period of one one-thousandth of a second. Only then was he satisfied.

"A thousandth is enough to give us a look around, due to persistence of vision; and it is short enough so that they won't see it unless they have a recording observer on us. Even if they still have rays on us, they can't possibly neutralize our screens in that short an exposure. All right, gang? We'll take five visiplates and cover the sphere. If any of you get a glimpse of him, mark the exact spot and outline on the glass. All set?"

He pressed the button. The stars flashed in the black void for an instant, then were again shut out.

"Here he is, Dick!" shrieked Margaret. "Right here—he covered almost half the visiplate!"

She outlined for him, as nearly as she could, the exact position of the object she had seen, and he calculated rapidly.

"Fine business!" he exulted. "He's within half a mile of us, three-quarters on—perfect! I thought he'd be so far away that I'd have to take photographs to locate him. He hasn't a single ray on us, either. That bird's goose is cooked right now, folks, unless every man on watch has his hand right on the controls of a generator and can get into action in less than a tenth of a second! Hang on, gang, I'm going to step on the gas!"

After making sure that everyone was fastened immovably in their seats he strapped himself in the pilot's seat, then set the bar toward the strange vessel and applied fully one-third of its full power. The *Skylark*, of course, did not move. Then, with bewildering rapidity, he went into action; face glued to the visiplate, hands moving faster than the eye could follow—the left closing and opening the switch controlling the zone of force, the right swinging the steering controls to all points of the sphere. The mighty vessel staggered this way and that, jerking and straining terribly as the zone was thrown on and off, lurching sickeningly about the central bearing as the gigantic power of the driving bar was exerted, now in one direction, now in another. After a second or two of this mad gyration, Seaton shut off the power. He then released the zone, after assuring himself that both inner and outer screens were operating at the highest possible rating.

"There, that'll hold 'em for a while, I guess. This battle was even shorter than the other one—and a lot more decisive. Let's turn on the flood-lights and see what the pieces look like."

The lights revealed that the zone of force had indeed sliced the enemy vessel into pieces. No fragment was large enough to be navigable or dangerous and each was sharply cut, as though sheared from its neighbor by some gigantic curved blade. Dorothy sobbed with relief in Seaton's arms as Crane, with one arm around his wife, grasped his hand.

"That was flawless, Dick. As an exhibition of perfect co-ordination and instantaneous timing under extreme physical difficulties, I have never seen its equal."

"You certainly saved all our lives," Margaret added.

"Only fifty-fifty, Peg," Seaton protested, and blushed vividly. "Mart did most of it, you know. I'd have gummed up everything back there if he had let me. Let's see what we can find out about them."

He touched the lever and the *Skylark* moved slowly toward the wreckage, the scattered fragments of which were beginning to move toward and around each other because of their mutual gravitational forces. Snapping on a searchlight, he swung its beam around, and as it settled upon one of the larger sections he saw a group of hooded figures; some of them upon the metal, others floating slowly toward it through space.

"Poor devils—they didn't have a chance," he remarked regretfully. "However, it was either they or we—look out! Sweet spirits of niter!"

He leaped back to the controls and the others were hurled bodily to the floor as he applied the power—for at a signal each of the hooded figures had leveled a tube and once more the outer screen had flamed into incandescence.

As the *Skylark* leaped away, Seaton focussed an attractor upon the one who had apparently signaled the attack. Rolling the vessel over in a short loop, so that the captive was hurled off into space upon the other side, he snatched the tube from the figure's grasp with one auxiliary attractor, and anchored head and limbs with others, so that the prisoner could scarcely move a muscle. Then, while Crane and the women scrambled up off the floor and hurried to the visiplates, Seaton cut in rays six, two-seven, and five-eight. Ray six, "the softener," was a band of frequencies extending from violet far up into the ultra-violet. When driven with sufficient power, this ray destroyed eyesight and nervous tissue, and its power increased still further, actually loosened the molecular structure of matter. Ray two-seven was operated in a range of frequencies far below the visible red. It was pure heat—under its action matter became hotter and hotter as long as it was applied, the upper limit being only the theoretical maximum of temperature. Ray five-eight was high-tension, high-frequency alternating current. Any conductor in its path behaved precisely as it would in the Ajax-Northrup induction furnace, which can boil platinum in ten seconds! These three rays composed the beam which Seaton directed upon the mass of metal from which the enemy had elected to continue the battle—and behind each ray, instead of the small energy at the command of its Osnomian inventor, were the untold millions of kilowatts developed by a one-hundred-pound bar of disintegrating copper!

There ensued a brief but appalling demonstration of the terrible effectiveness of those Osnomian weapons against anything not protected by ultra-powered ray screens. Metal and men—if men they were—literally vanished. One moment they were outlined starkly in the beam; there was a moment of searing, coruscating, blinding light—the next moment the beam bored on into the void, unimpeded. Nothing was visible save an occasional tiny flash, as some condensed or solidified droplet of the volatilized metal re-entered the path of that ravening beam.

"We'll see if there's any more of them loose," Seaton remarked, as he shut off the force and probed into the wreckage with a searchlight.

No sign of life or of activity was revealed, and the light was turned upon the captive. He was held motionless in the invisible grip of the attractors, at the point where the force of those peculiar magnets was exactly balanced by the outward thrust of the repellers. By manipulating the attractor holding it, Seaton brought the strange tubular weapon into the control-room through a small air-lock in the wall and examined it curiously, but did not touch it.

"I never heard of a hand-ray before, so I guess I won't play with it much until after I learn something about it."

"So you have taken a captive?" asked Margaret. "What are you going to do with him?"

"I'm going to drag him in here and read his mind. He's one of the officers of that ship, I believe, and I'm going to find out how to build one exactly like it. This old can is now as obsolete as a 1920 flivver, and I'm going to make us a later model. How about it, Mart, don't we want something really up-to-date if we're going to keep on space-hopping?"

"We certainty do. Those denizens seem to be particularly venomous, and we will not be safe unless we have the most powerful and most efficient space-ship possible. However, that fellow may be dangerous, even now—in fact, it is practically certain that he is."

"You chirped it, ace. I'd much rather touch a pound of dry nitrogen iodide. I've got him spread-eagled so that he can't destroy his brain until after we've read it, though, so there's no particular hurry about him. We'll leave him out there for a while, to waste his sweetness on the desert air. Let's all look around for the *Kondal.* I sure hope they didn't get her in that fracas."

They diffused the rays of eight giant searchlights into a vertical fan, and with it swept slowly through almost a semi-circle before anything was seen. Then there was revealed a cluster of cylindrical objects amid a mass of wreckage, which Crane recognized at once.

"The *Kondal* is gone, Dick. There is what is left of her, and most of her cargo of salt, in jute bags."

As he spoke, a series of green flashes played upon the bags, and Seaton yelled in relief.

"They got the ship all right, but Dunark and Sitar got away—they're still with their salt!"

The *Skylark* moved over to the wreck and Seaton, relinquishing the controls to Crane, donned a vacuum suit, entered the main air-lock and snapped on the motor which sealed off the lock, pumped the air into a pressure-tank, and opened the outside door. He threw a light line to the two figures and pushed himself lightly toward them. He then talked briefly to Dunark in the hand-language, and handed the end of the line to Sitar, who held it while the two men explored the fragments of the strange vessel, gathering up various things of interest as they came upon them.

Back in the control-room, Dunark and Sitar let their pressure decrease gradually to that of the terrestrial vessel and removed the face-plates from their helmets.

"Again, oh Karfedo of Earth, we thank you for our lives," Dunark began, gasping for breath, when Seaton leaped to the air-gauge with a quick apology.

"Never thought of the effect our atmospheric pressure would have on you two. We can stand yours all right, but you'd pretty nearly pass out on ours. There, that'll suit you better. Didn't you throw out your zone of force?"

"Yes, as soon as I saw that our screens were not going to hold." The Osnomians' labored breathing became normal as the air-pressure increased to a value only a little below that of the dense atmosphere of their native planet. "I then increased the power of the screens to the extreme limit and opened the zone for a moment to see how the screens would hold with the added power. That instant was enough. In that period a concentrated beam, such as I had no idea could ever be generated, went through the outer and inner screens as though they were not there, through the four-foot arenak of the hull, through the entire central installation, and through the hull on the other side. Sitar and I were wearing suits...."

"Say, Mart, that's one bet we overlooked. It's a good idea, too—those strangers wore them all the time as regular equipment, apparently. Next time we get into a jam, be sure we do it; they might come in handy. Excuse me, Dunark—go ahead."

"We had suits on, so as soon as the ray was shut off, which was almost instantly, I phoned the crew to jump, and we leaped out through the hole in the hull. The air rushing out gave us an impetus that carried us many miles out into space, and it required many hours for the slight attraction of the mass here to draw us back to it. We just got back a few minutes ago. That air-blast is probably what saved us, as they destroyed our vessel with atomic bombs and hunted down the four men of our crew, who stayed comparatively close to the scene. They rayed you for about an hour with the most stupendous beams imaginable—no such generators have ever been considered possible of construction—but couldn't make any impression upon you. Then they shut off their power and stood by, waiting. I wasn't looking at you when you released your zone. One moment it was there, and the next, the stranger had been cut in pieces. The rest you know."

"We're sure glad you two got away, Dunark. Well, Mart, what say we drag that guy in and give him the once-over?"

Seaton swung the attractors holding the prisoner until they were in line with the main air-lock, then reduced the power of the repellers. As he approached the lock various controls were actuated, and soon the stranger stood in the control room, held immovable against one wall, while Crane, with a 0.50-caliber elephant gun, stood against the other.

"Perhaps you girls should go somewhere else," suggested Crane.

"Not on your life!" protested Dorothy, who, eyes wide and flushed with excitement, stood near a door, with a heavy automatic pistol in her hand. "I wouldn't miss this for a farm!"

"Got him solid," declared Seaton, after a careful inspection of the various attractors and repellers he had bearing upon the prisoner, "Now let's get him out of that suit. No—better read his air first, temperature and pressure—might analyze it, too."

Nothing could be seen of the person of the stranger, since he was encased in vacuum armor, but it was plainly evident that he was very short and immensely broad and thick. By means of hollow needles forced through the leather-like material of the suit Seaton drew off a sample of the atmosphere within, into an Orsat apparatus, while Crane made pressure and temperature readings.

"Temperature, one hundred ten degrees. Pressure, twenty-eight pounds—about the same as ours is, now that we have stepped it up to keep the Osnomians from suffering."

Seaton soon reported that the atmosphere was quite similar to that of the *Skylark*, except that it was much higher in carbon dioxide and carried an extremely high percentage of water vapor. He took up a pair of heavy shears and laid the suit open full length, on both sides, knowing that the powerful attractors would hold the stranger immovable. He then wrenched off the helmet and cast the whole suit aside, revealing the enemy officer, clad in a tunic of scarlet silk.

He was less than five feet tall. His legs were merely blocks, fully as great in diameter as they were in length, supporting a torso of Herculean dimensions. His arms were as large as a strong man's thigh and hung almost to the floor. His astounding shoulders, fully a yard across, merged into and supported an enormous head. The being possessed recognizable nose, ears, and mouth; and the great domed forehead and huge cranium bespoke an immense and a highly developed brain.

But it was the eyes of this strange creature that fixed and held the attention. Large they were, and black—the dull, opaque, lusterless black of platinum sponge. The pupils were a brighter black, and in them flamed ruby lights: pitiless, mocking, cold. Plainly to be read in those sinister depths were the untold wisdom of unthinkable age, sheer ruthlessness, mighty power, and ferocity unrelieved. His baleful gaze swept from one member of the party to another, and to meet the glare of those eyes was to receive a tangible physical blow—it was actually ponderable force; that of embodied hardness and of ruthlessness incarnate, generated in that merciless brain and hurled forth through those flame-shot, Stygian orbs.

"If you don't need us for anything, Dick, I think Peggy and I will go upstairs," Dorothy broke the long silence.

"Good idea, Dot. This isn't going to be pretty to watch—or to do, either, for that matter."

"If I stay here another minute I'll see that thing as long as I live; and I might be very ill. Goodbye," and heartless and bloodthirsty Osnomian though she was, Sitar had gone to join the two Terrestrial women.

"I didn't want to say much before the girls, but I want to check a couple of ideas with you two. Don't you think it's a safe bet that this bird reported back to his headquarters?"

"I have been thinking that very thing," Crane spoke gravely, and Dunark nodded agreement. "Any race capable of developing such a vessel as this would almost certainly have developed systems of communication in proportion."

"That's the way I doped it out—and that's why I'm going to read his mind, if I have to burn out his brain to do it. We've got to know how far away from home he is, whether he has turned in any report about us, and all about it. Also, I'm going to get the plans, power, and armament of their most modern ships, if he knows them, so that your gang, Dunark, can build us one like them; because the next boat that tackles us will be warned and we won't be able to take it by surprise. We won't stand a chance in the *Skylark*. With a ship like theirs, however, we can run—or we can fight, if we have to. Any other ideas, fellows?"

As neither Crane nor Dunark had any other suggestions to offer, Seaton brought out the mechanical educator, watching the creature's eyes narrowly. As he placed one headset over that motionless head the captive sneered in pure contempt, but when the case was opened and the array of tubes and transformers was revealed, that expression disappeared; and when he added a super-power stage by cutting in a heavy-duty transformer and a five-kilowatt transmitting tube, Seaton thought that he saw an instantaneously suppressed flicker of doubt or fear.

"That headset thing was child's play to him, but he doesn't like the looks of this other stuff at all. I don't blame him a bit—I wouldn't like to be on the receiving end of this hook-up myself. I'm going to put him on the recorder and on the visualizer," Seaton continued as he connected spools of wire and tape, lamps, and lenses in an intricate system and donned a headset. "I'd hate to have much of that brain in my own skull—afraid I'd bite myself. I'm just going to look on, and when I see anything I want, I'll grab it and put it into my own brain. I'm starting off easy, not using the big tube."

He closed several switches, lights flashed, and the wires and tapes began to feed through the magnets.

"Well, I've got his language, folks, he seemed to want me to have it. It's got a lot of stuff in it that I can't understand yet, though, so guess I'll give him some English."

He changed several connections and the captive spoke, in a profoundly deep bass voice.

"You may as well discontinue your attempt, for you will gain no information from me. That machine of yours was out of date with us thousands of years ago."

"Save your breath or talk sense," said Seaton, coldly. "I gave you English so that you can give me the information I want. You already know what it is. When you get ready to talk, say so, or throw it on the screen of your own accord. If you don't, I'll put on enough voltage to burn your brain out. Remember, I can read your dead brain as well as though it were alive, but I want your thoughts, as well as your knowledge, and I'm going to have them. If you give them voluntarily, I will tinker up a lifeboat that you can navigate back to your own world and let you go; if you resist I intend getting them anyway and you shall not leave this vessel alive. You may take your choice."

"You are childish, and that machine is impotent against my will. I could have defied it a hundred years ago, when I was barely a grown man. Know you, American, that we supermen of the Fenachrone are as far above any of the other and lesser breeds of beings who spawn in their millions in their countless myriads of races upon the numberless planets of the Universe as you are above the inert metal from which this, your ship, was built. The Universe is ours, and in due course we shall take it—just as in due course I shall take this vessel. Do your worst; I shall not speak." The creature's eyes flamed, hurling a wave of hypnotic command through Seaton's eyes and deep into his brain. Seaton's very senses reeled for an instant under the impact of that awful mental force; but after a short, intensely bitter struggle he threw off the spell.

"That was close, fellow, but you didn't quite ring the bell," he said grimly, staring directly into those unholy eyes. "I may rate pretty low mentally, but I can't be hypnotized into turning you loose. Also I can give you cards and spades in certain other lines which I am about to demonstrate. Being superman didn't keep the rest of your men from going out in my ray, and being a superman isn't going to save your brain. I am not depending upon my intellectual or mental force—I've got an ace in the hole in the shape of five thousand volts to apply to the most delicate centers of your brain. Start giving me what I want, and start quick, or I'll tear it out of you."

The giant did not answer, merely glared defiance and bitter hate.

"Take it, then!" Seaton snapped, and cut in the super-power stage and began turning dials and knobs, exploring that strange mind for the particular area in which he was most interested. He soon found it, and cut in the visualizer—the stereographic device, in parallel with Solon's own brain recorder, which projected a three-dimensional picture into the "viewing-area" or dark space of the cabinet. Crane and Dunark, tense and silent, looked on in strained suspense as, minute after minute, the silent battle of wills raged. Upon one side was a horrible and gigantic brain, of undreamed of power; upon the other side a strong man, fighting for all that life holds dear, wielding against that monstrous and frightful brain a weapon wrought of high-tension electricity, applied with all the skill that earthly and Osnomian science could devise.

Seaton crouched over the amplifier, his jaw set and every muscle taut, his eyes leaping from one meter to another, his right hand slowly turning up the potentiometer which was driving more and ever more of the searing, torturing output of his super-power tube into that stubborn brain. The captive was standing utterly rigid, eyes closed, every sense and faculty mustered to resist that cruelly penetrant attack upon the very innermost recesses of his mind. Crane and Dunark scarcely breathed as the three-dimensional picture in the visualizer varied from a blank to the hazy outlines of a giant space-cruiser. It faded out as the unknown exerted himself to withstand that poignant inquisition, only to come back in, clearer than before, as Seaton advanced the potentiometer still farther. Finally, flesh and blood could no longer resist that lethal probe and the picture became sharp and clear. It showed the captain—for he was no less an officer than the commander of the vessel—at a great council table, seated, together with many other officers, upon very low, enormously strong metal stools. They were receiving orders from their Emperor; orders plainly understood by Crane and the Osnomian alike, for thought needs no translation.

"Gentlemen of the Navy," the ruler spoke solemnly, "Our preliminary expedition, returned some time ago, achieved its every aim, and we are now ready to begin fulfilling our destiny, the Conquest of the Universe. This Galaxy comes first. Our base of operations will be the largest planet of that group of brilliant green suns, for they can be seen from any point in the Galaxy and are almost in the exact center of it. Our astronomers," here the captain's thoughts shifted briefly to an observatory far out in space for perfect seeing, and portrayed a reflecting telescope with a mirror five miles in diameter, capable of penetrating unimaginable myriads of light-years into space, "have tabulated all the suns, planets, and satellites belonging to this Galaxy, and each of you has been given a complete chart and assigned a certain area which he is to explore. Remember, gentlemen, that this first major expedition is to be purely one of exploration; the one of conquest will set out after you have returned with complete information. You will each report by torpedo every tenth of the year. We do not anticipate any serious difficulty, as we are of course the highest type of life in the Universe; nevertheless, in the unlikely event of trouble, report it. We shall do the rest. In conclusion, I warn you again—let no people know that we exist. Make no conquests, and destroy all who by any chance may see you. Gentlemen, go with power."

The captain embarked in a small airboat and was shot to his vessel. He took his station at an immense control board and the warship shot off instantly, with unthinkable velocity, and with not the slightest physical shock.

At this point Seaton made the captain take them all over the ship. They noted its construction, its power-plant, its controls—every minute detail of structure, operation, and maintenance was taken from the captain's mind and was both recorded and visualized.

The journey seemed to be a very long one, but finally the cluster of green suns became visible and the Fenachrone began to explore the solar systems in the area assigned to that particular vessel. Hardly had the survey started, however, when the two globular space-cruisers were detected and located. The captain stopped the ship briefly, then attacked. They watched the attack, and saw the destruction of the *Kondal*. They looked on while the captain read the brain of one of Dunark's crew, gleaning from it all the facts concerning the two space-ships, and thought with him that the two absentees from the *Kondal* would drift back in a few hours, and would be disposed of in due course. They learned that these things were automatically impressed upon the torpedo next to issue, as was every detail of everything that happened in and around the vessel. They watched him impress a thought of his own upon the record—"the inhabitants of planet three of sun six four seven three Pilarone show unusual development and may cause trouble, as they have already brought knowledge of the metal of power and of the impenetrable shield to the Central System, which is to be our base. Recommend volatilization of this planet by vessel sent on special mission." They saw the raying of the *Skylark*. They sensed him issue commands:

"Ray it for a time; he will probably open the shield for a moment, as the other one did," then, after a time skipped over by the mind under examination. "Cease raying—no use wasting power. He must open eventually, as he runs out of power. Stand by and destroy him when he opens."

The scene shifted. The captain was asleep and was awakened by an alarm gong—only to find himself floating in a mass of wreckage. Making his way to the fragment of his vessel containing the torpedo port, he released the messenger, which flew, with ever-increasing velocity, back to the capital city of the Fenachrone, carrying with it a record of everything that had happened.

"That's what I want," thought Seaton. "Those torpedoes went home, fast. I want to know how far they have to go and how long it'll take them to get there. You know what distance a parsec is, since it is purely a mathematical concept; and you must have a watch or some similar instrument with which we can translate your years into ours. I don't want to have to kill you, fellow, and if you'll give up even now I'll spare you. I'll get it anyway, you know—and you also know that a few hundred volts more will kill you."

They saw the thought received, and saw its answer: "You shall learn no more. This is the most important of all, and I shall hold it to disintegration and beyond."

Seaton advanced the potentiometer still farther, and the brain picture waxed and waned, strengthened and faded. Finally, however, it was revealed by flashes that the torpedo had about a hundred and fifty-five thousand parsecs to go and that it would take two-tenths of a year to make the journey; that the warships which would come in answer to the message were as fast as the torpedo; that he did indeed have in his suit a watch—a device of seven dials, each turning ten times as fast as its successor; and that one turn of the slowest dial measured one year of his time. Seaton instantly threw off his headset and opened the power switch.

"Grab a stopwatch quick, Mart!" he called, as he leaped to the discarded vacuum suit and searched out the peculiar timepiece. They noted the exact time consumed by one complete revolution of one of the dials, and calculated rapidly.

"Better than I thought!" exclaimed Seaton. "That makes his year about four hundred ten of our days. That gives us eighty-two days before the torpedo gets there—longer than I'd dared hope. We've got to fight, too, not run. They figure on getting the *Skylark*, then volatilizing our world. Well, we can take time enough to grab off an absolutely complete record of this guy's brain. We'll need it for what's coming, and I'm going to get it, if I have to kill him to do it."

He resumed his place at the educator, turned on the power, and a shadow passed over his face.

"Poor devil, he's conked out—couldn't stand the gaff," he remarked, half-regretfully. "However that makes it easy to get what we want, and we'd have had to kill him anyway, I guess—Bad as it is, I'd hate to bump him off in cold blood."

He threaded new spools into the machine, and for three hours, mile after mile of tape sped between the magnets as Seaton explored every recess of that monstrous, yet stupendous brain.

"Well, that's that," he declared finally, as, the last bit of information gleaned and recorded upon the flying tape, he removed the body of the Fenachrone captain into space and rayed it out of existence. "Now what to do?"

"How can we get this salt to Osnome?" asked Dunark whose thoughts were never far from that store of the precious chemical. "You are already crowded, and Sitar and I will crowd you still more. You have no room for additional cargo, and yet much valuable time would be lost in going to Osnome for another vessel."

"Yes, and we've got to get a lot of 'X', too. Guess we'll have to take time to get another vessel. I'd like to drag in the pieces of that ship, too—his instruments and a lot of the parts could be used."

"Why not do it all at once?" suggested Crane. "We can start that whole mass toward Osnome by drawing it behind us until such a velocity has been attained that it will reach there at the desired time. We could then go to 'X,' and overtake this material near the green system."

"Right you are, ace—that's a sound idea. But say, Dunark, it wouldn't be good technique for you to eat our food for any length of time. While we're figuring this out you'd better hop over there and bring over enough to last you two until we get you home. Give it to Shiro—after a couple of lessons, you'll find he'll be as good as any of your cooks."

Faster and faster the *Skylark* flew, pulling behind her the mass of wreckage, held by every available attractor. When the calculated velocity had been attained, the attractors were shut off and the vessel darted away toward that planet, still in the Carboniferous Age, which possessed at least one solid ledge of metallic "X," the rarest of all earthly metals. As the automatic controls held the cruiser upon her course, the six wanderers sat long in discussion as to what should be done, what could be done, to avert the threatened destruction of all the civilization of the Galaxy except the monstrous and unspeakable culture of the Fenachrone. Nearing their destination, Seaton rose to his feet.

"Well, folks, it's like this. We've got our backs to the wall. Dunark has troubles of his own—if the Third Planet doesn't get him the Fenachrone will, and the Third Planet is the more pressing danger. That lets him out. We've got nearly six months before the Fenachrone can get back here...."

"But how can they possibly find us here, or wherever we'll be by that time, Dick?" asked Dorothy. "The battle was a long way from here."

"With that much start they probably couldn't find us," Seaton replied soberly. "It's the world I'm thinking about. They've got to be stopped, and stopped cold—and we've got only six months to do it in.... Osnome's got the best tools and the fastest workmen I know of...." his voice died away in thought.

"That sort of thing is in your department, Dick."

Crane was calm and judicial as always. "I will, of course, do anything I can. But you probably have a plan of campaign already laid out?"

"After a fashion. We've got to find out how to work through this zone of force or we're sunk without a trace. Even with rays, screens, and ships equal to theirs, we couldn't keep them from sending a vessel to destroy the earth; and they'd probably get us too, eventually. They've got a lot of stuff we don't know about, of course, since I took only one man's mind. While he was a very able man, he didn't know all that all the rest of them do, any more than any one man has all the earthly science known. Absolutely our only chance is to control that zone—it's the only thing they haven't got. Of course, it may be impossible, but I won't believe that, until I've exhausted a lot of possibilities. Dunark, can you spare a crew to build us a duplicate of that Fenachrone ship, besides those you are going to build for yourself?"

"Certainly. I will be only too glad to do so."

"Well, then, while Dunark is doing that, I suggest that we go to this Third Planet, abduct a few of their leading scientists, and read their minds. Then do the same, visiting every other highly advanced planet we can locate. There is a good chance that, by combining the best points of the warfares of many worlds, we can evolve something that will enable us to turn back these invaders."

"Why not send a copper torpedo to destroy their entire planet?" suggested Dunark.

"Wouldn't work. Their detecting screens would locate it a thousand million miles off in space, and they would ray it. With a zone of force that would get through their screens, that would be the first thing I'd do. You see, every thought comes back to that zone. We've got to get through it some way."

The course alarm sounded, and they saw that a planet lay directly in their path. It was "X," and enough negative acceleration was applied to make an easy landing possible.

"Isn't it going to be a long, slow job, chopping off two tons of that metal and fighting away those terrible animals besides?" asked Margaret.

"It'll take about a millionth of a second, Peg. I'm going to bite it off with the zone, just as I took that bite out of our field. The rotation of the planet will throw us away from the surface, then we'll release the zone and drag our prey off with us. See?"

The *Skylark* descended rapidly toward that well-remembered ledge of metal to which the object compass had led them.

"This is exactly where we landed before," Margaret commented in surprise, and Dorothy added:

"Yes, and there's that horrible tree that ate the dinosaur or whatever it was. I thought you blew it up for me, Dick?"

"I did, Dottie—blew it into atoms. Must be a good location for carnivorous trees—and they must grow awfully fast, too. As to its being the same place, Peg—sure it is. That's what object compasses are for."

Everything appeared as it had been at the time of their first visit. The rank Carboniferous vegetation, intensely, vividly green, was motionless in the still, hot, heavy air; the living nightmares inhabiting that primitive world were lying in the cooler depths of the jungle, sheltered from the torrid rays of that strange and fervent sun.

"How about it, Dot? Want to see some of your little friends again? If you do, I'll give them a shot and bring them out."

"Heavens, no! I saw them once—if I never see them again, that will be twenty minutes too soon!"

"All right—we'll grab us a piece of this ledge and beat it."

Seaton lowered the vessel to the ledge, focussed the main anchoring attractor upon it, and threw on the zone of force. Almost immediately he released the zone, pointed the bar parallel to the compass bearing upon Osnome, and slowly applied the power.

"How much did you take, anyway?" asked Dunark in amazement. "It looks bigger than the *Skylark*!"

"It is; considerably bigger. Thought we might as well take enough while we're here, so I set the zone for a seventy-five-foot radius. It's probably of the order of magnitude of half a million tons, since the stuff weighs more than half a ton to the cubic foot. However, we can handle it as easily as we could a smaller bite, and that much mass will help us hold that other stuff together when we catch up with it."

The voyage to Osnome was uneventful. They overtook the wreckage, true to schedule, as they were approaching the green system, and attached it to the mass of metal behind them by means of attractors.

"Where'll we land this junk, Dunark?" asked Seaton, as Osnome grew large beneath them. "We'll hold this lump of metal and the fragment of the ship carrying the salt; and we'll be able to hold some of the most important of the other stuff. But a lot of it is bound to get away from us—and the Lord help anybody who's under it when it comes down! You might yell for help—and say, you might ask somebody to have that astronomical data ready for us as soon as we land."

"The parade ground will be empty now, so we will land there," Dunark replied. "We should be able to land everything in a field of that size, I should think." He touched the sender at his belt, and in the general code notified the city of their arrival and warned everyone to keep away from the parade ground. He then sent several messages in the official code, concluding by asking that one or two space-ships come out and help lower the burden to the ground. As the peculiar, pulsating chatter of the Osnomian telegraph died out, Seaton called for help.

"Come here, you two, and grab some of these attractors. I need about twelve hands to keep this plunder in the straight and narrow path."

The course had been carefully laid, with allowance for the various velocities and forces involved, to follow the easiest path to the Kondalian parade ground. The hemisphere of "X" and the fragment of the *Kondal* which bore the salt were held immovably in place by the main attractor and one auxiliary; and many other auxiliaries held sections of the Fenachrone vessel. However, the resistance of the air seriously affected the trajectory of many of the irregularly shaped smaller masses of metal, and all three men were kept busy flicking attractors right and left; capturing those strays which threatened to veer off into the streets or upon the buildings of the Kondalian capital city, and shifting from one piece to another so that none should fall freely. Two sister-ships of the *Kondal* appeared as if by magic in answer to Dunark's call, and their attractors aided greatly in handling the unruly collection of wreckage. A few of the smaller sections and a shower of debris fell clear, however, in spite of all efforts, and their approach was heralded by a meteoric display unprecedented in that world of continuous daylight.

As the three vessels with their cumbersome convoy dropped down into the lower atmosphere, the guns of the city roared a welcome; banners and pennons waved; the air became riotous with color from hundreds of projectors and odorous with a bewildering variety of scents; while all around them played numberless aircraft of all descriptions and sizes. The space below them was carefully avoided, but on all sides and above them the air was so full that it seemed marvelous that no collision occurred. Tiny one-man helicopters, little more than single chairs flying about; beautiful pleasure-planes, soaring and wheeling; immense multiplane liners and giant helicopter freighters—everything in the air found occasion to fly as near as possible to the Skylark in order to dip their flags in salute to Dunark, their Kofedix, and to Seaton, the wearer of the seven disks—their revered Overlord.

Finally the freight was landed without serious mishap and the *Skylark* leaped to the landing dock upon the palace roof, where the royal family and many nobles were waiting, in full panoply of glittering harness. Dunark and Sitar disembarked and the four others stepped out and stood at attention as Seaton addressed Roban, the Karfedix.

"Sir, we greet you, but we cannot stop, even for a moment. You know that only the most urgent necessity would make us forego the pleasure of a brief rest beneath your roof—the Kofedix will presently give you the measure of that dire need. We shall endeavor to return soon. Greetings, and, for a time, farewell."

"Overlord, we greet you, and trust that soon we may entertain you and profit from your companionship. For what you have done, we thank you. May the great First Cause smile upon you until your return. Farewell."

CHAPTER VI

The Peace Conference

"Here's a chart of the green system, Mart, with all the motions and the rest of the dope that they've been able to get. How'd it be for you to navigate us over to the third planet of the fourteenth sun?"

"While you build a Fenachrone super-generator?"

"Right, the first time. Your deducer is hitting on all eight, as usual. That big ray is hot stuff, and their ray-screen is something to write home about, too."

"How can their rays be any hotter than ours, Dick?" Dorothy asked curiously. "I thought you said we had the very last word in rays."

"I thought we had, but those birds we met back there spoke a couple of later words. Their rays work on an entirely different system than the one we use. They generate an extremely short carrier wave, like the Millikan cosmic ray, by recombining some of the electrons and protons of their disintegrating metal, and upon this wave they impose a pure heat frequency of terrific power. The Millikan rays will penetrate anything except a special ray screen or a zone of force, and carry with them—somewhat as radio frequencies carry sound frequencies—the heat rays, which volatilize anything they touch. Their ray screens are a lot better than ours, too—they generate the entire spectrum. It's a sweet system and when we revamp ours so as to be just like it, we'll be able to talk turkey to those folks on the third planet."

"How long will it take you to build it?" asked Crane, who, dexterously turning the pages of "Vega's Handbuch" was calculating their course.

"A day or so—maybe less. I've got all the stuff and with my Osnomian tools it won't take long. If you find you'll get there before I get done, you'll have to loaf a while—kill a little time."

"Are you going to connect the power plant to operate on the entire vessel and all its contents?"

"No—can't do it without redesigning the whole thing and that's hardly worth while for the short time we'll use this old bus."

Building those generators would have been a long and difficult task for a corps of earthly mechanics and electricians, but to Seaton it was merely a job. The "shop" had been enlarged and had been filled to capacity with Osnomian machinery; machine tools that were capable of performing automatically and with the utmost precision and speed any conceivable mechanical operation. He put a dozen of them to work, and before the vessel reached its destination, the new offensive and defensive weapons had been installed and thoroughly tested. He had added a third screen-generator, so that now, in addition to the four-foot hull of arenak and the repellers, warding off any material projectile, the Skylark was also protected by an outer, an intermediate, and an inner ray-screen; each driven by the super-power of a four-hundred-pound bar and each covering the entire spectrum—capable of neutralizing any dangerous frequency known to those master-scientists, the Fenachrone.

As the *Skylark* approached the planet, Seaton swung number six visiplate upon it, and directed their flight toward a great army base. Darting down upon it, he snatched an officer into the airlock, closed the door, and leaped back into space. He brought the captive into the control room pinioned by auxiliary attractors, and relieved him of his weapons. He then rapidly read his mind, encountering no noticeable resistance, released the attractors, and addressed him in his own language.

"Please be seated, lieutenant," Seaton said courteously, motioning him to one of the seats. "We come in peace. Please pardon my discourtesy in handling you, but it was necessary in order to learn your language and thus to get in touch with your commanding officer."

The officer, overcome with astonishment that he had not been killed instantly, sank into the seat indicated, without a reply, and Seaton went on:

"Please be kind enough to signal your commanding officer that we are coming down at once, for a peace conference. By the way, I can read your signals, and will send them myself if necessary."

The stranger worked an instrument attached to his harness briefly, and the *Skylark* descended slowly toward the fortress.

"I know, of course, that your vessels will attack," Seaton remarked, as he noted a crafty gleam in the eyes of the officer. "I intend to let them use all their power for a time, to prove to them the impotence of their weapons. After that, I shall tell you what to say to them."

"Do you think this is altogether safe, Dick?" asked Crane as they saw a fleet of gigantic airships soaring upward to meet them.

"Nothing sure but death and taxes," returned Seaton cheerfully, "but don't forget that we've got Fenachrone armament now, instead of Osnomian. I'm betting that they can't begin to drive their rays through even our outer screen. And even if our outer screen should begin to go into the violet—I don't think it will even go cherry-red—out goes our zone of force and we automatically go up where no possible airship can reach. Since their only space-ships are rocket driven, and of practically no maneuverability, they stand a big chance of getting to us. Anyway, we must get in touch with them, to find out if they know anything we don't, and this is the only way I know of to do it. Besides, I want to head Dunark off from wrecking this world. They're exactly the same kind of folks he is, you notice, and I don't like civil war. Any suggestions? Keep an eye on that bird, then, Mart, and we'll go down."

The *Skylark* dropped down into the midst of the fleet, which instantly turned against her the full force of their giant guns and their immense ray batteries. Seaton held the *Skylark* motionless, staring into his visiplate, his right hand grasping the zone-switch.

"The outer screen isn't even getting warm!" he exulted after a moment. The repellers were hurling the shells back long before they reached even the outer screen, and they were exploding harmlessly in the air. The full power of the ray-generators, too, which had been so destructive to the Osnomian defenses, were only sufficient to bring the outer screen to a dull red glow. After fifteen minutes of passive acceptance of all the airships could do, Seaton spoke to the captive.

"Sir, please signal the commanding officer of vessel seven-two-four that I am going to cut it in two in the middle. Have him remove all men in that part of the ship to the ends, and have parachutes in readiness, as I do not wish to cause any loss of life."

The signal was sent, and, as the officer was already daunted by the fact that their utmost efforts could not even make the strangers' screens radiate, it was obeyed. Seaton then threw on the frightful power of the Fenachrone super-generators. The defensive screens of the doomed warship flashed once—a sparkling, coruscating display of incandescent brilliance—and in the same instant went down. Simultaneously the entire midsection of the vessel exploded into light and disappeared; completely volatilized.

"Sir, please signal the entire fleet to cease action, and to follow me down. If they do not do so, I will destroy the rest of them."

The *Skylark* dropped to the ground, followed by the fleet of warships, who settled in a ring about her—inactive, but ready.

"Will you please loan me your sending instrument, sir?" Seaton asked. "From this point on I can carry on negotiations better direct than through you."

The lieutenant found his voice as he surrendered the instrument.

"Sir, are you the Overlord of Osnome, of whom we have heard? We had supposed that one was a mythical character, but you must be he—no one else would spare lives that he could take, and the Overlord is the only being reputed to have a skin the color of yours."

"Yes, lieutenant, I am the Overlord—and I have decided to become the Overlord of the entire green system, as well as of Osnome."

He then sent out a call to the commander-in-chief of all the armies of the planet, informing him that he was coming to visit him at once, and the *Skylark* tore through the air to the capital city. No sooner had the earthly vessel alighted upon the palace grounds than she was surrounded by a ring of warships who, however, made no offensive move. Seaton again used the telegraph.

"Commander-in-Chief of the armed forces of the planet Urvania; greetings from the Overlord of this solar system. I invite you to come into my vessel, unarmed and alone, for a conference. I come in peace and, peace or war as you decide, no harm shall come to you, until after you have returned to your own command. Think well before you reply."

"If I refuse?"

"I shall destroy one of the vessels surrounding me, and shall continue to destroy them, one every ten seconds, until you agree to come. If you still do not agree. I shall destroy all the armed forces upon this planet, then destroy all your people who are at present upon Osnome. I wish to avoid bloodshed and destruction, but I can and I will do as I have said."

"I will come."

The general came out upon the field unarmed, escorted by a company of soldiers. A hundred feet from the vessel he halted the guards and came on alone, erect and soldierly. Seaton met him at the door and invited him to be seated.

"What can you have to say to me?" the general demanded, disregarding the invitation.

"Many things. First, let me say that you are not only a brave man; you are a wise general—your visit to me proves it."

"It is a sign of weakness, but I believed when I heard those reports, and still believe, that a refusal would have resulted in a heavy loss of our men," was the General's reply.

"It would have," said Seaton. "I repeat that your act was not weakness, but wisdom. The second thing I have to say is that I had not planned on taking any active part in the management of things, either upon Osnome or upon this planet, until I learned of a catastrophe that is threatening all the civilization in this Galaxy—thus threatening my own distant world as well as those of this solar system. Third, only by superior force can I make either your race or the Osnomians listen to reason sufficiently to unite against a common foe. You have been reared in unreasoning hatred for so many generations that your minds are warped. For that reason I have assumed control of this entire system, and shall give you your choice between co-operating with us or being rendered incapable of molesting us while our attention is occupied by this threatened invasion."

"We will have no traffic with the enemy whatever." said the general. "This is final."

"You just think so. Here is a mathematical statement of what is going to happen to your world, unless I intervene." He handed the general a drawing of Dunark's plan and described it in detail. "That is the answer of the Osnomians to your invasion of their planet. I do not want this world destroyed, but if you refuse to make common cause with us against a common foe, it may be necessary. Have you forces at your command sufficient to frustrate this plan?"

"No; but I cannot really believe that such a deflection of celestial bodies is possible. Possible or not, you realize that I could not yield to empty threats."

"Of course not," said Seaton, "but you were wise enough to refuse to sacrifice a few ships and men in a useless struggle against my overwhelming armament, therefore you are certainly wise enough to refuse to sacrifice your entire race. However, before you come to any definite conclusion, I will show you what threatens the Galaxy."

He handed the other a headset and ran through the section of the record showing the plans of the invaders. He then ran a few sections showing the irresistible power at the command of the Fenachrone.

"That is what awaits us all unless we combine against them."

"What are your requirements?" the general asked.

"I request immediate withdrawal of all your armed forces now upon Osnome and full co-operation with me in this coming war against the invaders. In return, I will give you the secrets I have just given the Osnomians—the power and the offensive and defensive weapons of this vessel."

"The Osnomians are now building vessels such as this one?" asked the general.

"They are building vessels a hundred times the size of this one, with the same armament."

"For myself, I would agree to your terms. However, the word of the Emperor is law."

"I understand," replied Seaton. "Would you be willing to seek an immediate audience with him? I would suggest that both you and he accompany me, and we shall hold a peace conference with the Osnomian Emperor and Commander-in-Chief upon this vessel. We shall be gone less than a day."

"I shall do so at once."

"You may accompany your general, lieutenant. Again I ask pardon for my necessary rudeness."

As the Urvanian officers hurried toward the palace, the other Terrestrials, who had been listening in from another room, entered.

"It sounded as though you convinced him, Dick; but that language is nothing like Kondalian. Why don't you teach it to us? Teach it to Shiro, too, so he can cook for, and talk to, our distinguished guests intelligently, if they're going back with us."

As he connected up the educator, Seaton explained what had happened, and concluded:

"I want to stop this civil war, keep Dunark from destroying this planet, preserve Osnome for Osnomians, and make them all co-operate with us against the Fenachrone. That's one tall order, since these folks haven't the remotest notion of anything except killing."

A company of soldiers approached, and Dorothy got up hastily.

"Stick around, folks. We can all talk to them."

"I believe that it would be better for you to be alone," Crane decided, after a moment's thought. "They are used to autocratic power, and can understand nothing but one-man control. The girls and I will keep out of it."

"That might be better at that," and Seaton went to the door to welcome the guests. Seaton instructed them to lie flat, and put on all the acceleration they could bear. It was not long until they were back in Kondal, where Roban, the Karfedix, and Tarnan, the Karbix, accepted Seaton's invitation and entered the Skylark, unarmed. Back out in space, the vessel stationary, Seaton introduced the emperors and commanders-in-chief to each other—introductions which were acknowledged almost imperceptibly. He then gave each a headset, and ran the complete record of the Fenachrone brain.

"Stop!" shouted Roban, after only a moment. "Would you, the Overlord of Osnome, reveal such secrets as this to the arch-enemies of Osnome?"

"I would. I have taken over the Overlordship of the entire green system for the duration of this emergency, and I do not want two of its planets engaged in civil war."

The record finished, Seaton tried for some time to bring the four green warriors to his way of thinking, but in vain. Roban and Tarnan remained contemptuous. They would have thrown themselves upon him, but for the knowledge that no fifty unarmed men of the green race could have overcome his strength—to them supernatural. The two Urvanians were equally obdurate. This soft earth-being had given them everything; they had given him nothing and would give him nothing. Finally Seaton rose to his full height and stared at them in turn, wrath and determination blazing in his eyes.

"I have brought you four together, here in a neutral vessel in neutral space, to bring about peace between you. I have shown you the benefits to be derived from the peaceful pursuit of science, knowledge, and power, instead of continuing this utter economic waste of continual war. You all close your senses to reason. You of Osnome accuse me of being an ingrate and a traitor; you of Urvania consider me a soft-headed, sentimental weakling, who may safely be disregarded—all because I think the welfare of the numberless peoples of the Universe more important than your narrow-minded, stubborn, selfish vanity. Think what you please. If brute force is your only logic, know now that I can, and will, use brute force. Here are the seven disks," and he placed the bracelet upon Roban's knee.

"If you four leaders are short-sighted enough to place your petty enmity before the good of all civilization, I am done with you forever. I have deliberately given Urvanians precisely the same information that I have given the Osnomians—no more and no less. I have given neither of you all that I know, and I shall know much more than I do now, before the time of the conquest shall have arrived. Unless you four men, here and now, renounce this war and agree to a perpetual peace between your worlds, I shall leave you to your mutual destruction. You do not yet realize the power of the weapons I have given you. When you do realize it, you will know that mutual destruction is inevitable if you continue this internecine war. I shall continue upon other worlds my search for the one secret standing between me and a complete mastery of power. That I shall find that secret I am confident; and, having found it, I shall, without your aid, destroy the Fenachrone.

"You have several times remarked with sneers that you are not to be swayed by empty threats. What I am about to say is no empty threat—it is a most solemn promise, given by one who has both the will and the power to fulfill his every given word. Now listen carefully to this, my final utterance. If you continue this warfare and if the victor should not be utterly destroyed in its course, I swear as I stand here, by the great First Cause, that I shall myself wipe out every trace of the surviving nation as soon as the Fenachrone shall have been obliterated. Work with each other and me and we all may live—fight on and both your nations, to the last person, will most certainly die. Decide now which it is to be. I have spoken."

Roban took up the bracelet and clasped it again about Seaton's arm, saying, "You are more than ever our Overlord. You are wiser than are we, and stronger. Issue your commands and they shall be obeyed."

"Why did not you say those things first, Overlord?" asked the Urvanian emperor, as he saluted and smiled. "We could not in honor submit to a weakling, no matter what the fate in store. Having convinced us of your strength, there can be no disgrace in fighting beneath your screens. An armlet of seven symbols shall be cast and ready for you when you next visit us. Roban of Osnome, you are my brother."

The two emperors saluted each other and stared eye to eye for a long moment, and Seaton knew that the perpetual peace had been signed. Then all four spoke, in unison:

"Overlord, we await your commands."

"Dunark of Osnome is already informed as to what Osnome is to do. Say to him that it will not be necessary for him to build the vessel for me; the Urvanians will do that. Urvan of Urvania, you will accompany Roban to Osnome, where you two will order instant cessation of hostilities. Osnome has many ships of this type, and upon some of them you will return your every soldier and engine of war to your own planet. As soon as possible you will build for me a vessel like that of the Fenachrone, except that it shall be ten times as large, in every dimension, and except that every instrument, control, and weapon is to be left out."

"Left out? It shall be so built—but of what use will it be?"

"The empty spaces shall be filled after I have returned from my quest. You will build this vessel of dagal. You will also instruct the Osnomian commander in the manufacture of that metal, which is so much more resistant than their arenak."

"But, Overlord, we have...."

"I have just brought immense stores of the precious chemical and of the metal of power to Osnome. They will share it with you. I also advise you to build for yourselves many ships like those of the Fenachrone, with which to do battle with the invaders, in case I should fail in my quest. You will, of course, see to it that there will be a corps of your most efficient mechanics and artisans within call at all times in case I should return and have sudden need for them."

"All these things shall be done."

The conference ended, the four nobles were quickly landed upon Osnome and once more the *Skylark* traveled out into her element, the total vacuum and absolute zero of the outer void, with Crane at the controls.

"You certainly sounded savage, Dick. I almost thought you really meant it!" Dorothy chuckled.

"I did mean it, Dot. Those fellows are mighty keen on detecting bluffs. If I hadn't meant it, and if they hadn't known that I meant it, I'd never have got away with it."

"But you *couldn't* have meant it, Dick! You wouldn't have destroyed the Osnomians, surely—you know you wouldn't."

"No, but I would have destroyed what was left of the Urvanians, and all five of us knew exactly how it would have turned out and exactly what I would have done about it—that's why they all pulled in their horns."

"I don't know what would have happened," interjected Margaret. "What would have?"

"With this new stuff the Urvanians would have wiped the Osnomians out. They are an older race, and so much better in science and mechanics that the Osnomians wouldn't have stood much chance, and knew it. Incidentally, that's why I'm having them build our new ship. They'll put a lot of stuff into it that Dunark's men would miss—maybe some stuff that even the Fenachrone haven't got. However, though it might seem that the Urvanians had all the best of it, Urvan knew that I had something up my sleeve besides my bare arm—and he knew that I'd clean up what there was left of his race if they polished off the Osnomians."

"What a frightful chance you were taking, Dick!" gasped Dorothy.

"You have to be hard to handle those folks—and believe me, I was a forty-minute egg right then. They have such a peculiar mental and moral slant that we can hardly understand them at all. This idea of co-operation is so new to them that it actually dazed all four of them even to consider it."

"Do you suppose they will fight, anyway?" asked Crane.

"Absolutely not. Both nations have an inflexible code of honor, such as it is, and lying is against both codes. That's one thing I like about them—I'm sort of honest myself, and with either of these races you need nothing signed or guaranteed."

"What next, Dick?"

"Now the real trouble begins. Mart, oil up the massive old intellect. Have you found the answer to the problem?"

"What problem?" asked Dorothy. "You didn't tell us anything about a problem."

"No, I told Mart. I want the best physicist in this entire solar system—and since there are only one hundred and twenty-five planets around these seventeen suns, it should be simple to yon phenomenal brain. In fact, I expect to hear him say 'elementary, my dear Watson, elementary'!"

"Hardly that, Dick, but I have found out a few things. There are some eighty planets which are probably habitable for beings like us. Other things being equal, it seems reasonable to assume that the older the sun, the longer its planets have been habitable, and therefore the older and more intelligent the life...."

"'Ha! ha! It was elementary,' says Sherlock." Seaton interrupted. "You're heading directly at that largest, oldest, and most intelligent planet, then, I take it, where I can catch me my physicist?"

"Not directly at it, no. I am heading for the place where it will be when we reach it. That is elementary."

"Ouch! That got to me, Mart, right where I live. I'll be good."

"But you are getting ahead of me, Dick—it is not as simple as you have assumed from what I have said so far. The Osnomian astronomers have done wonders in the short time they have had, but their data, particularly on the planets of the outer suns, is as yet necessarily very incomplete. Since the furthermost outer sun is probably the oldest, it is the one in which we are most interested. It has seven planets, four of which are probably habitable, as far as temperature and atmosphere are concerned. However, nothing exact is yet known of their masses, motions, or places. Therefore I have laid our course to intercept the closest one to us, as nearly as I can from what meager data we have. If it should prove to be inhabited by intelligent beings, they can probably give us more exact information concerning their neighboring planets. That is the best I can do."

"That's a darn fine best, old top—narrowing down to four from a hundred and twenty-five. Well, until we get there, what to do? Let's sing us a song, to keep our fearless quartette in good voice."

"Before you do anything," said Margaret seriously, "I would like to know if you really think there is a chance of defeating those monsters."

"In all seriousness, I do. In fact, I am quite confident of it. If we had two years, I know that we could lick them cold; and by stepping on the gas I believe we can get the dope in less than the six months we have to work in."

"I know that you are serious, Dick. Now you know that I do not want to discourage any one, but I can see small basis for optimism," Crane spoke slowly and thoughtfully. "I hope that you will be able to control the zone of force—but you are not studying it yourself. You seem to be certain that somewhere in this system there is a race who already knows all about it. I would like to know your reasons for thinking that such a race exists."

"They may not be upon this system; they may have been outsiders, as we are—but I have reasons for believing them to be natives of this system, since they were green. You are as familiar with Osnomian mythology as I am—you girls in particular have read Osnomian legends to Osnomian children for hours. Also identically the same legends prevail upon Urvania. I read them in that lieutenant's brain—in fact, I looked for them. You also know that every folk-legend has some basis, however tenuous, in fact. Now, Dottie, tell about the battle of the gods, when Osnome was a pup."

"The gods came down from the sky," Dorothy recited. "They were green, as were men. They wore invisible armor of polished metal, which appeared and disappeared. They stayed inside the armor and fought outside it with swords and lances of fire. Men who fought against them cut them through and through with swords, and they struck the men with lances of flame so that they were stunned. So the gods fought in days long gone and vanished in their invisible armor, and——"

"That's enough," interrupted Seaton. "The little red-haired girl has her lesson perfectly. Get it, Mart?"

"No, I cannot say that I do."

"Why, it doesn't even make sense!" exclaimed Margaret.

"All right, I'll elucidate. Listen!" and Seaton's voice grew tense with earnestness. "Visitors came down out of space. They were green. They wore zones of force, which they flashed on and off. They stayed inside the zones and projected their images outside, and used rays *through the zones*. Men who fought against the images cut them through and through with swords, but could not harm them since they were not actual substance; and the images directed rays against the men so that they were stunned. So the visitors fought in days long gone, and vanished in their zones of force. How does that sound?"

"You have the most stupendous imagination the world has ever seen—but there may be some slight basis of fact there, after all," said Crane, slowly.

"I'm convinced of it, for one reason in particular. Notice that it says specifically that the visitors stunned the natives. Now that thought is absolutely foreign to all Osnomian nature—when they strike they kill, and always have. Now if that myth has come down through so many generations without having that 'stunned' changed to 'killed', I'm willing to bet a few weeks of time that the rest of it came down fairly straight, too. Of course, what they had may not have been the zone of force as we know it, but it must have been a ray of some kind—and believe me, that was one educated ray. Somebody sure had something, even 'way back in those days. And if they had anything at all back there, they must know a lot by now. That's why I want to look 'em up."

"But suppose they want to kill us off at sight?" objected Dorothy. "They might be able to do it, mightn't they?"

"Sure, but they probably wouldn't want to—any more than you would step on an ant who asked you to help him move a twig. That's about how much ahead of us they probably are. Of course, we struck a pure mentality once, who came darn near dematerializing us entirely, but I'm betting that these folks haven't got that far along yet. By the way, I've got a hunch about those pure intellectuals."

"Oh, tell us about it!" laughed Margaret. "Your hunches are the world's greatest brainstorms!"

"Well, I pumped out and rejeweled the compass we put on that funny planet—as a last resort, I thought we might maybe visit them and ask that bozo we had the argument with to help us out. I think he—or it—would show us everything about the zone of force we want to know. I don't think that we'd be dematerialized, either, because the situation would give him something more to think about for another thousand cycles; and thinking seemed to be his main object in life. However, to get back to the subject, I found that even with the new power of the compass the entire planet was still out of reach. Unless they've dematerialized it, that means about ten billion light-years as an absolute minimum. Think about that for a minute!... I've just got a kind of a hunch that maybe they don't belong in this Galaxy at all—that they might be from some other Galaxy, planet and all; just riding around on it, as we are riding in the *Skylark*. Is the idea conceivable to a sane mind, or not?"

"Not!" decided Dorothy, promptly. "We'd better go to bed. One more such idea, in progression with the last two you've had, would certainly give you a compound fracture of the skull. 'Night, Cranes."

CHAPTER VII

DuQuesne's Voyage

Far from our solar system a cigar-shaped space-car slackened its terrific acceleration to a point at which human beings could walk, and two men got up, exercised vigorously to restore the circulation to their numbed bodies, and went into the galley to prepare their meal—the first since leaving the Earth some eight hours or more before.

Because of the long and arduous journey he had decided upon, DuQuesne had had to abandon his custom of working alone, and had studied all the available men with great care before selecting his companion and relief pilot. He finally had chosen "Baby Doll" Loring—so called because of his curly yellow hair, his pink and white complexion, his guileless blue eyes, his slight form of rather less than medium height. But never did outward attributes more belie the inner man! The yellow curls covered a brain agile, keen, and hard; the girlish complexion neither paled nor reddened under stress; the wide blue eyes had glanced along the barrels of so many lethal weapons, that in various localities the noose yawned for him; the slender body was built of rawhide and whalebone, and responded instantly to the dictates of that ruthless brain. Under the protection of Steel he flourished, and in return for that protection he performed, quietly and with neatness and despatch, such odd jobs as were in his line, with which he was commissioned.

When they were seated at an excellent breakfast of ham and eggs, buttered toast, and strong, aromatic coffee, DuQuesne broke the long silence.

"Do you want to know where we are?"

"I'd say we were a long way from home, by the way this elevator of yours has been climbing all night."

"We are a good many million miles from the Earth, and we are getting farther away at a rate that would have to be measured in millions of miles per second." DuQuesne, watching the other narrowly as he made this startling announcement and remembering the effect of a similar one upon Perkins, saw with approval that the coffee-cup in midair did not pause or waver in its course. Loring noted the bouquet of his beverage and took an appreciative sip before he replied.

"You certainly can make coffee, Doctor; and good coffee is nine-tenths of a good breakfast. As to where we are—that's all right with me. I can stand it if you can."

"Don't you want to know where we're going, and why?"

"I've been thinking about that. Before we started I didn't want to know anything, because what a man doesn't know he can't be accused of spilling in case of a leak. Now that we are on our way, though, maybe I should know enough about things to act intelligently, if something unforeseen should develop. If you'd rather keep it dark and give me orders when necessary, that's all right with me, too. It's your party, you know."

"I brought you along because one man can't stay on duty twenty-four hours a day, continuously. Since you are in as deep as you can get, and since this trip is dangerous, you should know everything there is to know. You are one of the higher-ups now, anyway: and we understand each other thoroughly, I believe?"

"I believe so."

Back in the bow control-room DuQuesne applied more power, but not enough to render movement impossible.

"You don't have to drive her as hard all the way, then, as you did last night?"

"No, I'm out of range of Seaton's instrument now, and we don't have to kill ourselves. High acceleration is punishment for anyone and we must keep ourselves fit. To begin with, I suppose that you are curious about that object-compass?"

"That and other things."

"An object-compass is a needle of specially-treated copper, so activated that it points always toward one certain object, after being once set upon it. Seaton undoubtedly has one upon me; but, sensitive as they are, they can't hold on a mass as small as a man at this distance. That was why we left at midnight, after he had gone to bed—so that we'd be out of range before he woke up. I wanted to lose him, as he might interfere if he knew where I was going. Now I'll go back to the beginning and tell you the whole story."

Tersely, but vividly, he recounted the tale of the interstellar cruise, the voyage of the *Skylark of Space*. When he had finished, Loring smoked for a few minutes in silence.

"There's a lot of stuff there that's hard to understand all at once. Do you mind if I ask a few foolish questions, to get things straightened out in my mind?"

"Go ahead—ask as many as you want to. It is hard to understand a lot of that Osnomian stuff—a man can't get it all at once."

"Osnome is so far away—how are you going to find it?"

"With one of the object-compasses I mentioned. I had planned on navigating from notes I took on the trip back to the Earth, but it wasn't necessary. They tried to keep me from finding out anything, but I learned all about the compasses, built a few of them in their own shop, and set one on Osnome. I had it, among other things, in my pocket when I landed. In fact, the control of that explosive copper bullet is the only thing they had that I wasn't able to get—and I'll get that on this trip."

"What is that arenak armor they're wearing?"

"Arenak is a synthetic metal, almost perfectly transparent. It has practically the same refractive index as air, therefore it is, to all intents and purposes, invisible. It's about five hundred times as strong as chrome-vanadium steel, and even when you've got it to the yield-point, it doesn't break, but stretches out and snaps back, like rubber, with the strength unimpaired. It's the most wonderful thing I saw on the whole trip. They make complete suits of it. Of course they aren't very comfortable, but since they are only a tenth of an inch they can be worn."

"And a tenth of an inch of that stuff will stop a steel-nosed machine-gun bullet?"

"Stop it! A tenth of an inch of arenak is harder to pierce than fifty inches of our hardest, toughest armor steel. A sixteenth-inch armor-piercing projectile couldn't get through it. It's hard to believe, but nevertheless it's a fact. The only way to kill Seaton with a gun would be to use one heavy enough so that the shock of the impact would kill him—and it wouldn't surprise me a bit if he had his armor anchored with an attractor against that very contingency. Even if he hasn't, you can imagine the chance of getting action against him with a gun of that size."

"Yes, I've heard that he is fast."

"That doesn't tell half of it. You know that I'm handy with a gun myself?"

"You're faster than I am, and that's saying something. You're chain lightning."

"Well, Seaton is at least that much faster than I am. You've never seen him work—I have. On that Osnomian dock he shot twice before I started, and shot twice to my once from then on. I must have been shooting a quarter of a second after he had his side all cleaned up. To make it worse I missed once with my left hand—he didn't. There's absolutely no use tackling Richard Seaton without an Osnomian ray-generator or something better; but, as you know, Brookings always has been and always will be a fool. He won't believe anything new until after he has actually been shown. Well, I imagine he will be shown plenty by this evening."

"Well, I'll never tackle him with heat. How does he get that way?"

"He's naturally fast, and has practiced sleight-of-hand work ever since he was a kid. He's one of the best amateur magicians in the country, and I will say that his ability along that line has come in handy for him more than once."

"I see where you're right in wanting to get something, since we have only ordinary weapons and they have all that stuff. This trip is to get a little something for ourselves, I take it?"

"Exactly, and you know enough now to understand what we are out here to get for ourselves. You have guessed that we are headed for Osnome?"

"I suspected it. However, if you were going only to Osnome, you would have gone alone; so I also suspect that that's only half of it. I have no idea what it is, but you've got something else on your mind."

"You're right—I knew you were keen. When I was on Osnome I found out something that only four other men—all—dead—ever knew. There is a race of men far ahead of the Osnomians in science, particularly in warfare. They live a long way beyond Osnome. It is my plan to steal an Osnomian airship and mount all its ray screens, generators, guns, and everything else, upon this ship, or else convert their vessel into a space-ship. Instead of using their ordinary power, however, we will do as Seaton did, and use intra-atomic power, which is practically infinite. Then we'll have everything Seaton's got, but that isn't enough. I want enough more than he's got to wipe him out. Therefore, after we get a ship armed to suit us, we'll visit this strange planet and either come to terms with them or else steal a ship from them. Then we'll have their stuff and that of the Osnomians, as well as our own. Seaton won't last long after that."

"Do you mind if I ask how you got that dope?"

"Not at all. Except when right with Seaton I could do pretty much as I pleased, and I used to take long walks for exercise. The Osnomians tired very easily, being so weak, and because of the light gravity of the planet, I had to do a lot of work or walking to keep in any kind of condition at all. I learned Kondalian quickly, and got so friendly with the guards, that pretty soon they quit trying to keep me in sight, but waited at the edge of the palace grounds until I came back and joined them.

"Well, on one trip I was fifteen miles or so from the city when an airship crashed down in a woods about half a mile from me. It was in an uninhabited district and nobody else saw it. I went over to investigate, thinking probably I could find out something useful. It had the whole front end cut or broken off, and that made me curious, because no imaginable fall will break an arenak hull. I walked in through the hole and saw that it was one of their fighting tenders—a combination warship and repair shop, with all of the stuff in it that I've been telling you about. The generators were mostly burned out and the propelling and lifting motors were out of commission. I prowled around, getting acquainted with it, and found a lot of useful instruments and, best of all, one of Dunark's new mechanical educators, with complete instructions for its use. Also, I found three bodies, and thought I'd try it out...."

"Just a minute. Only three bodies on a warship? And what good could a mechanical educator do you if the men were all dead?"

"Three is all I found then, but there was another one. Three men and a captain compose an Osnomian crew for any ordinary vessel. Everything is automatic, you, know. As for the men being dead, that doesn't make any difference—you can read their brains just the same, if they haven't been dead too long. However, when I tried to read theirs, I found only blanks—their brains had been destroyed so that nobody could read them. That did look funny, so I ransacked the ship from truck to keelson, and finally found another body, wearing an air-helmet, in a sort of closet off the control room. I put the educator on it...."

"This is getting good. It sounds like a page of the old 'Arabian Nights' that I used to read when I was a boy. You know, it really isn't surprising that Brookings didn't believe a lot of this stuff."

"As I have said, a lot of it is hard to understand, but I'm going to show it to you—all that, and more."

"Oh, I believe it, all right. After riding in this boat and looking out of the windows, I'll believe anything. Reading a dead man's brain is steep, though."

"I'll let you do it after we get there. I don't understand exactly how it works, myself, but I know how to operate one. Well, I found out that this man's brain was in good shape, and I got a shock when I read it. Here's what he had been through. They had been flying very high on their way to the front when their ship was seized by an invisible force and thrown upward. He must have thought faster than the others, because he put on an air-helmet and dived into this locker where he hid under a pile of gear, fixing things so that he could see out through the transparent arenak of the wall. No sooner was he hidden that the front end of the ship went up in a blaze of light, in spite of their ray screens going full blast. They were up so high by that time that when the bow was burned off the other three fainted from lack of air. Then their generators went out, and pretty soon two peculiar-looking strangers entered. They were wearing vacuum suits and were very short and stocky, giving the impression of enormous strength. They brought an educator of their own with them and read the brains of the three men. Then they dropped the ship a few thousand feet and revived the three with a drink of something out of a flask."

"Must have been different from the kind handled by most booties I know, then. The stuff we've been getting lately would make a man more unconscious than ever."

"Some powerful drug, probably, but the Osnomian didn't know anything about it. After the men were revived, the strangers, apparently from sheer cruelty and love of torturing their victims, informed them in the Osnomian language that they were from another world, on the far edge of the Galaxy. They even told them, knowing that the Osnomians knew nothing of astronomy, exactly where they were from. Then they went on to say that they wanted the entire green system for themselves, and that in something like two years of our time they were going to wipe out all the present inhabitants of the system and take it over, as a base for further operations. After that they amused themselves by describing exactly the kinds of death and destruction they were going to use. They described most of it in great detail. It's too involved to tell you about now, but they've got rays, generators, and screens that even the Osnomians never heard of. And of course they've got intra-atomic energy the same as we have. After telling them all this and watching them suffer, they put a machine on their heads and they dropped dead. That's probably what disintegrated their brains. Then they looked the ship over rather casually, as though they didn't see anything they were interested in; crippled the motors; and went away. The vessel was then released, and crashed. This man, of course, was killed by the fall. I buried the men—I didn't want anybody else reading that brain—hid some of the stuff I wanted most, and camouflaged the ship so that I'm fairly sure that it's there yet. I decided then to make this trip."

"I see." Loring's mind was grappling with these new and strange facts. "That news is staggering, Doctor. Think of it. Everybody thinks our own world is everything there is!"

"Our world is simply a grain of dust in the Universe. Most people know it, academically, but very few ever give the fact any actual consideration. But now that you've had a little time to get used to the idea of there being other worlds, and some of them as far ahead of us in science as we are ahead of the monkeys, what do you think of it?"

"I agree with you, that we've got their stuff," said Loring. "However, it occurs to me as a possibility that they may have so much stuff that we won't be able to make the approach. However, if the Osnomian fittings we're going to get are as good as you say they are, I think that two such men as you and I can get at least a lunch while any other crew, no matter who they are, are getting a square meal."

"I like your style, Loring. You and I will have the world eating out of our hands shortly after we get back. As far as actual procedure over there is concerned, of course, I haven't made any definite plans. We'll have to size up the situation after we get there before we can know exactly what we'll have to do. However, we are not coming back empty-handed."

"You said something, Chief!" and the two men, so startlingly unlike physically, but so alike inwardly, shook hands in token of their mutual dedication to a single purpose.

Loring was then instructed in the simple navigation of the ship of space, and thereafter the two men took their regular shifts at the controls. In due time they approached Osnome, and DuQuesne studied the planet carefully through a telescope before he ventured down into the atmosphere.

"This half of it used to be Mardonale. I suppose it's all Kondal now. No, there's a war on down there yet—at least, there's a disturbance of some kind, and on this planet that means war."

"What are you looking for, exactly?" asked Loring, who was also examining the terrain with a telescope.

"They've got some spherical space-ships, like Seaton's. I know they had one, and they've probably built more of them since that time. Their airships can't touch us, but those ball-shaped cruisers would be pure poison for us, the way we are fixed now. Can you see any of them?"

"Not yet. Too far away to make out details. They're certainly having a hot time down there, though, in that one spot."

They dropped lower, toward the stronghold which was being so stubbornly defended by the inhabitants of the third planet of the fourteenth sun, and so savagely attacked by the Kondalian forces.

"There, we can see what they're doing now," and DuQuesne anchored the vessel with an attractor. "I want to see if they've got many of those space-ships in action, and you will want to see what war is like, when it is fought by people, who have been making war steadily for ten thousand years."

Poised at the limit of clear visibility, the two men studied the incessant battle being waged beneath them. They saw not one, but fully a thousand of the globular craft high in the air and grouped in a great circle around an immense fortification upon the ground below. They saw no airships in the line of battle, but noticed that many such vessels were flying to and from the front, apparently carrying supplies. The fortress was an immense dome of some glassy, transparent material, partially covered with slag, through which they saw that the central space was occupied by orderly groups of barracks, and that round the circumference were arranged gigantic generators, projectors, and other machinery at whose purposes they could not even guess. From the base of the dome a twenty-mile-wide apron of the same glassy substance spread over the ground, and above this apron and around the dome were thrown the mighty defensive ray-screens, visible now and then in scintillating violet splendor as one of the copper-driven Kondalian projectors sought in vain for an opening. But the Earth-men saw with surprise that the main attack was not being directed at the dome; that only an occasional ray was thrown against it in order to make the defenders keep their screens up continuously. The edge of the apron was bearing the brunt of that vicious and never-ceasing attack, and most concerned the desperate defense.

For miles beyond that edge, and as deep under it as frightful rays and enormous charges of explosive copper could penetrate, the ground was one seething, flaming volcano of molten and incandescent lava; lava constantly being volatilized by the unimaginable heat of those rays and being hurled for miles in all directions by the inconceivable power of those explosive copper projectiles—the heaviest projectiles that could be used without endangering the planet itself—being directed under the exposed edge of that unbreakable apron, which was in actuality anchored to the solid core of the planet itself; lava flowing into and filling up the vast craters caused by the explosions. The attack seemed fiercest at certain points, perhaps a quarter of a mile apart around the circle, and after a time the watchers perceived that at those points, under the edge of the apron, in that indescribable inferno of boiling lava, destructive rays, and disintegrating copper, there were enemy machines at work. These machines were strengthening the protecting apron and extending it, very slowly, but ever wider and ever deeper as the ground under it and before it was volatilized or hurled away by the awful forces of the Kondalian attack. So much destruction had already been wrought that the edge of the apron and its molten moat were already fully a mile below the normal level of that cratered, torn, and tortured plain.

Now and then one of the mechanical moles would cease its labors, overcome by the concentrated fury of destruction centered upon it. Its shattered remnants would be withdrawn and shortly, repaired or replaced, it would be back at work. But it was not the defenders who had suffered most heavily. The fortress was literally ringed about with the shattered remnants of airships, and the riddled hulls of more than a few of those mighty globular cruisers of the void bore mute testimony to the deadliness and efficiency of the warfare of the invaders.

Even as they watched, one of the spheres, unable for some reason to maintain its screens or overcome by the awful forces playing upon it, flared from white into and through the violet and was hurled upward as though shot from the mouth of some Brobdingnagian howitzer. A door opened, and from its flaming interior four figures leaped out into the air, followed by a puff of orange-colored smoke. At the first sign of trouble, the ship next it in line leaped in front of it and the four figures floated gently to the ground, supported by friendly attractors and protected from enemy rays by the bulk and by the screens of the rescuing vessel. Two great airships soared upward from back of the lines and hauled the disabled vessel to the ground by means of their powerful attractors. The two observers saw with amazement that after brief attention from an ant-like ground-crew, the original four men climbed back into their warship and she again shot into the fray, apparently as good as ever.

"What do you know about that!" exclaimed DuQuesne. "That gives me an idea, Loring. They must get to them that way fairly often, to judge by the teamwork they use when it does happen. How about waiting until they disable another one like that, and then grabbing it while its in the air, deserted and unable to fight back? One of those ships is worth a thousand of this one, even if we had everything known to the Osnomians."

"That's a real idea—those boats certainly are brutes for punishment," agreed Loring, and as both men again settled down to watch the battle, he went on: "So this is war out this way? You're right. Seaton, with half this stuff, could whip the combined armies and navies of the world. I don't blame Brookings much, though, at that—nobody could believe half of this unless they could actually see it, as we are doing."

"I can't understand it," DuQuesne frowned as he considered the situation. "The attackers are Kondalians, all right—those ships are developments of the *Skylark*—but I don't get that fort at all. Wonder if it can be the strangers already? Don't think so—they aren't due for a couple of years yet, and I don't think the Kondalians could stand against them a minute. It must be what is left of Mardonale, although I never heard of anything like that. Probably it is some new invention they dug up at the last minute. That's it, I guess," and his brow cleared. "It couldn't be anything else."

They waited long for the incident to be repeated, and finally their patience was rewarded. When the next vessel was disabled and hurled upward by the concentration of enemy forces, DuQuesne darted down, seized it with his most powerful attractor, and whisked it away into space at such a velocity that to the eyes of the Kordalians it simply disappeared. He took the disabled warship far out into space and allowed it to cool off for a long time before deciding that it was safe to board it. Through the transparent walls they could see no sign of life, and DuQuesne donned a vacuum suit and stepped into the airlock. As Loring held the steel vessel close to the stranger, DuQuesne leaped lightly through the open door into the interior. Shutting the door, he opened an auxiliary air-tank, adjusting the gauge to one atmosphere as he did so. The pressure normal, he divested himself of the suit and made a thorough examination of the vessel. He then signaled Loring to follow him, and soon both ships were over Kondal, so high as to be invisible from the ground. Plunging the vessel like a bullet towards the grove in which he had left the Kondalian airship, he slowed abruptly just in time to make a safe landing. As he stepped out upon Osnomian soil, Loring landed the Earthly ship hardly less skillfully.

"This saves us a lot of trouble, Loring. This is undoubtedly one of the finest space-ships of the Universe, and just about ready for anything."

"How did they get to it?"

"One of the screen generators apparently weakened a trifle, probably from weeks of continuous use. That let some of the rays come through; everything got hot, and the crew had to jump or roast. Nothing is hurt, though, as the ship was thrown up and out of range before the arenak melted at all. The copper repellers are gone, of course, and most of the bars that were in use are melted down, but there was enough of the main bar left to drive the ship and we can replace the melted stuff easily enough. Nothing else was hurt, as there's absolutely nothing in the structure of these vessels that can be burned. Even the insulation in the coils and generators has a melting-point higher than that of porcelain. And not all the copper was melted, either. Some of these storerooms are lined with two feet of insulation and are piled full of bars and explosive ammunition."

"What was the smoke we saw, then?"

"That was their food-supply. It's cooked to an ash, and their water was all boiled away through the safety-valves. Those rays certainly can put out a lot of heat in a second or two!"

"Can the two of us put on those copper repeller-bands? This ship must be seventy-five feet in diameter."

"Yes, it's a lot bigger than the *Skylark* was. It's one of their latest models, or it wouldn't have been on the front line. As to banding on the repellers—that's easy. That airship is half full of metal-working machinery that can do everything but talk. I know how to use most of it, from seeing it in use, and we can figure out the rest."

In that unfrequented spot there was little danger of detection from the air. And none whatsoever of detection from the ground—of ground-travel upon Osnome there is none. Nevertheless, the two men camouflaged the vessels so that they were visible only to keen and direct scrutiny, and drove their task through to completion on the shortest possible time. The copper repellers were banded on, and much additional machinery was installed in the already well-equipped shop. This done, they transferred to their warship food, water, bedding, instruments, and everything else they needed or wanted from their own ship and from the disabled Kondalian airship. They made a last tour of inspection to be sure they had overlooked nothing useful, then embarked.

"Think anybody will find those ships? They could get a good line on what we've done."

"Probably, eventually, Loring, so we'd better destroy them. We'd better take a short hop first, though, to test everything out. Since you're not familiar with the controls of a ship of this type, you need practise. Shoot us up around that moon over there and bring us back to this spot."

"She's a sweet-handling boat—easy like a bicycle," declared Loring as he brought the vessel lightly to a landing upon their return. "We can burn the old one up now. We'll never need her again, any more than a snake needs his last year's skin."

"She's good, all right. Those two hulks must be put out of existence, but we shouldn't do it here. The rays would set the woods afire, and the metal would condense all around. We don't want to leave any tracks, so we'd better pull them out into space to destroy them. We could turn them loose, and as you've never worked a ray, it'll be good practice for you. Also, I want you to see for yourself just what our best armour-plate amounts to compared with arenak."

When they towed the two vessels far out into space, Loring put into practise the instruction he had received from DuQuesne concerning the complex armament of their vessel. He swung the beam-projector upon the Kondalian airship, pressed the connectors of the softener ray, the heat ray, and the induction ray, and threw the master switch. Almost instantly the entire hull became blinding white, but it was several seconds before the extremely refractory material began to volatilize. Though the metal was less than an inch think, it retained its shape and strength stubbornly, and only slowly did it disappear in flaming, flaring gusts of incandescent gas.

"There, you've seen what an inch of arenak is like," said DuQuesne when the destruction was complete. "Now shine it on that sixty-inch chrome-vanadium armor hull of our old bus and see what happens."

Loring did so. As the beam touched it, the steel disappeared in one flare of radiance—as he swung the projector in one flashing arc from the stem to the stern there was nothing left. Loring, swinging the beam, whistled in amazement.

"Wow! What a difference! And this ship of ours has a skin of arenak six feet thick!"

"Yes. Now you understand why I didn't want to argue with anybody out here as long as we were in our steel ship."

"I understand, all right; but I can't understand the power of these rays. Suppose I had had all twenty of them on instead of only three?"

"In that case, I think that we could have whipped even the short, thick strangers."

"You and me both. But say, every ship's got to have a name. This new one of ours is such a sweet, harmless, inoffensive little thing, we'd better name her the *Violet*, hadn't we?"

DuQuesne started the *Violet* off in the direction of the solar system occupied by the warlike strangers, but he did not hurry. He and Loring practiced incessantly for days at the controls, darting here and there, putting on terrific acceleration until the indicators showed a velocity of hundreds of thousand of miles per second, then reversing the acceleration until the velocity was zero. They studied the controls and alarm system until each knew perfectly every instrument, every tiny light, and the tone of each bell. They practiced with the rays, singly and in combination, with the visiplates, and with the many levers and dials, until each was so familiar with the complex installation that his handling of every control had become automatic. Not until then did DuQuesne give the word to start out in earnest toward their goal, at an unthinkable distance.

They had not been under way long when an alarm bell sounded its warning and a brilliant green light began flashing upon the board.

"Hm ... m," DuQuesne frowned as he reversed the bar. "Outside intra-atomic energy detector. Somebody's using power out here. Direction, about dead ahead—straight down. Let's see if we can see anything."

He swung number six, the telescopic visiplate, into connection. After what seemed to them a long time they saw a sudden sharp flash, apparently an immense distance ahead, and simultaneously three more alarm bells rang and three colored lights flashed briefly.

"Somebody got quite a jolt then. Three rays in action at once for three or four seconds," reported DuQuesne, as he applied still more negative acceleration.

"I'd like to know what this is all about!" he exclaimed after a time, as they saw a subdued glow, which lasted a minute or two. As the warning light was flashing more and more slowly and with diminishing intensity, the *Violet* was once more put upon her course. As she proceeded, however, the warnings of the liberation of intra-atomic energy grew stronger and stronger, and both men scanned their path intensely for a sight of the source of the disturbance, while their velocity was cut to only a few hundred miles an hour. Suddenly the indicator swerved and pointed behind them, showing that they had passed the object, whatever it was. DuQuesne instantly applied power and snapped on a small searchlight.

"If it's so small that we couldn't see it when we passed it, it's nothing to be afraid of. We'll be able to find it with a light."

After some search, they saw an object floating in space-apparently a vacuum suit!

"Shall one of us get in the airlock, or shall we bring it in with an attractor?" asked Loring.

"An attractor, by all means. Two or three of them, in fact, to spread-eagle whatever it is. Never take any chances. It's probably an Osnomian, but you never can tell. It may be one of those other people. We know they were around here a few weeks ago, and they're the only ones I know of that have intra-atomic power besides us and the Osnomians."

"That's no Osnomian," he continued, as the stranger was drawn into the airlock. "He's big enough around for four Osnomians, and very short. We'll take no chances at all with that fellow."

The captive was brought into the control room pinioned head, hand, and foot with attractors and repellers, before DuQuesne approached him. He then read the temperature and pressure of the stranger's air-supply, and allowed the surplus air to escape slowly before removing the stranger's suit and revealing one of the Fenachrone—eyes closed, unconscious or dead.

DuQuesne leaped for the educator and handed Loring a headset.

"Put this on quick. He may be only unconscious, and we might not be able to get a thing from him if he were awake."

Loring donned the headset, still staring at the monstrous form with amazement, not unmixed with awe, while DuQuesne, paying no attention to anything except the knowledge he was seeking, manipulated the controls of the instrument. His first quest was for the weapons and armament of the vessel. In this he was disappointed, as he learned that the stranger was one of the navigating engineers, and as such, had no detailed knowledge of the matters of prime importance to the inquisitor. He did have a complete knowledge of the marvelous Fenachrone propulsion system, however, and this DuQuesne carefully transferred to his own brain. He then rapidly explored other regions of that fearsome organ of thought.

As the gigantic and inhuman brain was spread before them, DuQuesne and Loring read not only the language, customs, and culture of the Fenachrone, but all their plans for the future, as well as the events of the past. Plainly in his mind they perceived how he had been cast adrift in the emptiness of the void. They saw the Fenachrone cruiser lying in wait for the two globular vessels. Looking through an extraordinarily powerful telescope with the eyes of their prisoner, they saw them approach, all unsuspecting. DuQuesne recognized all five persons in the *Skylark* and Dunark and Sitar in the Kondal; such was that unearthly optical instrument and so clear was the impression upon the mind before him. They saw the attack and the battle. They saw the *Skylark* throw off her zone of force and attack; saw this one survivor standing directly in line with a huge projector-spring, and saw the spring severed by the zone. The free end, under its thousands of pounds of tension, had struck the being upon the side of the head, and the force of the blow, only partially blocked by the heavy helmet, had hurled him out through the yawning gap in the wall and hundreds of miles out into space.

Suddenly the clear view of the brain of the Fenachrone became blurred and meaningless and the flow of knowledge ceased—the prisoner had regained consciousness and was trying with all his gigantic strength to break from those intangible bonds that held him. So powerful were the forces upon him, however, that only a few twitching muscles gave evidence that he was struggling at all. Glancing about him he recognized the attractors and repellers bearing upon him, ceased his efforts to escape, and hurled the full power of his baleful gaze into the black eyes so close to his own. But DuQuesne's mind, always under perfect control and now amply reenforced by a considerable proportion of the stranger's own knowledge and power, did not waver under the force of even that hypnotic glare.

"It is useless, as you observe," he said coldly, in the stranger's own tongue, and sneered. "You are perfectly helpless. Unlike you of the Fenachrone, however, men of my race do not always kill strangers at sight, merely because they are strangers. I will spare your life, if you can give me anything of enough value to me to make extra time and trouble worth while."

"You read my mind while I could not resist your childish efforts. I will have no traffic whatever with you who have destroyed my vessel. If you have mentality enough to understand any portion of my mind—which I doubt—you already know the fate in store for you. Do with me what you will." This from the stranger.

DuQuesne pondered long before he replied; considering whether it was to his advantage to inform this stranger of the facts. Finally he decided.

"Sir, neither I nor this vessel had anything to do with the destruction of your warship. Our detectors discovered you floating in empty space; we stopped and rescued you from death. We have seen nothing else, save what we saw pictured in your own brain. I know that, in common with all of your race, you possess neither conscience nor honor, as we understand the terms. An automatic liar by instinct and training whenever you think lies will best serve your purpose, you may yet have intelligence enough to recognize simple truth when you hear it. You already have observed that we are of the same race as those who destroyed your vessel, and have assumed that we are with them. In that you are wrong. It is true that I am acquainted with those others, but they are my enemies. I am here to kill them, not to aid them. You have already helped me in one way—I know as much as does my enemy concerning the impenetrable shield of force. If I will return you unharmed to your own planet, will you assist me in stealing one of your ships of space, so that I may destroy that Earth-vessel?"

The Fenachrone, paying no attention to DuQuesne's barbed comments concerning his honor and veracity, did not hesitate an instant in his reply.

"I will not. We supermen of the Fenachrone will allow no vessel of ours, with its secrets unknown to any others of the Universe, to fall into the hands of any of the lesser breeds of men."

"Well, you didn't try to lie that time, anyway," said DuQuesne, "but think a minute. Seaton, my enemy, already has one of your vessels—don't think he is too much of a fool to put it back together and to learn its every secret. Then, too, remember that I have your mind, and can get along without you; even though I am willing to admit that you could be of enough help to me so that I would save your life in exchange for that help. Also remember that, superman though you may be, your mentality cannot cope with the forces I have bearing upon you. Neither will your being a superman enable your body to retain life after I have pushed you through yonder door, dressed as you are in a silken tunic."

"I have the normal love of life," was the reply, "but some things cannot be done, even with life at stake. Stealing a vessel of the Fenachrone is one of those things. I can, however, do this much—if you will return me to my own planet, you two shall be received as guests aboard one of our vessels and shall be allowed to witness the vengeance of the Fenachrone upon your enemy. Then you shall be returned to your vessel and allowed to depart unharmed."

"Now you are lying by rote—I know just what you'd do," said DuQuesne. "Get that idea out of your head right now. The attractors now holding you will not be released until after you have told all. Then, and then only, will we try to discover a way of returning you to your own world safely, and yet in a manner which will in no way jeopardize my own safety. Incidentally, I warn you that the first sign of an attempt to play false with me in any way will mean your instant death."

The prisoner remained silent, analyzing every feature of the situation, and DuQuesne continued, coldly:

"Here's something else for you to think about. If you are unwilling to help us, what is to prevent me from killing you, and then hunting up Seaton and making peace with him for the duration of this forthcoming war? With the fragments of your vessel, which he has; with my knowledge of your mind, reenforced by your own dead brain; and with the vast resources of all the planets of the green system; there is no doubt that the plans of the Fenachrone will be seriously interfered with. Myriads of your race will certainly lose their lives, and it is quite possible that your entire race would be destroyed. Understand that I care nothing for the green system. You are welcome to it if you do as I ask. If you do not, I shall warn them and help them simply to protect my world, which is now my own personal property."

"In return for our armament and equipment, you promise not to warn the green system against us? The death of your enemy takes first place in your mind?" The stranger spoke thoughtfully. "In that I understand your viewpoint thoroughly. But, after I have remodeled your power-plant into ours and have piloted you to our planet, what assurance have I that you will liberate me, as you have said?"

"None whatever—I have made and am asking no promises, since I cannot expect you to trust me, any more than I can trust you. Enough of this argument! I am master here, and I am dictating terms. We can get along without you. Therefore you must decide quickly whether you would rather die suddenly and surely, here in space and right now, or help us as I demand and live until you get back home—enjoying meanwhile your life and whatever chance you think you may have of being liberated within the atmosphere of your own planet."

"Just a minute, Chief!" Loring said, in English, his back to the prisoner. "Wouldn't we gain more by killing him and going back to Seaton and the green system, as you suggested?"

"No." DuQuesne also turned away, to shield his features from the mind-reading gaze of the Fenachrone. "That was pure bluff. I don't want to get within a million miles of Seaton until after we have the armament of this fellow's ships. I couldn't make peace with Seaton now, even if I wanted to—and I haven't the slightest intention of trying. I intend killing him on sight. Here's what we're going to do. First, we'll get what we came after. Then we'll find the *Skylark* and blow her clear out of space, and take over the pieces of that Fenachrone ship. After that we'll head for the green system, and with their own stuff and what we'll give them, they'll be able to give those fiends a hot reception. By the time they finally destroy the Osnomians—if they do—we'll have the world ready for them." He turned to the Fenachrone. "What is your decision?"

"I submit, in the hope that you will keep your promise, since there is no alternative but death," and the awful creature, still loosely held by the attractors and carefully watched by DuQuesne and Loring, fairly tore into the task of rebuilding the Osnomian power-plant into the space-annihilating drive of the Fenachrone—for he well knew one fact that DuQuesne's hurried inspection had failed to glean from the labyrinthine intricacies of that fearsome brain: that once within the detector screens of that distant solar system these Earth-beings would be utterly helpless before the forces which would inevitably be turned upon them. Also, he realized that time was precious, and resolved to drive the *Violet* so unmercifully that she would overtake that fleeing torpedo, now many hours upon its way—the torpedo bearing news, for the first time in Fenachrone history, of the overwhelming defeat and capture of one of its mighty engines of interstellar war.

In a very short time, considering the complexity of the undertaking, the conversion of the power-plant was done and the repellers, already supposed the ultimate in protection, were reenforced by a ten-thousand-pound mass of activated copper, effective for untold millions of miles. Their monstrous pilot then set the bar and advanced both levers of the dual power control out to the extreme limit of their travel.

There was no sense of motion or of acceleration, since the new system of propulsion acted upon every molecule of matter within the radius of activity of the bar, which had been set to include the entire hull. The passengers felt only the utter lack of all weight and the other peculiar sensations with which they were already familiar, as each had had previous experience of free motion in space. But in spite of the lack of apparent motion, the *Violet* was now leaping through the unfathomable depths of interstellar space with the unthinkable speed of five times the velocity of light!

CHAPTER VIII

The Porpoise-Men of Dasor

"How long do you figure it's going to take us to get there, Mart?" Seaton asked from a corner, where he was bending over his apparatus-table.

"About three days at this acceleration. I set it at what I thought the safe maximum for the girls. Should we increase it?"

"Probably not—three days isn't bad. Anyway, to save even one day we'd have to more than double the acceleration, and none of us could do anything, so we'd better let it ride. How're you making it, Peg?"

"I'm getting used to weighing a ton now. My knees buckled only once this morning from my forgetting to watch them when I tried to walk. Don't let me interfere, though! if I am slowing us down, I'll go to bed and stay there!"

"It'd hardly pay," said Seaton. "We can use the time to good advantage. Look here, Mart—I've been looking over this stuff I got out of their ship and here's something I know you'll eat up. They refer to it as a chart, but it's three-dimensional and almost incredible. I can't say that I understand it, but I get an awful kick out of looking at it. I've been studying it a couple of hours, and haven't started yet. I haven't found our solar system, the green one, or their own. It's too heavy to move around now, because of the acceleration we're using—come on over here and give it a look."

The "chart" was a strip of some parchment-like material, or film, apparently miles in length, wound upon reels at each end of the machine. One section of the film was always under the viewing mechanism—an optical system projecting an undistorted image into a visiplate plate somewhat similar to their own—and at the touch of a lever, a small atomic motor turned the reels and moved the film through the projector.

It was not an ordinary star-chart: it was three-dimensional, ultra-stereoscopic. The eye did not perceive a flat surface, but beheld an actual, extremely narrow wedge of space as seen from the center of the galaxy. Each of the closer stars was seen in its true position in space and in its true perspective, and each was clearly identified by number. In the background were faint stars and nebulous masses of light, too distant to be resolved into separate stars—a true representation of the actual sky. As both men stared, fascinated, into the visiplate, Seaton touched the lever and they apparently traveled directly along the center line of that ever-widening wedge. As they proceeded, the nearer stars grew brighter and larger, soon becoming suns, with their planets and then the satellites of the planets plainly visible, and finally passing out of the picture behind the observers. The fainter stars became bright, grew into suns and solar systems, and were passed in turn. The chart unrolled, and the nebulous masses of light were approached, became composed of faint stars, which developed as had the others, and were passed.

Finally, when the picture filled the entire visiplate, they arrived at the outermost edge of the galaxy. No more stars were visible: they saw empty space stretching for inconceivably vast distances before them. But beyond that indescribable and incomprehensible vacuum they saw faint lenticular bodies of light, which were also named, and which each man knew to be other galaxies, charted and named by the almost unlimited power of the Fenachrone astronomers, but not as yet explored. As the magic scroll unrolled still farther, they found themselves back in the center of the galaxy, starting outward in the wedge adjacent to the one which they had just traversed. Seaton cut off the motor and wiped his forehead.

"Wouldn't that break you off at the ankles, Mart? Did you ever conceive the possibility of such a thing?

"It would, and I did not. There are literally miles and miles of film in each of those reels, and I see that there is a magazine full of reels in the cabinet. There must be an index or a master-chart."

"Yeah, there's a book in this slot here," said Seaton, "but we don't know any of their names or numbers—wait a minute! How did he report our Earth on that torpedo? Planet number three of sun six four something Pilarone, wasn't it? I'll get the record.

"Six four seven three Pilarone, it was."

"Pilarone ... let's see...." Seaton studied the index volume. "Reel twenty, scene fifty-one, I'd translate it."

They found the reel, and "scene fifty-one" did indeed show that section of space in which our solar system is. Seaton stopped the chart when star six four seven three was at its closest range, and there was our sun; with its nine planets and their many satellites accurately shown and correctly described.

"They know their stuff, all right—you've got to hand it to 'em. I've been straightening out that brain record—cutting out the hazy stretches and getting his knowledge straightened out so we can use it, and there's a lot of this kind of stuff in the record you can get. Suppose that you can figure out exactly where he comes from with this dope and with his brain record?"

"Certainly. I may be able to get more complete information upon the green system than the Osnomians have, which will be very useful indeed. You are right—I am intensely interested in this material, and if you do not care particularly about studying it any more at this time, I believe that I should begin to study it now."

"Hop to it. I'm going to study that record some more. No human brain can take it all, I'm afraid, especially all at once, but I'm going to kinda peck around the edges and get me some dope that I want pretty badly. We got a lot of stuff from that wampus."

About sixty hours out, Dorothy, who had been observing the planet through number six visiplate, called Seaton away from the Fenachrone brain-record, upon which he was still concentrating.

"Come here a minute, Dickie! Haven't you got that knowledge all packed away in your skull yet?"

"I'll say I haven't. That bird's brain would make a dozen of mine, and it was loaded until the scuppers were awash. I'm just nibbling around the edges yet."

"I've always heard that the capacity of even the human brain was almost infinite. Isn't that true?" asked Margaret.

"Maybe it is, if the knowledge were built up gradually over generations. I think maybe I can get most of this stuff into my peanut brain so I can use it, but it's going to be an awful job."

"Is their brain really as far ahead of ours as I gathered from what I saw of it?" asked Crane.

"It sure is," replied Seaton, "as far as knowledge and intelligence are concerned, but they have nothing else in common with us. They don't belong to the genus 'homo' at all, really. Instead of having a common ancestor with the anthropoids, as they say we had, they evolved from a genus which combined the worst traits of the cat tribe and the carnivorous lizards—the most savage and bloodthirsty branches of the animal kingdom—and instead of getting better as they went along, they got worse, in that respect at least. But they sure do know something. When you get a month or so to spare, you want to put on this harness and grab his knowledge, being very careful to steer clear of his mental traits and so on. Then, when we get back to the Earth, we'll simply tear it apart and rebuild it. You'll know what I mean when you get this stuff transplanted into your own skull. But to cut out the lecture, what's on your mind, Dottie Dimple?"

"This planet Martin picked out is all wet, literally. The visibility is fine—very few clouds—but this whole half of it is solid ocean. If there are any islands, even, they're mighty small."

All four looked into the receiver. With the great magnification employed, the planet almost filled the visiplate. There were a few fleecy wisps of cloud, but the entire surface upon which they gazed was one sheet of the now familiar deep and glorious blue peculiar to the waters of that cuprous solar system, with no markings whatever.

"What d'you make of it, Mart? That's water all right—copper-sulphate solution, just like the Osnomian and Urvanian oceans—and nothing else visible. How big would an island have to be for us to see it from here?"

"So much depends upon the contour and nature of the island, that it is hard to say. If it were low and heavily covered with their green-blue vegetation, we might not be able to see even a rather large one, whereas if it were hilly and bare, we could probably see one only a few miles in diameter."

"Well, one good thing, anyway, we're approaching it from the central sun, and almost in line with their own sun, so it's daylight all over it. As it turns and as we get closer, we'll see what we can see. Better take turns watching it, hadn't we?" asked Seaton.

It was decided, and while the *Skylark* was still some distance away, several small islands became visible, and the period of rotation of the planet was determined to be in the neighborhood of fifty hours. Margaret, then at the controls, picked out the largest island visible and directed the bar toward it. As they dropped down close to their objective, they found that the air was of the same composition as that of Osnome, but had a pressure of seventy-eight centimeters of mercury, and that the surface gravity of the planet was ninety-five hundredths that of the Earth.

"Fine business!" exulted Seaton. "Just about like home, but I don't see much of any place to land without getting wet, do you? Those reflectors are probably solar generators, and they cover the whole island except for that lagoon right under us."

The island, perhaps ten miles long and half that in width, was entirely covered with great parabolic reflectors, arranged so closely together that little could be seen between them. Each reflector apparently focussed upon an object in the center, a helix which seemed to writhe luridly in that flaming focus, glowing with a nacreous, opalescent green light.

"Well, nothing much to see there—let's go down," remarked Seaton as he shot the *Skylark* over to the edge of the island and down to the surface of the water. But here again nothing was to be seen of the land itself. The wall was one vertical plate of seamless metal, supporting huge metal guides, between which floated metal pontoons. From these gigantic floats metal girders and trusses went through slots in the wall into the darkness of the interior. Close scrutiny revealed that the large floats were rising steadily, although very slowly; while smaller floats bobbed up and down upon each passing wave.

"Solar generators, tide-motors, and wave-motors, all at once!" ejaculated Seaton. "*Some* power-plant! Folks, I'm going to take a look at that if I have to drill in with a ray!"

Some power plant! Folks, I'm going to take a look at that....

They circumnavigated the island without revealing any door or other opening—the entire thirty miles was one stupendous battery of the generators. Back at the starting point, the *Skylark* hopped over the structure and down to the surface of the small central lagoon previously noticed. Close to the water, it was seen that there was plenty of room for the vessel to move about beneath the roof of reflectors, and that the island was one solid stand of tide-motors. At one end of the lagoon was an open metal structure, the only building visible, and Seaton brought the space-cruiser up to it and through the huge opening—for door there was none. The interior of the room was lighted by long, tubular lights running around in front of the walls, which were veritable switchboards. Row after row and tier upon tier stood the instruments, plainly electrical meters of enormous capacity and equally plainly in full operation, but no wiring or bus-bar could be seen. Before each row of instruments there was a narrow walk, with steps leading down into the water of the lagoon. Every part of the great room was plainly visible, and not a living being was even watching that vast instrument-board.

"What do you make of it, Dick?" asked Crane, slowly.

"No wiring—tight beam transmission. The Fenachrone do it with two matched-frequency separable units. Millions and millions of kilowatts there, if I'm any judge. Absolutely automatic too, or else——" Seaton's voice died away.

"Or else what?" asked Dorothy.

"Just a hunch. I wouldn't wonder if——"

"Hold it, Dicky! Remember I had to put you to bed after that last hunch you had!"

"Here it is, anyway. Mart, what would be the logical line of evolution when the planet has become so old that all the land has been eroded to a level below that of the ocean? You picked us out an old one, all right—so old that there's no land left. Would a highly civilized people revert to fish? That seems like a backward move to me, but what other answer is possible?"

"Probably not to true fishes—although they might easily develop some fish-like traits. I do not believe, however, that they would go back to gills or to cold blood."

"What *are* you two saying?" interrupted Margaret. "Do you mean to say that you think *fish* live here instead of people, and that *fish* did all this?" as she waved her hand at the complicated machinery about them.

"Not fish exactly, no." Crane paused in thought. "Merely a people who have adjusted themselves to their environment through conscious or natural selection. We had a talk about this very thing in our first trip, shortly after I met you. Remember? I commented on the fact that there must be life throughout the Universe, much of it that we could not understand; and you replied that there would be no reason to suppose them awful because incomprehensible. That may be the case here."

"Well, I'm going to find out," declared Seaton, as he appeared with a box full of coils, tubes, and other apparatus.

"How?" asked Dorothy, curiously.

"Fix me up a detector and follow up one of those beams. Find its frequency and direction, first, you know, then pick it up outside and follow it to where it's going. It'll go through anything, of course, but I can trap off enough of it to follow it, even if it's tight enough to choke itself," said Seaton.

"That's one thing I got from that brain reçord."

He worked deftly and rapidly, and soon was rewarded by a flaring crimson color in his detector when it was located in one certain position in front of one of the meters. Noting the bearing on the great circles, he then moved the *Skylark* along that exact line, over the reflectors, and out beyond the island, where he allowed the vessel to settle directly downwards.

"Now folks, if I've done this just right, we'll get a red flash directly."

As he spoke the detector again burst into crimson light, and he set the bar into the line and applied a little power, keeping the light at its reddest while the other three looked on in fascinated interest.

"This beam is on something that's moving, Mart—can't take my eyes off it for a second or I'll lose it entirely. See where we're going, will you?"

"We are about to strike the water," replied Crane quietly.

"The water!" exclaimed Margaret.

"Fair enough—why not?"

"Oh, that's right—I forgot that the *Skylark* is as good a submarine as she is an airship."

Crane pointed number six visiplate directly into the line of flight and started into the dark water.

"Mow deep are we, Mart?" asked Seaton after a time.

"Only about a hundred feet, and we do not seem to be getting any deeper."

"That's good. Afraid this beam might be going to a station on the other side of the planet—through the ground. If so, we'd have had to go back and trace another. We can follow it any distance under water, but not through rock. Need a light?"

"Not unless we go deeper."

For two hours Seaton held the detector upon that tight beam of energy, traveling at a hundred miles an hour, the highest speed he could use and still hold the beam.

"I'd like to be up above watching us. I bet we're making the water boil behind us," remarked Dorothy.

"Yeah, we're kicking up quite a wake, I guess. It sure takes power to drive the old can through this wetness."

"Slow down!" commanded Crane. "I see a submarine ahead. I thought it might be a whale at first, but it is a boat and it is what we are aiming for. You are constantly swinging with it, keeping it exactly in the line."

"O.K." Seaton reduced the power and swung the visiplate over in front of him, whereupon the detector lamp went out. "It's a relief to follow something I can see, instead of trying to guess which way that beam's going to wiggle next. Lead on, Macduff—I'm right on your tail!"

The *Skylark* fell in behind the submersible craft, close enough to keep it plainly visible in the telescopic visiplate. Finally the stranger stopped and rose to the surface between two rows of submerged pontoons which, row upon row, extended in every direction as far as the telescope could reach.

"Well, Dot, we're where we're going, wherever that is."

"What do you suppose it is? It looks like a floating isleport, like what it told about in that wild-story magazine you read so much."

"Maybe—but if so they can't be fish," answered Seaton. "Let's go—I want to look it over," and water flew in all directions as the *Skylark* burst out of the ocean and leaped into the air far above what was in truth a floating city.

Rectangular in shape, it appeared to be about six miles long and four wide. It was roofed with solar generators like those covering the island just visited, but the machines were not spaced quite so closely together, and there were numerous open lagoons. The water around the entire city was covered with wave-motors. From their great height the visitors could see an occasional submarine moving slowly under the city, and frequently small surface craft dashed across the lagoons. As they watched, a seaplane with short, thick wings curved like those of a gull, rose from one of the lagoons and shot away over the water.

"Quite a place," remarked Seaton as he swung a visiplate upon one of the lagoons. "Submarines, speedboats, and fast seaplanes. Fish or not, they're not so slow. I'm going to grab off one of those folks and see how much they know. Wonder if they're peaceable or warlike?"

"They look peaceable, but you know the proverb," Crane cautioned his impetuous friend.

"Yes, and I'm going to be timid like a mice," Seaton returned as the *Skylark* dropped rapidly toward a lagoon near the edge of the island.

"You ought to put that in a gag book, Dick," Dorothy chuckled. "You forget all about being timid until an hour afterwards."

"Watch me, Red-top! If they even point a finger at us, I'm going to run a million miles a minute."

No hostile demonstration was made as they dropped lower and lower, however, and Seaton, with one hand upon the switch actuating the zone of force, slowly lowered the vessel down past the reflectors and to the surface of the water. Through the visiplate he saw the crowd of people coming toward them—some swimming in the lagoon, some walking along narrow runways. They seemed to be of all sizes, and unarmed.

"I believe they're perfectly peaceable, and just curious, Mart. I've already got the repellers on close range—believe I'll cut them off altogether."

"How about the ray-screens?"

"All three full out. They don't interfere with anything solid, though, and won't hurt anything. They'll stop any ray attack and this arenak hull will stop anything else we are apt to get there. Watch this board, will you, and I'll see if I can't negotiate with them."

Seaton opened the door. As he did so, a number of the smaller beings dived headlong into the water, and a submarine rose quietly to the surface less than fifty feet away with a peculiar tubular weapon and a huge ray-generator trained upon the *Skylark*. Seaton stood motionless, his right hand raised in the universal sign of peace, his left holding at his hip an automatic pistol charged with X-plosive shells—while Crane, at the controls, had the Fenachrone super-generator in line, and his hand lay upon the switch, whose closing would volatilize the submarine and cut an incandescent path of destruction through the city lengthwise.

After a moment of inaction, a hatch opened, a man stepped out upon the deck of the submarine, and the two tried to converse, but with no success. Seaton then brought out the mechanical educator, held it up for the other's inspection, and waved an invitation to come aboard. Instantly the other dived, and came to the surface immediately below Seaton, who assisted him into the *Skylark*. Tall and heavy as Seaton was, the stranger was half a head taller and almost twice as heavy. His thick skin was of the characteristic Osnomian green and his eyes were the usual black, but he had no hair whatever. His shoulders, though broad and enormously strong, were very sloping, and his powerful arms were little more than half as long as would have been expected had they belonged to a human being of his size. The hands and feet were very large and very broad, and the fingers and toes were heavily webbed. His high domed forehead appeared even higher because of the total lack of hair, otherwise his features were regular and well-proportioned. He carried himself easily and gracefully, and yet with the dignity of one accustomed to command as he stepped into the control room and saluted gravely the three other Earth-beings. He glanced quickly around the room, and showed unmistakable pleasure as he saw the power-plant of the cruiser of space. Languages were soon exchanged and the stranger spoke, in a bass voice vastly deeper than Seaton's own.

"In the name of our city and planet—I may say in the name of our solar system, for you are very evidently from one other than our green system—I greet you. I would offer you refreshment, as is our custom, but I fear that your chemistry is but ill adapted to our customary fare. If there be aught in which we can be of assistance to you, our resources are at your disposal—but before you leave us, I shall wish to ask from you a great gift."

"Sir, we thank you. We are in search of knowledge concerning forces which we cannot as yet control. From the power systems you employ, and from what I have learned of the composition of your suns and planets, I assume you have none of the metal of power, and it is a quantity of that element that is your greatest need?"

"Yes. Power is our only lack. We generate all we can with the materials and knowledge at our disposal, but we never have enough. Our development is hindered, our birth-rate must be held down to a minimum, many new cities which we need cannot be built and many new projects cannot be started, all for lack of power. For one gram of that metal I see plated upon that copper cylinder, of whose very existence no scientist upon Dasor has had even an inkling, we would do almost anything. In fact, if all else failed, I would be tempted to attack you, did I not know that our utmost power could not penetrate even your outer screen, and that you could volatilize the entire planet if you so desired."

"Great Cat!" In his surprise Seaton lapsed from the formal language he had been employing. "Have you figured us all out already, from a standing start?"

"We know electricity, chemistry, physics, and mathematics fairly well. You see, our race is many millions of years older than is yours."

"You're the man I've been looking for, I guess," said Seaton. "We have enough of this metal with us so that we can spare you some as well as not. But before you get it, I'll introduce you. Folks, this is Sacner Carfon, Chief of the Council of the planet Dasor. They saw us all the time, and when we headed for this, the Sixth City, he came over from the capital, or First City, in the flagship of his police fleet, to welcome us or to fight us, as we pleased. Carfon, this is Martin Crane—or say, better than introductions, put on the headsets, everybody, and get acquainted right."

Acquaintance made and the apparatus put away, Seaton went to one of the store-rooms and brought out a lump of "X," weighing about a hundred pounds.

"There's enough to build power-plants from now on. It would save time if you were to dismiss your submarine. With you to pilot us, we can take you back to the First City a lot faster than your vessel can travel."

Carfon took a miniature transmitter from a pouch under his arm and spoke briefly, then gave Seaton the course. In a few minutes, the First City was reached, and the *Skylark* descended rapidly to the surface of a lagoon at one end of the city. Short as had been the time consumed by their journey from the Sixth City, they found a curious and excited crowd awaiting them. The central portion of the lagoon was almost covered by the small surface craft, while the sides, separated from the sidewalks by the curbs, were full of swimmers. The peculiar Dasorian equivalents of whistles, bells, and gongs were making a deafening uproar, and the crowd was yelling and cheering in much the same fashion as do earthly crowds upon similar occasions. Seaton stopped the *Skylark* and took his wife by the shoulder, swinging her around in front of the visiplate.

"Look at that, Dot. Talk about rapid transit! They could give the New York subway a flying start and beat them hands down!"

Dorothy looked into the visiplate and gasped. Six metal pipes, one above the other, ran above and parallel to each sidewalk-lane of water. The pipes were full of ocean water, water racing along at fully fifty miles an hour and discharging, each stream a small waterfall, into the lagoon. Each pipe was lighted in the interior, and each was full of people, heads almost touching feet, unconcernedly being borne along, completely immersed in that mad current. As the passenger saw daylight and felt the stream begin to drop, he righted himself, apparently selecting an objective point, and rode the current down into the ocean. A few quick strokes, and he was either at the surface or upon one of the flights of stairs leading up to the platform. Many of the travelers did not even move as they left the orifice. If they happened to be on their backs, they entered the ocean backward and did not bother about righting themselves or about selecting a destination until they were many feet below the surface.

"Good heavens, Dick! They'll kill themselves or drown!"

"Not these birds. Notice their skins? They've got a hide like a walrus, and a terrific layer of subcutaneous fat. Even their heads are protected that way—you could hardly hit one of them enough with a baseball bat to hurt him. And as for drowning—they can out-swim a fish, and can stay under water almost an hour without coming up for air. Even one of those youngsters can swim the full length of the city without taking a breath."

"How do you get that velocity of flow, Carfon?" asked Crane.

"By means of pumps. These channels run all over the city, and the amount of water running in each tube and the number of tubes in use are regulated automatically by the amount of traffic. When any section of tube is empty of people, no water flows through it. This was necessary in order to save power. At each intersection there are four stand pipes and automatic swim-counters that regulate the volume of water and the number of tubes in use. This is ordinarily a quiet pool, as it is in a residence section, and this channel—our channels correspond to your streets, you know—has only six tubes each way. If you will look on the other side of the channel, you will see the intake end of the tubes going down-town."

Seaton swung the visiplate around and they saw six rapidly-moving stairways, each crowded with people, leading from the ocean level up to the top of a tall metal tower. As the passengers reached the top of the flight they were catapulted head-first into the chamber leading to the tube below.

"Well, that is some system for handling people!" exclaimed Seaton. "What's the capacity of the system?"

"When running full pressure, six tubes will handle five thousand people a minute. It is only very rarely, on such occasions as this, that they are ever loaded to capacity. Some of the channels in the middle of the city have as many as twenty tubes, so that it is always possible to go from one end of the city to the other in less than ten minutes."

"Don't they ever jam?" asked Dorothy curiously. "I've been lost more than once in the New York subway, and been in some perfectly frightful jams, too—and they weren't moving ten thousand people a minute either."

"No jams ever have occurred. The tubes are perfectly smooth and well-lighted, and all turns and intersections are rounded. The controlling machines allow only so many persons to enter any tube—if more should try to enter than can be carried comfortably, the surplus passengers are slid off down a chute to the swim-ways, or sidewalks, and may either wait a while or swim to the next intersection."

"That looks like quite a jam down there now." Seaton pointed to the receiving pool, which was now one solid mass except for the space kept clear by the six mighty streams of humanity-laden water.

"If the newcomers can't find room to come to the surface they'll swim over to some other pool." Carfon shrugged indifferently. "My residence is the fifth cubicle on the right side of this channel. Our custom demands that you accept the hospitality of my home, if only for a moment and only for a beaker of distilled water. Any ordinary visitor could be received in my office, but you must enter my home."

Seaton steered the *Skylark* carefully, surrounded as she was by a tightly packed crowd of swimmers, to the indicated dwelling, and anchored her so that one of the doors was close to a flight of steps leading from the corner of the building down into the water. Carfon stepped out, opened the door of his house, and preceded his guests within. The room was large and square, and built of a synthetic, non-corroding metal, as was the entire city. The walls were tastefully decorated with striking geometrical designs in many-colored metal, and upon the floor was a softly woven rug. Three doors leading into other rooms could be seen, and strange pieces of furniture stood here and there. In the center of the floor-space was a circular opening some four feet in diameter, and there, only a few inches below the level of the floor, was the surface of the ocean.

Carfon introduced his guests to his wife—a feminine replica of himself, although she was not of quite such heroic proportions.

"I don't suppose that Seven is far away, is he?" Carfon asked of the woman.

"Probably he is outside, near the flying ball. If he has not been touching it ever since it came down, it is only because someone stronger than he pushed him aside. You know how boys are," turning to Dorothy with a smile as she spoke, "boy nature is probably universal."

"Pardon my curiosity, but why 'Seven'?" asked Dorothy, as she returned the smile.

"He is the two thousand three hundred and forty-seventh Sacner Carfon in direct male line of descent," she explained. "But perhaps Six has not explained these things to you. Our population must not be allowed to increase, therefore each couple can have only two children. It is customary for the boy to be born first, and is given the name of his father. The girl is younger, and is given her mother's name."

"That will now be changed," said Carfon feelingly. "These visitors have given us the secret of power, and we shall be able to build new cities and populate Dasor as she should he populated."

"Really?——" She checked herself, but a flame leaped to her eyes, and her voice was none too steady as she addressed the visitors. "For that we Dasorians thank you more than words can express. Perhaps you strangers do not know what it means to want a dozen children with every fiber of your being and to be allowed to have only two—we do, all too well—I will call Seven."

She pressed a button, and up out of the opening in the middle of the floor there shot a half-grown boy, swimming so rapidly that he scarcely touched the coaming as he came to his feet. He glanced at the four visitors, then ran up to Seaton and Crane.

"Please, sirs, may I ride, just a little short ride, in your vessel before you go away?" This was said in their language.

"Seven!" boomed Carfon sternly, and the exuberant youth subsided.

"Pardon me, sirs, but I was so excited——"

"All right, son, no harm done at all. You bet you'll have a ride in the *Skylark* if your parents will let you." He turned to Carfon. "I'm not so far beyond that stage myself that I'm not in sympathy with him. Neither are you, unless I'm badly mistaken."

"I am very glad that you feel as you do. He would be delighted to accompany us down to the office, and it will be something to remember all the rest of his life."

"You have a little girl, too?" Dorothy asked the woman.

"Yes—would you like to see her? She is asleep now," and without waiting for an answer, the proud Dasorian mother led the way into a bedroom—a bedroom without beds, for Dasorians sleep floating in thermostatically controlled tanks, buoyed up in water of the temperature they like best, in a fashion that no Earthly springs and mattresses can approach. In a small tank in a corner reposed a baby, apparently about a year old, over whom Dorothy and Margaret made the usual feminine ceremony of delight and approbation.

Back in the living room, after an animated conversation in which much information was exchanged concerning the two planets and their races of peoples, Carfon drew six metal goblets of distilled water and passed them around. Standing in a circle, the six touched goblets and drank.

They then embarked, and while Crane steered the *Skylark* slowly along the channel toward the offices of the Council, and while Dorothy and Margaret showed the eager Seven all over the vessel, Seaton explained to Carfon the danger that threatened the Universe, what he had done, and what he was attempting to do.

"Doctor Seaton, I wish to apologize to you," the Dasorian said when Seaton had done. "Since you are evidently still land animals, I had supposed you of inferior intelligence. It is true that your younger civilization is deficient in certain respects, but you have shown a depth of vision, a sheer power of imagination and grasp, that no member of our older civilization could approach. I believe that you are right in your conclusions. We have no such rays nor forces upon this planet, and never have had; but the sixth planet of our own sun has. Less than fifty of your years ago, when I was but a small boy, such a projection visited my father. It offered to 'rescue' us from our watery planet, and to show us how to build rocket-ships to move us to Three, which is half land, inhabited by lower animals."

"And he didn't accept?"

"Certainly not. Then as now our sole lack was power, and the strangers did not show us how to increase our supply. Perhaps they had more power than we, perhaps, because of the difficulty of communication, our want was not made clear to them. But, of course, we did not want to move to Three, and we had already had rocket-ships for hundreds of generations. We have never been able to reach Six with them, but we visited Three long ago; and every one who went there came back as soon as he could. We detest land. It is hard, barren, unfriendly. We have everything, here upon Dasor. Food is plentiful, synthetic or natural, as we prefer. Our watery planet supplies our every need and wish, with one exception; and now that we are assured of power, even that one exception vanishes, and Dasor becomes a very Paradise. We can now lead our natural lives, work and play to our fullest capacity—we would not trade our world for all the rest of the Universe."

"I never thought of it in that way, but you're right, at that," Seaton conceded. "You are ideally suited to your environment. But how do I get to planet Six? Its distance is terrific, even as cosmic distances go. You won't have any night until Dasor swings outside the orbit of your sun, and until then Six will be invisible, even to our most powerful telescope."

"I do not know, myself," answered Carfon, "but I will send out a call for the chief astronomer. He will meet us, and give you a chart and the exact course."

At the office, the earthly visitors were welcomed formally by the Council—the nine men in control of the entire planet. The ceremony over and their course carefully plotted, Carfon stood at the door of the *Skylark* a moment before it closed.

"We thank you with all force, Earthmen, for what you have done for us this day. Please remember, and believe that this is no idle word—if we can assist you in any way in this conflict which is to come, the resources of this planet are at your disposal. We join Osnome and the other planets of this system in declaring you, Doctor Seaton, our Overlord."

CHAPTER IX

The Welcome to Norlamin

The *Skylark* was now days upon her way toward the sixth planet, Seaton gave the visiplates and the instrument board his customary careful scrutiny and rejoined the others.

"Still talking about the human fish, Dottie Dimple?" he asked, as he stoked his villainous pipe. "Peculiar tribe of porpoises, but I'm strong for 'em. They're the most like our own kind of folks, as far as ideas go, of anybody we've seen yet—in fact, they're more like us than a lot of human beings we all know."

"I like them immensely——"

"You couldn't like 'em any other way, their size——"

"Terrible, Dick, terrible! Easy as I am, I can't stand for any such joke as that was going to be. But really, I think they're just perfectly fine, in spite of their being so funny-looking. Mrs. Carfon is just simply sweet, even if she does look like a walrus, and that cute little seal of a baby was just too perfectly cunning for words. That boy Seven is keen as mustard, too."

"He should be," put in Crane, dryly. "He probably has as much intelligence now as any one of us."

"Do you think so?" asked Margaret. "He acted like any other boy, but he did seem to understand things remarkably well."

"He would—they're 'way ahead of us in most things." Seaton glanced at the two women quizzically and turned to Crane. "And as for their being bald, this was one time, Mart, when those two phenomenal heads of hair our two little girl-friends are so proud of didn't make any kind of hit at all. They probably regard that black thatch of Peg's and Dot's auburn mop as relics of a barbarous and prehistoric age—about as we would regard the hirsute hide of a Neanderthal man."

"That may be so, too," Dorothy replied, unconcernedly, "but we aren't planning on living there, so why worry about it? I like them, anyway, and I believe that they like us."

"They acted that way. But say, Mart, if that planet is so old that all their land area has been eroded away, how come they've got so much water left? And they've got quite an atmosphere, too."

"The air-pressure," said Crane, "while greater than that now obtaining upon Earth, was probably of the order of magnitude of three meters of mercury, originally. As to the erosion, they might have had more water to begin with than our Earth had."

"Yeah, that'd account for it, all right," said Dorothy.

"There's one thing I want to ask you two scientists," Margaret said. "Everywhere we've gone, except on that one world that Dick thinks is a wandering planet, we've found the intelligent life quite remarkably like human beings. How do you account for that?"

"There, Mart, is one for the massive old bean to concentrate on," challenged Seaton: then, as Crane considered the question in silence for some time he went on: "I'll answer it myself, then, by asking another. Why not? Why shouldn't they be? Remember, man is the highest form of earthly life—at least, in our own opinion and as far as we know. In our wanderings, we have picked out planets quite similar to our own in point of atmosphere and temperature and, within narrow limits, of mass as well. It stands to reason that under such similarity of conditions, there would be a certain similarity of results. How about it, Mart? Reasonable?"

"It seems plausible, in a way," conceded Crane, "but it probably is not universally true."

"Sure not—couldn't be, hardly. No doubt we could find a lot of worlds inhabited by all kinds of intelligent things—freaks that we can't even begin to imagine now—but they probably would be occupying planets entirely different from ours in some essential feature of atmosphere, temperature, or mass."

"But the Fenachrone world is entirely different," Dorothy argued, "and they're more or less human—they're bipeds, anyway, with recognizable features. I've been studying that record with you, you know, and their world has so much more mass than ours that their gravitation is simply frightful!"

"That much difference is comparatively slight, not a real fundamental difference. I meant a hundred or so times either way—greater or less. And even their gravitation has modified their structure a lot—suppose it had been fifty times as great as it is? What would they have been like? Also, their atmosphere is very similar to ours in composition, and their temperature is bearable. It is my opinion that atmosphere and temperature have more to do with evolution than anything else, and that the mass of the planet runs a poor third."

"You may be right," admitted Crane, "but it seems to me that you are arguing from insufficient premises."

"Sure I am—almost no premises at all. I would be just about as well justified in deducing the structure of a range of mountains from a superficial study of three pebbles picked up in a creek near them. However, we can get an idea some time, when we have a lot of time."

"How?"

"Remember that planet we struck on the first trip, that had an atmosphere composed mostly of gaseous chlorin? In our ignorance we assumed that life there was impossible, and didn't stop. Well, it may be just as well that we didn't. If we go back there, protected as we are with our rays and stuff, it wouldn't surprise me a bit to find life there, and lots of it—and I've got a hunch that it'll be a form of life that'd make your grandfather's whiskers curl right up into a ball!"

"You do get the weirdest ideas, Dick!" protested Dorothy. "I hope you aren't planning on exploring it, just to prove your point?"

"Never thought of it before. Can't do it now, anyway—got our hands full already. However, after we get this Fenachrone mess cleaned up we'll have to do just that little thing, won't we, Mart? As that intellectual guy said while he was insisting upon dematerializing us, 'Science demands it.'"

"By all means. We should be in a position to make contributions to science in fields as yet untouched. Most assuredly we shall investigate those points."

"Then they'll go alone, won't they, Peggy?"

"Absolutely! We've seen some pretty middling horrible things already, and if these two men of ours call the frightful things we have seen normal, and are planning on deliberately hunting up things that even they will consider monstrous, you and I most certainly shall stay at home!"

"Yeah? You say it easy. Bounce back, Peg, you've struck a rubber fence! Rufus, you red-headed little fraud, you know you wouldn't let me go to the corner store after a can of tobacco without insisting on tagging along!"

"You're a...." began Dorothy hotly, but broke off in amazement and gasped, "For Heaven's sake, what was that?"

"What was what? It missed me."

"It went right through you! It was a kind of funny little cloud, like smoke or something. It came right through the ceiling like a flash—went right through you and on down through the floor. There it comes back again!"

Before their staring eyes a vague, nebulous something moved rapidly upward through the floor and passed upward through the ceiling. Dorothy leaped to Seaton's side and he put his arm around her reassuringly.

"'Sall right folks—I know what that thing is."

"Well, shoot it, quick!" Dorothy implored.

"It's one of those projections from where we're heading for, trying to get our range; and it's the most welcome sight these weary old eyes have rested upon for full many a long and dreary moon. They've probably located us from our power-plant rays. We're an awful long ways off yet, though, and going like a streak of greased lightning, so they're having trouble in holding us. They're friendly, we already know that—they probably want to talk to us. It'd make it easier for them if we'd shut off our power and drift at constant velocity, but we'd use up valuable time and throw our calculations all out of whack. We'll let them try to match our acceleration If they can do that, they're good."

The apparition reappeared, oscillating back and forth irregularly—passing through the arenak walls, through the furniture and the instrument boards, and even through the mighty power-plant itself, as though nothing was there. Eventually, however, it remained stationary a foot or so above the floor of the control-room. Then it began to increase in density until apparently a man stood before them. His skin, like that of all the inhabitants of the planets of the green suns, was green. He was tall and well-proportioned when judged by Earthly standards, except for his head, which was overly large, and which was particularly massive above the eyes and backward from the ears. He was evidently of great age, for what little of his face was visible was seamed and wrinkled, and his long, thick mane of hair and his square-cut, yard-long beard were a dazzling white, only faintly tinged with green.

While not in any sense transparent, nor even translucent, it was evident that the apparition before them was not composed of flesh and blood. He looked at each of the four Earth-beings intensely for a moment, then pointed toward the table upon which stood the mechanical educator, and Seaton placed it in front of the peculiar visitor. As Seaton donned a headset and handed one to the stranger, the latter stared at him, impressing upon his consciousness that he was to be given a knowledge of English. Seaton pressed the lever, receiving as he did so a sensation of an unbroken calm, a serenity profound and untroubled, and the projection spoke.

"Dr. Seaton, Mr. Crane, and ladies—welcome to Norlamin, the planet toward which you are now flying. We have been awaiting you for more than five thousand years of your time. It has been a mathematical certainty—it has been graven upon the very Sphere itself—that in time someone would come to us from without this system, bringing a portion, however small, of Rovolon—of the metal of power, of which there is not even the most minute trace in our entire solar system. For more than five thousand years our instruments have been set to detect the vibrations which would herald the advent of the user of that metal. Now you have come, and I perceive that you have vast stores of it. Being yourselves seekers after truth, you will share it with us gladly as we will instruct you in many things you wish to know. Allow me to operate the educator—I would gaze into your minds and reveal my own to your sight. But first I must tell you that your machine is too rudimentary to work at all well, and with your permission I shall make certain minor alterations."

Seaton nodded permission, and from the eyes and from the hands of the figure there leaped visible streams of force, which seized the transformers, coils and tubes, and reformed and reconnected them, under Seaton's bulging eyes, into an entirely different mechanism.

"Oh, I see!" he gasped. "Say, what are you anyway?"

"Pardon me; in my eagerness I became forgetful. I am Orlon, the First of Astronomy of Norlamin, in my observatory upon the surface of the planet. This that you see is simply my projection, composed of forces for which you have no name in your language. You can cut it off, if you wish, with your ray-screens, which even I can see are of a surprisingly high order of efficiency. There, this educator will now work very well. Please put on the remodeled headsets, all four of you."

They did so, and the rays of force moved levers, switches, and dials as positively as human hands could have moved them, and with infinitely greater speed and precision. As the dials moved, each brain received clearly and plainly a knowledge of the customs, language, and manners of the inhabitants of Norlamin. Each mind became suffused with a vast, immeasurable peace, calm power, and a depth and breadth of mental vision theretofore undreamed of. Looking deep into his mind they sensed a quiet, placid certainty, beheld power and knowledge to them illimitable, perceived depths of wisdom to them unfathomable.

Then from his mind into theirs there flowed smoothly a mighty stream of comprehension of cosmic phenomena. They hazily saw infinitely small units grouped into planetary formations to form practically dimensionless particles. These particles in turn grouped to form slightly larger ones, and after a long succession of such grouping they knew that the comparatively gigantic aggregates which then held their attention were in reality electrons and protons, the smallest units recognized by Earthly science. They clearly understood the combination of these electrons and protons into atoms.

They perceived plainly the way in which atoms build up molecules, and comprehended the molecular structure of matter. In mathematical thoughts, only dimly grasped even by Seaton and Crane, were laid before them the fundamental laws of physics, of electricity, of gravitation, and of chemistry. They saw globular aggregations of matter, the suns and their planets, comprising solar systems; saw solar systems, in accordance with those immutable laws, grouped into galaxies, galaxies in turn—here the flow was suddenly shut off as though a valve had been closed, and the astronomer spoke.

"Pardon me. Your brains should be stored only with the material you desire most and can use to the best advantage, for your mental capacity is even more limited than my own. Please understand that I speak in no derogatory sense; it is only that your race has many thousands of generations to go before your minds should be stored with knowledge indiscriminately. We ourselves have not yet reached that stage, and we are perhaps millions of years older than you. And yet," he continued musingly, "I envy you. Knowledge is, of course, relative, and I can know *so* little! Time and space have yielded not an iota of their mystery to our most penetrant minds. And whether we delve baffled into the unknown smallness of the small, or whether we peer, blind and helpless, into the unknown largeness of the large, it is the same—infinity is comprehensible only to the Infinite One: the all-shaping Force directing and controlling the Universe and the unknowable Sphere. The more we know, the vaster the virgin fields of investigation open to us, and the more infinitesimal becomes our knowledge. But I am perhaps keeping you from more important activities. As you approach Norlamin more nearly, I shall guide you to my observatory. I am glad indeed that it is in my lifetime that you have come to us, and I await anxiously the opportunity of greeting you in the flesh. The years remaining to me of this cycle of existence are few, and I had almost ceased hoping to witness your coming."

The projection vanished instantaneously, and the four stared at each other in an incredulous daze of astonishment. Seaton finally broke the stunned silence. "Well, I'll be kicked to death by little red spiders!" he ejaculated. "Mart, did you see what I saw, or did I get tight on something without knowing it? That sure burned me up—it breaks me right off at the ankles, just to think of it!"

Crane walked to the educator in silence. He examined it, felt the changed coils and transformers, and gently shook the new insulating base of the great power-tube. Still in silence he turned his back, walked around the instrument board, read the meters, then went back and again inspected the educator.

"It was real, and not a higher development of hypnotism, as at first I thought it must be," he reported seriously. "Hypnotism, if sufficiently advanced, might have affected us in that fashion, even to teaching us all a strange language, but by no possibility could it have had such an effect upon copper, steel, bakelite, and glass. It was certainly real, and while I cannot begin to understand it, I will say that your imagination has certainly vindicated itself. A race of beings, who can do such things as that, can do almost anything—you have been right, from the start."

"Then you can beat those horrible Fenachrone, after all!" cried Dorothy, and threw herself into her husband's arms.

"Do you remember, Dick, that I hailed you once as Columbus at San Salvador?" asked Margaret unsteadily from Crane's encircling arm. "What could a man be called who from the sheer depths of his imagination called forth the means of saving from destruction all the civilization of millions of entire worlds?"

"Don't talk that way, please, folks," Seaton was plainly very uncomfortable. He blushed intensely, the burning red tide rising in waves up to his hair as he wriggled in embarrassment, like any schoolboy. "Mart's done most of it, anyway, you know; and even at that, we ain't out of the woods yet, by forty-seven rows of apple trees."

"You will admit, will you not, that we can see our way out of the woods, at least, and that you yourself feel rather relieved?" asked Crane.

"I think we'll be able to pull their corks now, all right, after we get some dope. It's a cinch they've either got the stuff we need or know how to get it—and if that zone is impenetrable, I'll bet they'll be able to dope out something just as good. Relieved? That doesn't half tell it, guy—I feel as if I had just pitched off the Old Man of the Sea who's been sitting on my neck! What say you girls get your fiddle and guitar and we'll sing us a little song? I feel kind of relieved—they had me worried some—it's the first time I've felt like singing since we cut that warship up."

Dorothy brought out her "fiddle"—the magnificent Stradivarius, formerly Crane's, which he had given her—Margaret her guitar, and they sang one rollicking number after another. Though by no means a Metropolitan Opera quartette, their voices were all better than mediocre, and they had sung together so much that they harmonized readily.

"Why don't you play us some real music, Dottie?" asked Margaret, after a time. "You haven't practiced for ages."

"I haven't felt like playing lately, but I do now," and Dorothy stood up and swept the bow over the strings. Doctor of Music in violin, an accomplished musician, playing upon one of the finest instruments the world has ever known, she was lifted out of herself by relief from the dread of the Fenachrone invasion and that splendid violin expressed every subtle nuance of her thought.

She played rhapsodies and paeans, and solos by the great masters. She played vivacious dances, then "Traumerei" and "Liebestraum." At last she swept into the immortal "Meditation," and as the last note died away Seaton held out his arms.

"You're a blinding flash and a deafening report, Dottie Dimple, and I love you," he declared—and his eyes and his arms spoke volumes that his light utterance had left unsaid.

Norlamin close enough so that its image almost filled number six visiplate, the four wanderers studied it with interest. Partially obscured by clouds and with its polar regions two glaring caps of snow—they would be green in a few months, when the planet would swing inside the orbit of its sun around the vast central luminary of that complex solar system—it made a magnificent picture. They saw sparkling blue oceans and huge green continents of unfamiliar outlines. So terrific was the velocity of the space-cruiser, that the image grew larger as they watched it, and soon the field of vision could not contain the image of the whole disk.

"Well, I expect Orlon'll be showing up pretty quick now," remarked Seaton; and it was not long until the projection appeared in the air of the control room.

"Hail, Terrestrials!" he greeted them. "With your permission, I shall direct your flight."

Permission granted, the figure floated across the room to the board and the rays of force centered the visiplate, changed the direction of the bar a trifle, decreased slightly their negative acceleration, and directed a stream of force upon the steering mechanism.

"We shall alight upon the grounds of my observatory upon Norlamin in seven thousand four hundred twenty-eight seconds," he announced presently. "The observatory will be upon the dark side of Norlamin when we arrive, but I have a force operating upon the steering mechanism which will guide the vessel along the required curved path. I shall remain with you until we land, and we may converse upon any topic of most interest to you."

"We've got a topic of interest, all right. That's what we came out here for. But it would take too long to tell you about it—I'll show you!"

He brought out the magnetic brain record, threaded it into the machine and handed the astronomer a head-set. Orlon put it on, touched the lever, and for an hour there was unbroken silence as the monstrous brain of the menace was studied by the equally capable intellect of the Norlaminian scientist. There was no pause in the motion of the magnetic tape, no repetition—Orlon's brain absorbed the information as fast as it could be sent, and understood that frightful mind in every particular.

As the end of the tape was reached and the awful record ended, a shadow passed over Orlon's face.

"Truly a depraved evolution—it is sad to contemplate such a perversion of a really excellent brain. They have power, even as you have, and they have the will to destroy, which is a thing that I cannot understand. However, if it is graven upon the Sphere that we are to pass, it means only that upon the next plane we shall continue our searches—let us hope with better tools and with greater understanding than we now possess."

"'Smatter?" snapped Seaton gravely. "Going to take it lying down, without putting up any fight at all?"

"What can we do? Violence is contrary to our very natures. No man of Norlamin could offer any but passive resistance."

"You can do a lot if you will. Put on that headset again and get my plan, offering any suggestions your far abler brain may suggest."

As the human scientist poured his plan of battle into the brain of the astronomer, Orlon's face cleared.

"It is graven upon the Sphere that the Fenachrone shall pass," he said finally. "What you ask of us we can do. I have only a general knowledge of rays, as they are not in the province of the Orlon family; but the student Rovol, of the family Rovol of Rays, has all present knowledge of such phenomena. Tomorrow I will bring you together, and I have little doubt that he will be able, with the help of your metal of power, to solve your problem."

"I don't quite understand what you said about a whole family studying one subject, and yet having only one student in it," said Dorothy, in perplexity.

"A little explanation is perhaps necessary," replied Orlon. "First, you must know that every man of Norlamin is a student, and most of us are students of science. With us, 'labor' means mental effort, that is, study. We perform no physical or manual labor save for exercise, as all our mechanical work is done by forces. This state of things having endured for many thousands of years, it long ago became evident that specialization was necessary in order to avoid duplication of effort and to insure complete coverage of the field. Soon afterward, it was discovered that very little progress was being made in any branch, because so much was known that it took practically a lifetime to review that which had already been accomplished, even in a narrow and highly specialized field. Many points were studied for years before it was discovered that the identical work had been done before, and either forgotten or overlooked. To remedy this condition the mechanical educator had to be developed. Once it was perfected a new system was begun. One man was assigned to each small subdivision of scientific endeavor, to study it intensively. When he became old, each man chose a successor—usually a son—and transferred his own knowledge to the younger student. He also made a complete record of his own brain, in much the same way as you have recorded the brain of the Fenachrone upon your metallic tape. These records are all stored in a great central library, as permanent references.

"All these things being true, now a young person may need only finish an elementary education—just enough to learn to think, which takes only about twenty-five or thirty years—and then he is ready to begin actual work. When that time comes, he receives in one day all the knowledge of his specialty which has been accumulated by his predecessors during many thousands of years of intensive study."

"Whew!" Seaton whistled, "no wonder you folks know something! With that start, I believe I might know something myself! As an astronomer, you may be interested in this star-chart and stuff—or do you know all about that already?"

"No, the Fenachrone are far ahead of us in that subject, because of their observatories out in open space and because of their gigantic reflectors, which cannot be used through any atmosphere. We are further hampered in having darkness for only a few hours at a time and only in the winter, when our planet is outside the orbit of our sun around the great central sun of our entire system. However, with the Rovolon you have brought us, we shall have real observatories far out in space; and for that I personally will be indebted to you more than I can ever express. As for the chart, I hope to have the pleasure of examining it while you are conferring with Rovol of Rays."

"How many families are working on rays—just one?"

"One upon each kind of ray. That is, each of the ray families knows a great deal about all kinds of vibrations of the ether, but is specializing upon one narrow field. Take, for instance, the rays you are most interested in; those able to penetrate a zone of force. From my own very slight and general knowledge I know that it would of necessity be a ray of the fifth order. These rays are very new—they have been under investigation only a few hundred years—and the Rovol is the only student who would be at all well informed upon them. Shall I explain the orders of rays more fully than I did by means of the educator?"

"Please. You assumed that we knew more than we do, so a little explanation would help."

"All ordinary vibrations—that is, all molecular and material ones, such as light, heat, electricity, radio, and the like—were arbitrarily called waves of the first order; in order to distinguish them from waves of the second order, which are given off by particles of the second order, which you know as protons and electrons, in their combination to form atoms. Your scientist Millikan discovered these rays for you, and in your language they are known as Millikan, or Cosmic, rays.

"Some time later, when sub-electrons were identified the rays given off by their combination into electrons, or by the disruption of electrons, were called rays of the third order. These rays are most interesting and most useful; in fact, they do all our mechanical work. They as a class are called protelectricity, and bear the same relation to ordinary electricity that electricity does to torque—both are pure energy, and they are inter-convertible. Unlike electricity, however, it may be converted into many different forms by fields of force, in a way comparable to that in which white light is resolved into colors by a prism—or rather, more like the way alternating current is changed to direct current by a motor-generator set, with attendant changes in properties. There is a complete spectrum of more than five hundred factors, each as different from the others as red is different from green.

"Continuing farther, particles of the fourth order give rays of the fourth order; those of the fifth, rays of the fifth order. Fourth-order rays have been investigated quite thoroughly, but only mathematically and theoretically, as they are of excessively short wave-length and are capable of being generated only by the breaking down of matter itself into the corresponding particles. However, it has been shown that they are quite similar to protelectricity in their general behavior. Thus, the power that propels your space-vessel, your attractors, your repellers, your object-compass, your zone of force—all these things are simply a few of the many hundreds of wave-bands of the fourth order, all of which you doubtless would have worked out for yourselves in time. Very little is known, even in theory, of the rays of the fifth order, although they have been shown to exist."

"For a man having no knowledge, you seem to know a lot about rays. How about the fifth order—is that as far as they go?"

"My knowledge is slight and very general; only such as I must have in order to understand my own subject. The fifth order certainly is not the end—it is probably scarcely a beginning. We think now that the orders extend to infinite smallness, just as the galaxies are grouped into larger aggregations, which are probably in their turn only tiny units in a scheme infinitely large.

"Over six thousand years ago the last third order rays were worked out; and certain peculiarities in their behavior led the then Rovol to suspect the existence of the fourth order. Successive generations of the Rovol proved their existence, determined the conditions of their liberation, and found that this metal of power was the only catalyst able to decompose matter and thus liberate the rays. This metal, which was called Rovolon after the Rovol, was first described upon theoretical grounds and later was found, by spectroscopy, in certain stars, notably in one star only eight light-years away, but not even the most infinitesimal trace of it exists in our entire solar system. Since these discoveries, the many Rovol have been perfecting the theory of the fourth order, beginning that of the fifth, and waiting for your coming. The present Rovol, like myself and many others whose work is almost at a standstill, is waiting with all-consuming interest to greet you, as soon as the *Skylark* can be landed upon our planet."

"Neither your rocket-ships nor your projections could get you any Rovolon?"

"No. Every hundred years or so someone develops a new type of rocket that he thinks may stand a slight chance of making the journey, but not one of these venturesome youths has as yet returned. Either that sun has no planets or else the rocket-ships have failed. Our projections are useless, as they can be driven only a very short distance upon our present carrier wave. With a carrier of the fifth order we could drive a projection to any point in the galaxy, since its velocity would be millions of times that of light and the power necessary reduced accordingly—but as I have said before, such waves cannot be generated without metal Rovolon."

"I hate to break this up—I'd like to listen to you talk for a week—but we're going to land pretty quick, and it looks as though we were going to land pretty hard."

"We will land soon, but not hard," replied Orlon confidently, and the landing was as he had foretold. The *Skylark* was falling with an ever-decreasing velocity, but so fast was the descent that it seemed to the watchers as though they must crash through the roof of the huge brilliantly lighted building upon which they were dropping and bury themselves many feet in the ground beneath it. But they did not strike the observatory. So incredibly accurate were the calculations of the Norlaminian astronomer and so inhumanly precise were the controls he had set upon their bar, that, as they touched the ground after barely clearing the domed roof and he shut off their power, the passengers felt only a sudden decrease in acceleration, like that following the coming to rest of a rapidly moving elevator, after it has completed a downward journey.

"I shall join you in person very shortly," Orlon said, and the projection vanished.

"Well, we're here, folks, on another new world. Not quite as thrilling as the first one was, is it?" and Seaton stepped toward the door.

"How about the air composition, density, gravity, temperature, and so on?" asked Crane. "Perhaps we should make a few tests."

"Didn't you get that on the educator? Thought you did. Gravity a little less than seven-tenths. Air composition, same as Osnome and Dasor. Pressure, half-way between Earth and Osnome. Temperature, like Osnome most of the time, but fairly comfortable in the winter. Snow now at the poles, but this observatory is only ten degrees from the equator. They don't wear clothes enough to flag a hand-car with here, either, except when they have to. Let's go!"

He opened the door and the four travelers stepped out upon a close-cropped lawn—a turf whose blue-green softness would shame an Oriental rug. The landscape was illuminated by a soft and mellow, yet intense green light which emanated from no visible source. As they paused and glanced about them, they saw that the *Skylark* had alighted in the exact center of a circular enclosure a hundred yards in diameter, walled by row upon row of shrubbery, statuary, and fountains, all bathed in ever-changing billows of light. At only one point was the circle broken. There the walls did not come together, but continued on to border a lane leading up to the massive structure of cream-and-green marble, topped by its enormous, glassy dome—the observatory of Orlon.

"Welcome to Norlamin, Terrestrials," the deep, calm voice of the astronomer greeted them, and Orlon in the flesh shook hands cordially in the American fashion with each of them in turn, and placed around each neck a crystal chain from which depended a small Norlaminian chronometer-radiophone. Behind him there stood four other old men.

"These men are already acquainted with each of you, but you do not as yet know them. I present Fodan, Chief of the Five of Norlamin. Rovol, about whom you know. Astron, the First of Energy. Satrazon, the First of Chemistry."

Orlon fell in beside Seaton and the party turned toward the observatory. As they walked along the Earth-people stared, held by the unearthly beauty of the grounds. The hedge of shrubbery, from ten to twenty feet high, and which shut out all sight of everything outside it, was one mass of vivid green and flaring crimson leaves; each leaf and twig groomed meticulously into its precise place in a fantastic geometrical scheme. Just inside this boundary there stood a ring of statues of heroic size. Some of them were single figures of men and women; some were busts; some were groups in natural or allegorical poses—all were done with consummate skill and feeling. Between the statues there were fountains, magnificent bronze and glass groups of the strange aquatic denizens of this strange planet, bathed in geometrically shaped sprays, screens, and columns of water. Winding around between the statues and the fountains there was a moving, scintillating wall, and upon the waters and upon the wall there played torrents of color, cataracts of harmoniously blended light. Reds, blues, yellows, greens—every color of their peculiar green spectrum and every conceivable combination of those colors writhed and flamed in ineffable splendor upon those deep and living screens of falling water and upon that shimmering wall.

As they entered the lane, Seaton saw with amazement that what he had supposed a wall, now close at hand, was not a wall at all. It was composed of myriads of individual sparkling jewels, of every known color, for the most part self-luminous; and each gem, apparently entirely unsupported, was dashing in and out and along among its fellows, weaving and darting here and there, flying at headlong speed along an extremely tortuous, but evidently carefully calculated course.

"What can that be, anyway, Dick?" whispered Dorothy, and Seaton turned to his guide.

"Pardon my curiosity, Orlon, but would you mind explaining the why of that moving wall? We don't get it."

"Not at all. This garden has been the private retreat of the family of Orlon for many thousands of years, and women of our house have been beautifying it since its inception. You may have observed that the statuary is very old. No such work has been done for ages. Modern art has developed along the lines of color and motion, hence the lighting effects and the tapestry wall. Each gem is held upon the end of a minute pencil of force, and all the pencils are controlled by a machine which has a key for every jewel in the wall."

Crane, the methodical, stared at the innumerable flashing jewels and asked, "It must have taken a prodigious amount of time to complete such an undertaking?"

"It is far from complete; in fact, it is scarcely begun. It was started only about four hundred years ago."

"*Four hundred years!*" exclaimed Dorothy. "Do you live that long? How long will it take to finish it, and what will it be like when it is done?"

"No, none of us live longer than about one hundred and sixty years—at about that age most of us decide to pass. When this tapestry wall is finished, it will not be simply form and color, as it is now. It will be a portrayal of the history of Norlamin from the first cooling of the planet. It will, in all probability, require thousands of years for its completion. You see, time is of little importance to us, and workmanship is everything. My companion will continue working upon it until we decide to pass; my son's companion may continue it. In any event, many generations of the women of the Orlon will work upon it until it is complete. When it is done, it will be a thing of beauty as long as Norlamin shall endure."

"But suppose that your son's wife isn't that kind of an artist? Suppose she should want to do music or painting or something else?" asked Dorothy, curiously.

"That is quite possible; for, fortunately, our art is not yet entirely intellectual, as is our music. There are many unfinished artistic projects in the house of Orlon, and if the companion of my son should not find one to her liking, she will be at liberty to continue anything else she may have begun, or to start an entirely new project of her own."

"You have a family, then?" asked Margaret, "I'm afraid I didn't understand things very well when you gave them to us over the educator."

"I sent things too fast for you, not knowing that your educator was new to you; a thing with which you were not thoroughly familiar. I will therefore explain some things in language, since you are not familiar with the mechanism of thought transference. The Five, a self-perpetuating body, do what governing is necessary for the entire planet. Their decrees are founded upon self-evident truth, and are therefore the law. Population is regulated according to the needs of the planet, and since much work is now in progress, an increase in population was recommended by the Five. My companion and I therefore had three children, instead of the customary two. By lot it fell to us to have two boys and one girl. One of the boys will assume my duties when I pass; the other will take over a part of some branch of science that has grown too complex for one man to handle as a specialist should. In fact, he has already chosen his specialty and been accepted for it—he is to be the nine hundred and sixty-seventh of Chemistry, the student of the asymmetric carbon atom, which will thus be his specialty from this time henceforth.

"It was learned long ago that the most perfect children were born of parents in the full prime of mental life, that is, at one hundred years of age. Therefore, with us each generation covers one hundred years. The first twenty-five years of a child's life are spent at home with his parents, during which time he acquires his elementary education in the common schools. Then boys and girls alike move to the Country of Youth, where they spend another twenty-five years. There they develop their brains and initiative by conducting any researches they choose. Most of us, at that age, solve all the riddles of the Universe, only to discover later that our solutions have been fallacious. However, much really excellent work is done in the Country of Youth, primarily because of the new and unprejudiced viewpoints of the virgin minds there at work. In that country also each finds his life's companion, the one necessary to round out mere existence into a perfection of living that no person, man or woman, can ever know alone. I need not speak to you of the wonders of love or of the completion and fullness of life that it brings, for all four of you, children though you are, know love in full measure.

"At fifty years of age the man, now mentally mature, is recalled to his family home, as his father's brain is now losing some of its vigor and keenness. The father then turns over his work to the son by means of the educator—and when the weight of the accumulated knowledge of a hundred thousand generations of research is impressed upon the son's brain, his play is over."

"What does the father do then?"

"Having made his brain record, about which I have told you, he and his companion—for she has in similar fashion turned over her work to her successor—retire to the Country of Age, where they rest and relax after their century of effort. They do whatever they care to do, for as long as they please to do it. Finally, after assuring themselves that all is well with the children, they decide that they are ready for the Change. Then, side by side as they have labored, they pass."

Now at the door of the observatory, Dorothy paused and shrank back against Seaton, her eyes widening as she stared at Orlon.

"No, daughter, why should we fear the Change?" he answered her unspoken question, calm serenity in every inflection of his quiet voice. "The life-principle is unknowable to the finite mind, as is the All-Controlling Force. But even though we know nothing of the sublime goal toward which it is tending, any person ripe for the Change can, and of course does, liberate the life-principle so that its progress may be unimpeded."

In a spacious room of the observatory, in which the Terrestrials and their Norlaminian hosts had been long engaged in study and discussion, Seaton finally rose and extended a hand toward his wife.

"Well, that's that, then, Orlon, I guess. We've been thirty hours without sleep, and for us that's a long time. I'm getting so dopey I can't think a lick. We'd better go back to the *Skylark* and turn in, and after we've slept nine hours or so I'll go over to Rovol's laboratory and Crane'll come back here to you."

"You need not return to your vessel," said Orlon. "I know that its somewhat cramped quarters have become irksome. Apartments have been prepared here for you. We shall have a meal here together, and then we shall retire, to meet again tomorrow."

As he spoke, a tray laden with appetizing dishes appeared in the air in front of each person. As Seaton resumed his seat the tray followed him, remaining always in the most convenient position.

Crane glanced at Seaton questioningly, and Satrazon, the First of Chemistry, answered his thought before he could voice it.

"The food before you, unlike that which is before us of Norlamin, is wholesome for you. It contains no copper, no arsenic, no heavy metals—in short, nothing in the least harmful to your chemistry. It is balanced as to carbohydrates, proteins, fats and sugars, and contains the due proportion of each of the various accessory nutritional factors. You will also find the flavors are agreeable to each of you."

"Synthetic, eh? You've got us analyzed," Seaton stated, rather than asked, as with knife and fork he attacked the thick, rare, and beautifully broiled steak which, with its mushrooms and other delicate trimmings, lay upon his rigid although unsupported tray—noticing as he did so that the Norlaminians ate with tools entirely different from those they had supplied to their Earthly guests.

"Entirely synthetic," Satrazon made answer, "except for the sodium chloride necessary. As you already know, sodium and chlorin are very rare throughout our system, therefore the force upon the food-supply took from your vessel the amount of salt required for the formula. We have been unable to synthesize atoms, for the same reason that the labors of so many others have been hindered—because of the lack of Rovolon. Now, however, my science shall progress as it should; and for that I join with my fellow scientists in giving you thanks for the service you have rendered us."

"We thank you instead," replied Seaton, "for the service we have been able to do you is slight indeed compared to what you are giving us in return. But it seems that you speak quite impersonally of the force upon the food supply. Did you yourself direct the preparation of these meats and vegetables?"

"Oh, no. I merely analyzed your tissues, surveyed the food-supplies you carried, discovered your individual preferences, and set up the necessary integrals in the mechanism. The forces did the rest, and will continue to do so as long as you remain upon this planet."

"Fruit salad always my favorite dish," Dorothy said, after a couple of bites, "and this one is just too perfectly divine! It doesn't taste like any other fruit I ever ate, either—I think it must be the same ambrosia that the old pagan gods used to eat."

"If all you did was to set up the integrals, how do you know what you are going to have for the next meal?" asked Crane.

"We have no idea what the form, flavor, or consistency of any dish will be," was the surprising answer. "We know only that the flavor will be agreeable and that it will agree with the form and consistency of the substance, and that the composition will be well-balanced chemically. You see, all the details of flavor, form, texture, and so on are controlled by a device something like one of your kaleidoscopes. The integrals render impossible any unwholesome, unpleasant, or unbalanced combination of any nature, and everything else is left to the mechanism, which operates upon pure chance."

"Some system, I'd rise to remark," and Seaton, with the others, resumed his vigorous attack upon the long-delayed supper.

The meal over, the Earthly visitors were shown to their rooms, and fell into a deep, dreamless sleep.

CHAPTER X

Norlaminian Science

Breakfast over, Seaton watched intently as his tray, laden with empty containers, floated away from him and disappeared into an opening in the wall.

"How do you do it, Orlon?" he asked, curiously. "I can hardly believe it, even after seeing it done."

"Each tray is carried upon the end of a beam or rod of force, and supported rigidly by it. Since the beam is tuned to the individual wave of the instrument you wear upon your chest, your tray is, of course, placed in front of you, at a predetermined distance, as soon as the sending force is actuated. When you have finished your meal, the beam is shortened. Thus the tray is drawn back to the food laboratory, where other forces cleanse and sterilize the various utensils and place them in readiness for the next meal. It would be an easy matter to have this same mechanism place your meals before you wherever you may go upon this planet, provided only that a clear path can be plotted from the laboratory to your person."

"Thanks, but it wouldn't pay. No telling where we'd be. Besides, we'd better eat in the *Skylark* most of the time, to keep our cook good-natured. Well, I see Rovol's got his boat here for me, so guess I'd better turn up a few r. p. m. Coming along, Dot, or have you got something else on your mind?"

"I'm going to leave you for a while. I can't really understand even a radio, and just thinking about those funny, complicated rays and things you are going after makes me dizzy in the head. Mrs. Orlon is going to take us over to the Country of Youth—she says Margaret and I can play around with her daughter and her bunch and have a good time while you scientists are doing your stuff."

"All right. 'Bye till tonight," and Seaton stepped out into the grounds, where the First of Rays was waiting.

The flier was a torpedo-shaped craft of some transparent, glassy material, completely enclosed except for one circular opening or doorway. From the midsection, which was about five feet in diameter and provided with heavily-cushioned seats capable of carrying four passengers in comfort, the hull tapered down smoothly to a needle point at each end. As Seaton entered and settled himself into the cushions, Rovol touched a lever. Instantly a transparent door slid across the opening, locking itself into position flush with the surface of the hull, and the flier darted into the air and away. For a few minutes there was silence, as Seaton studied the terrain beneath them. Fields or cities there were none; the land was covered with dense forests and vast meadows, with here and there great buildings surrounded by gracious, park-like areas. Rovol finally broke the silence.

"I understand your problem, I believe, since Orlon has transferred to me all the thoughts he had from you. With the aid of the Rovolon you have brought us, I am confident that we shall be able to work out a satisfactory solution of the various problems involved. It will take us some few minutes to traverse the distance to my laboratory, and if there are any matters upon which your mind is not quite clear, I shall try to clarify them."

"That's letting me down easy," Seaton grinned, "but you don't need to be afraid of hurting my feelings—I know just exactly how ignorant and dumb I am compared to you. There's a lot of things I don't get at all. First, and nearest, this airboat. It has no power-plant at all. I assume that it, like so many other things hereabouts, is riding on the end of a rod of force?"

"Exactly. The beam is generated and maintained in my laboratory. All that is here in the flier is a small sender, for remote control."

"How do you obtain your power?" asked Seaton. "Solar generators and tide motors? I know that all your work is done by protelectricity, but Orlon did not inform us as to the sources."

"We have not used such inefficient generators for many thousands of years. Long ago it was shown by research that these rays were constantly being generated in abundance in outer space, and that they could be collected upon spherical condensers and transmitted without loss to the surface of the planet by means of matched and synchronized crystals. Several millions of these condensers have been built and thrown out to become tiny satellites of Norlamin."

"How did you get them far enough out?"

"The first ones were forced out to the required distance upon beams of force produced by the conversion of electricity, which was in turn produced from turbines, solar motors, and tide motors. With a few of them out, however, it was easy to obtain sufficient power to send out more; and now, whenever one of us requires more power than he has at his disposal, he merely sends out such additional collectors as he needs."

"Now about those fifth-order rays, which will penetrate a zone of force. I am told that they are not ether waves at all?"

"They are not ether waves. The fourth order rays, of which the theory has been completely worked out, are the shortest vibrations that can be propagated through the ether; for the ether itself is not a continuous medium. We do not know its nature exactly, but it is an actual substance, and is composed of discrete particles of the fourth order. Now the zone of force, which is itself a fourth-order phenomenon, sets up a condition of stasis in the particles composing the ether. These particles are relatively so coarse, that rays and particles of the fifth order will pass through the fixed zone without retardation. Therefore, if there is anything between the particles of the ether—this matter is being debated hotly among us at the present time—it must be a sub-ether, if I may use that term. We have never been able to investigate any of these things experimentally, not even such a coarse aggregation as is the ether; but now, having Rovolon, it will not be many thousands of years until we shall have extended our knowledge many orders farther, in both directions."

"Just how will Rovolon help you?"

"It will enable us to generate a force of the ninth magnitude—that much power is necessary to set up what you have so aptly named a zone of force—and will give us a source of fourth, fifth, and probably higher orders of rays which, if they are generated in space at all, are beyond our present reach. The zone of force is necessary to shield certain items of equipment from ether vibrations; as any such vibration inside the controlling fields of force renders observation or control of the higher orders of rays impossible."

"Hm ... m, I see—I'm learning something," Seaton replied cordially. "Just as the higher-powered a radio set is, the more perfect must be its shielding?"

"Yes. Just as a trace of any gas will destroy the usefulness of your most sensitive vacuum tubes, and just as imperfect shielding will allow interfering waves to enter sensitive electrical apparatus—in that same fashion will even the slightest ether vibration interfere with the operation of the extremely sensitive fields and lenses of force which must be used in controlling forces of the higher orders."

"You haven't tested the theory of the fourth order yet, have you?"

"No, but that is unnecessary. The theory of the fourth order is not really theory at all—it is mathematical fact. Although we have never been able to generate them, we know exactly the forces you use in your ship of space, and we can tell you of some thousands of others more or less similar and also highly useful forces which you have not yet discovered, but are allowing to go to waste. We know exactly what they are, how to liberate and control them, and how to use them. In fact, in the work which we are to begin today, we shall use but little ordinary power: almost all our work will be done by fourth-order forces, liberated from copper by means of the

Rovolon you have given me. But here we are at my laboratory. You already know that the best way to learn is by doing, and we shall begin at once."

The flier alighted upon a lawn quite similar to the one before the observatory of Orlon, and the scientist led his Earthly guest through the main entrance of the imposing structure of vari-colored marble and gleaming metal and into the vast, glass-lined room that was his laboratory. Great benches lined the walls, and there were hundreds of dials, meters, tubes, transformers and other instruments, whose uses Seaton could not even guess.

Rovol first donned a suit of transparent, flexible material, of a deep golden color, instructing Seaton to do the same; explaining that much of the work would be with dangerous frequencies and with high pressures, and that the suits were not only absolute insulators against electricity, heat, and sound, but were also ray-filters proof against any harmful radiations. As each helmet was equipped with radiophones, conversation was not interfered with in the least.

Rovol took up a tiny flash-pencil, and with it deftly cut off a bit of Rovolon, almost microscopic in size. This he placed upon a great block of burnished copper, and upon it played a force. As he manipulated two levers, two more beams of force flattened out the particle of metal, spread it out over the copper, and forced it into the surface of the block until the thin coating was at every point in molecular contact with the copper beneath it—a perfect job of plating, and one done in the twinkling of an eye. He then cut out a piece of the treated copper the size of a pea, and other forces rapidly built around it a structure of coils and metallic tubes. This apparatus he suspended in the air at the extremity of a small beam of force. The block of copper was next cut in two, and Rovol's fingers moved rapidly over the keys of a machine which resembled slightly an overgrown and exceedingly complicated book-keeping machine. Streams and pencils of force flashed and crackled, and Seaton saw raw materials transformed into a complete power-plant, in its center the two-hundred-pound lump of plated copper, where an instant before there had been only empty space upon the massive metal bench. Rovol's hands moved rapidly from keys to dials and back, and suddenly a zone of force, as large as a basketball appeared around the apparatus poised in the air.

"But it'll fly off and we can't stop it with anything," Seaton protested, and it did indeed dart rapidly upward.

The old man shook his head as he manipulated still more controls, and Seaton gasped as nine stupendous beams of force hurled themselves upon that brilliant spherical mirror of pure energy, seized it in mid-flight, and shaped it resistlessly, under his bulging eyes, into a complex geometrical figure of precisely the desired form.

Lurid violet light filled the room, and Seaton turned towards the bar. That two-hundred-pound mass of copper was shrinking visibly, second by second, so vast were the forces being drawn from it, and the searing, blinding light would have been intolerable but for the protective color-filters of his helmet. Tremendous flashes of lightning ripped and tore from the relief-points of the bench to the ground-rods, which flared at blue-white temperature under the incessant impacts. Knowing that this corona-loss was but an infinitesimal fraction of the power being used, Seaton's very mind staggered as he strove to understand the magnitude of the forces at work upon that stubborn sphere of energy.

The aged scientist used no tools whatever, as we understand the term. His laboratory was a power-house; at his command were the stupendous forces of a battery of planetoid accumulators, and added to these were the fourth-order, ninth-magnitude forces of the disintegrating copper bar. Electricity, protelectricity, and fourth-order rays, under millions upon millions of kilovolts of pressure, leaped to do the bidding of that wonderful brain, stored with the accumulated knowledge of countless thousands of years of scientific research. Watching the ancient physicist work, Seaton compared himself to a schoolboy mixing chemicals indiscriminately and ignorantly, with no knowledge whatever of their properties, occasionally obtaining a reaction by pure chance. Whereas he had worked with intra-atomic energy schoolboy fashion, the master craftsman before him knew every reagent, every reaction, and worked with known and thoroughly familiar agencies to bring about his exactly predetermined ends—just as calmly certain of the results as Seaton himself would have been in his own laboratory, mixing equivalent quantities of solutions of barium chloride and of sulphuric acid to obtain a precipitate of barium sulphate.

Hour after hour Rovol labored on, oblivious to the passage of time in his zeal of accomplishment, the while carefully instructing Seaton, who watched every step with intense interest....

Hour after hour Rovol labored on, oblivious to the passage of time in his zeal of accomplishment, the while carefully instructing Seaton, who watched every step with intense interest and did everything possible for him to do. Bit by bit a towering structure arose in the middle of the laboratory. A metal foundation supported a massive compound bearing, which in turn carried a tubular network of latticed metal, mounted like an immense telescope. Near the upper, outer end of this openwork tube a group of nine forces held the field of force rigidly in place in its axis; at the lower extremity were mounted seats for two operators and the control panels necessary for the operation of the intricate system of forces and motors which would actuate and control that gigantic projector. Immense hour and declination circles could be read by optical systems from the operators' seats—circles fully forty feet in diameter, graduated with incredible delicacy and accuracy into decimal fractions of seconds of arc, and each driven by variable-speed motors through gear-trains and connections having no backlash whatever.

While Rovol was working upon one of the last instruments to be installed upon the controlling panel a mellow note sounded throughout the building, and he immediately ceased his labors and opened the master-switches of his power plants.

"You have done well, youngster," he congratulated his helper, as he began to take off his protective covering, "Without your aid I could not have accomplished nearly this much during one period of labor. The periods of exercise and of relaxation are at hand—let us return to the house of Orlon, where we all shall gather to relax and to refresh ourselves for the labors of tomorrow."

"But it's almost done!" protested Seaton. "Let's finish it up and shoot a little juice through it, just to try it out."

"There speaks the rashness and impatience of youth," rejoined the scientist, calmly removing the younger man's suit and leading him out to the waiting airboat. "I read in your mind that you are often guilty of laboring continuously until your brain loses its keen edge. Learn now, once and for all, that such conduct is worse than foolish—it is criminal. We have labored the full period. Laboring for more than that length of time without recuperation results in a loss of power which, if persisted in, wreaks permanent injury to the mind; and by it you gain nothing. We have more than ample time to do that which must be done—the fifth-order projector shall be completed before the warning torpedo shall have reached the planet of the Fenachrone—therefore over-exertion is unwarranted. As for testing, know now that only mechanisms built by bunglers require testing. Properly built machines work properly."

"But I'd have liked to see it work just once, anyway," lamented Seaton as the small airship tore through the air on its way back to the observatory.

"You must cultivate calmness, my son, and the art of relaxation. With those qualities your race can easily double its present span of useful life. Physical exercise to maintain the bodily tissues at their best, and mental relaxation following mental toil—these things are the secrets of a long and productive life. Why attempt to do more than can be accomplished efficiently? There is always tomorrow. I am more interested in that which we are now building than you can possibly be, since many generations of the Rovol have anticipated its construction; yet I realize that in the interest of our welfare and for the progress of civilization, today's labors must not be prolonged beyond today's period of work. Furthermore, you yourself realize that there is no optimum point at which any task may be interrupted. Short of final completion of any project, one point is the same as any other. Had we continued, we would have wished to continue still farther, and so on without end."

"You're probably right, at that," the impetuous chemist conceded, as their craft came to earth before the observatory.

Crane and Orlon were already in the common room, as were the scientists Seaton already knew, as well as a group of women and children still strangers to the Terrestrials. In a few minutes Orlon's companion, a dignified, white-haired woman, entered; accompanied by Dorothy, Margaret, and a laughing, boisterous group of men and women from the Country of Youth. Introductions over, Seaton turned to Crane.

"How's every little thing, Mart?"

"Very well indeed. We are building an observatory in space—or rather, Orlon is building it and I am doing what little I can to help him. In a few days we shall be able to locate the system of the Fenachrone. How is your work progressing?"

"Smoother than a kitten's ear. Got the fourth-order projector about done. We're going to project a fourth-order force out to grab us some dense material, a pretty close approach to pure neutronium. There's nothing dense enough around here, even in the core of the central sun, so we're going out to a white dwarf star—one a good deal like the companion star to Sirius in Canis Major—get some material of the proper density from its core, and convert our sender into a fifth-order machine. Then we can really get busy—go places and do things."

"Neutronium? Pure mass?" queried Crane, "I have been under the impression that it does not exist. Of what use can such a substance be to you?"

"Can't get pure neutronium, of course—couldn't use it if we could. What we need and are going to get is a material of about two and a half million specific gravity. Got to have it for lenses and controls for the fifth-order forces. Those rays go right through anything less dense without measurable refraction. But I see Rovol's giving me a nasty look. He's my boss on this job, and I imagine this kind of talk's barred during the period of relaxation, as being work. That so, chief?"

"You know that it is barred, you incorrigible young cub!" answered Rovol, with a smile.

"All right, boss; one more little infraction and I'll shut up like a clam. I'd like to know what the girls have been doing."

"We've been having a wonderful time!" Dorothy declared. "We've been designing fabrics and ornaments and jewels and things. Wait 'til you see 'em!"

"Fine! All right, Orlon, it's your party—what to do?"

"This is the time of exercise. We have many forms, most of which are unfamiliar to you. You all swim, however, and as that is one of the best of exercises, I suggest that we all swim."

"Lead us to it!" Seaton exclaimed, then his voice changed abruptly. "Wait a minute—I don't know about our swimming in copper sulphate solution."

"We swim in fresh water as often as in salt, and the pool is now filled with distilled water."

The Terrestrials quickly donned their bathing suits and all went through the observatory and down a winding path, bordered with the peculiarly beautiful scarlet and green shrubbery, to the "pool"—an artificial lake covering a hundred acres, its polished metal bottom and sides strikingly decorated with jewels and glittering tiles in tasteful yet contrasting inlaid designs. Any desired depth of water was available and plainly marked, from the fenced-off shallows where the smallest children splashed to the forty feet of liquid crystal which received the diver who cared to try his skill from one of the many spring-boards, flying rings, and catapults which rose high into the air a short distance away from the entrance.

Orlon and the others of the older generation plunged into the water without ado and struck out for the other shore, using a fast double-overarm stroke. Swimming in a wide circle they came out upon the apparatus and went through a series of methodical dives and gymnastic performances. It was evident that they swam, as Orlon had intimated, for exercise. To them, exercise was a necessary form of labor—labor which they performed thoroughly and well—but nothing to call forth the whole-souled enthusiasm they displayed in their chosen fields of mental effort.

The visitors from the Country of Youth, however, locked arms and sprang to surround the four Terrestrials, crying, "Let's do a group dive!"

"I don't believe that I can swim well enough to enjoy what's coming," whispered Margaret to Crane, and they slipped into the pool and turned around to watch. Seaton and Dorothy, both strong swimmers, locked arms and laughed as they were encircled by the green phalanx and swept out to the end of a dock-like structure and upon a catapult.

"Hold tight, everybody!" someone yelled, and interlaced, straining arms and legs held the green and white bodies in one motionless group as a gigantic force hurled them fifty feet into the air and out over the deepest part of the pool. There was a mighty splash and a miniature tidal wave as that mass of humanity struck the water. Many feet they went down before the cordon was broken and the individual units came to the surface. Then pandemonium reigned. Vigorous informal games, having to do with floating and sinking balls and effigies: pushball, in which the players never seemed to know, or to care, upon which side they were playing; water-fights and ducking contests.... A green mermaid, having felt the incredible power of Seaton's arms as he tossed her lightly away from a goal he was temporarily defending, put both her small hands around his biceps wonderingly, amazed at a strength unknown and impossible upon her world; then playfully tried to push him under. Failing, she called for help.

"He's needed a good ducking for ages!" Dorothy cried, and she and several other girls threw themselves upon him. Over and around him the lithe forms flashed, while the rest of the young people splashed water impartially over all the combatants and cheered them on. In the midst of the battle the signal sounded to end the period of exercise.

"Saved by the bell," Seaton laughed as, thoroughly ducked and almost half drowned, he was allowed to swim ashore.

When all had returned to the common room of the observatory and had seated themselves, Orlon took out his miniature ray-projector, no larger than a fountain pen, and flashed it briefly upon one of the hundreds of button-like lenses upon the wall. Instantly each chair converted itself into a form-fitting divan, inviting complete repose.

"I believe that you of Earth would perhaps enjoy some of our music during this, the period of relaxation and repose—it is so different from your own," Orlon remarked, as he again manipulated his tiny force-tube.

Every light was extinguished and there was felt a profoundly deep vibration—a note so low as to be palpable rather than audible; and simultaneously the utter darkness was relieved by a tinge of red so dark as to be barely perceptible, while a peculiar somber fragrance pervaded the atmosphere. The music rapidly ran the gamut to the limit of audibility and, in the same tempo, the lights traversed the visible spectrum and disappeared. Then came a crashing chord and a vivid flare of blended light; ushering in an indescribable symphony of sound and color, accompanied by a slower succession of shifting, blending odors.

The quality of tone was now that of a gigantic orchestra, now that of a full brass band, now that of a single unknown instrument—as though the composer had had at his command every overtone capable of being produced by any possible instrument, and with them had woven a veritable tapestry of melody upon an incredibly complex loom of sound. As went the harmony, so the play of light accompanied it. Neither music nor illumination came from any apparent source; they simply pervaded the entire room. When the music was fast—and certain passages were of a rapidity impossible for any human fingers to attain—the lights flashed in vivid, tiny pencils, intersecting each other in sharply drawn, brilliant figures, which changed with dizzying speed; when the tempo was slow, the beams were soft and broad, blending into each other to form sinuous, indefinite, writhing patterns, whose very vagueness was infinitely soothing.

"What do you think of it, Mrs. Seaton?" Orlon asked.

"Marvelous!" breathed Dorothy, awed. "I never imagined anything like it. I can't begin to tell you how much I like it. I never dreamed of such absolute perfection of execution, and the way the lighting accompanies the theme is just too perfectly wonderful for words! It was incredibly brilliant."

"Brilliant—yes. Perfectly executed—yes. But I notice that you say nothing of depth of feeling or of emotional appeal." Dorothy blushed uncomfortably and started to say something, but Orlon silenced her and continued: "You need not apologize. I had a reason for speaking as I did, for in you I recognize a real musician, and our music is indeed entirely soulless. That is the result of our ancient civilization. We are so old that our music is purely intellectual, entirely mechanical, instead of emotional. It is perfect, but, like most of our other arts, it is almost completely without feeling."

"But your statues are wonderful!"

"As I told you, those statues were made myriads of years ago. At that time we also had real music, but, unlike statuary, music at that time could not be preserved for posterity. That is another thing you have given us. Attend!"

At one end of the room, as upon a three-dimensional screen, the four Terrestrials saw themselves seated in the control-room of the *Skylark*. They saw and heard Margaret take up her guitar, and strike four sonorous chords in "A." Then, as if they had been there in person, they heard themselves sing "The Bull-Frog" and all the other songs they had sung, far off in space. They heard Margaret suggest that Dorothy play some "real music," and heard Seaton's comments upon the quartette.

"In that, youngster, you were entirely wrong," said Orlon, stopping the reproduction for a moment. "The entire planet was listening to you very attentively—we were enjoying it as no music has been enjoyed for thousands of years."

"The whole planet!" gasped Margaret. "Were you broadcasting it? How could you?"

"Easy," grinned Seaton. "They can do most anything with these rays of theirs."

"When you have time, in some period of labor, we would appreciate it very much if you four would sing for us again, would give us more of your vast store of youthful music, for we can now preserve it exactly as it is sung. But much as we enjoyed the quartette, Mrs. Seaton, it was your work upon the violin that took us by storm. Beginning with tomorrow, my companion intends to have you spend as many periods as you will, playing for our records. We shall now have your music."

"If you like it so well, wouldn't you rather I'd play you something I hadn't played before?"

"That is labor. We could not...."

"Piffle!" Dorothy interrupted. "Don't you see that I could really play right now, with somebody to listen, who really enjoys music; whereas, if I tried to play in front of a record, I'd be perfectly mechanical?"

"'At-a-girl, Dot! I'll get your fiddle."

"Keep your seat, son," instructed Orlon, as the case containing the Stradivarius appeared before Dorothy, borne by a pencil of force. "While that temperament is incomprehensible to every one of us, it is undoubtedly true that the artistic mind does work in that manner. We listen."

Dorothy swept into "The Melody in F," and as the poignantly beautiful strains poured forth from that wonderful violin, she knew that she had her audience with her. Though so intellectual that they themselves were incapable of producing music of real depth of feeling, they could understand and could enjoy such music with an appreciation impossible to a people of lesser mental attainments; and their profound enjoyment of her playing, burned into her mind by the telepathic, almost hypnotic power of the Norlaminian mentality, raised her to heights of power she had never before attained. Playing as one inspired, she went through one tremendous solo after another—holding her listeners spellbound, urged on by their intense feeling to carry them further and ever further into the realm of pure emotional harmony. The bell which ordinarily signaled the end of the period of relaxation did not sound; for the first time in thousands of years the planet of Norlamin deserted its rigid schedule of life—to listen to one Earth-woman, pouring out her very soul upon her incomparable violin.

The final note of "Memories" died away in a diminuendo wail, and the musician almost collapsed into Seaton's arms. The profound silence, more impressive far than any possible applause, was soon broken by Dorothy.

"There—I'm all right now, Dick. I was about out of control for a minute. I wish they could have had that on a recorder—I'll never be able to play like that again if I live to be a thousand years old."

"It is on record, daughter. Every note and every inflection is preserved, precisely as you played it," Orlon assured her. "That is our only excuse for allowing you to continue as you did, almost to the point of exhaustion. While we cannot really understand an artistic mind of the peculiar type to which yours belongs, yet we realized that each time you play you are doing something that no one, not even yourself, can ever do again in precisely the same subtle fashion. Therefore we allowed, in fact encouraged, you to go on as long as that creative impulse should endure—not merely for our pleasure in hearing it, great though that pleasure was, but in the hope that our workers in music could, by a careful analysis of your product, determine quantitatively the exact vibrations or overtones which make the difference between emotional and intellectual music."

CHAPTER XI

Into a Sun

As Rovol and Seaton approached the physics laboratory at the beginning of the period of labor, another small airboat occupied by one man drew up beside them and followed them to the ground. The stranger, another white-bearded ancient, greeted Rovol cordially and was introduced to Seaton as "Caslor, the First of Mechanism."

"Truly, this is a high point in the course of Norlaminian science, my young friend," Caslor acknowledged the introduction smilingly. "You have enabled us to put into practice many things which our ancestors studied in theory for many a wearisome cycle of time." Turning to Rovol, he went on: "I understand that you require a particularly precise directional mechanism? I know well that it must indeed be one of exceeding precision and delicacy, for the controls you yourself have built are able to hold upon any point, however moving, within the limits of our immediate solar system."

"We require controls a million times as delicate as any I have constructed," said Rovol, "therefore I have called your surpassing skill into co-operation. It is senseless for me to attempt a task in which I would be doomed to failure. We intend to send out a fifth-order projection, something none of our ancestors ever even dreamed of, which, with its inconceivable velocity of propagation, will enable us to explore any region in the galaxy as quickly as we now visit our closest sister planet. Knowing the dimensions of this, our galaxy, you can readily understand the exact degree of precision required to hold upon a point at its outermost edge."

"Truly, a problem worthy of any man's brain," Caslor replied after a moment's thought. "Those small circles," pointing to the forty-foot hour and declination circles which Seaton had thought the ultimate in precise measurement of angular magnitudes, "are of course useless. I shall have to construct large and accurate circles, and in order to produce the slow and fast motions of the required nature, without creep, slip, play, or backlash, I shall require a pure torque, capable of being increased by infinitesimal increments.... Pure torque."

He thought deeply for a time, then went on: "No gear-train or chain mechanism can be built of sufficient tightness, since in any mechanism there is some freedom of motion, however slight, and for this purpose the director must have no freedom of motion whatever. We must have a pure torque—and the only possible force answering our requirements is the four hundred sixty-seventh band of the fourth order. I shall therefore be compelled to develop that band. The director must, of course, have a full equatorial mounting, with circles some two hundred and fifty feet in diameter. Must your projector tube be longer than that, for correct design?"

"That length will be ample."

"The mounting must be capable of rotation through the full circle of arc in either plane, and must be driven in precisely the motion required to neutralize the motion of our planet, which, as you know, is somewhat irregular. Additional fast and slow motions must, of course, be provided to rotate the mechanism upon each graduated circle at the will of the operator. It is my idea to make the outer supporting tube quite large, so that you will have full freedom with your inner, or projector tube proper. It seems to me that dimensions X37 B42 J867 would perhaps be as good as any."

"Perfectly satisfactory. You have the apparatus well in mind."

"These things will consume some time. How soon will you require this mechanism?" asked Caslor.

"We also have much to do. Two periods of labor, let us say: or, if you require them, three."

"It is well. Two periods will be ample time: I was afraid that you might need it today, and the work cannot be accomplished in one period of labor. The mounting will, of course, be prepared in the Area of Experiment. Farewell."

"You aren't going to build the final projector here, then?" Seaton asked as Caslor's flier disappeared.

"We shall build it here, then transport it to the Area, where its dirigible housing will be ready to receive it. All mechanisms of that type are set up there. Not only is the location convenient to all interested, but there are to be found all necessary tools, equipment and material. Also, and not least important for such long-range work as we contemplate, the entire Area of Experiment is anchored immovably to the solid crust of the planet, so that there can be not even the slightest vibration to affect the direction of our beams of force, which must, of course, be very long."

He closed the master switches of his power-plants and the two resumed work where they had left off. The control panel was soon finished. Rovol then plated an immense cylinder of copper and placed it in the power-plant. He next set up an entirely new system of refractory relief-points and installed additional ground-rods, sealed through the floor and extending deep into the ground below, explaining as he worked.

"You see, son, we must lose one one-thousandth of one per cent of our total energy, and provision must be made for its dissipation in order to avoid destruction of the laboratory. These air-gap resistances are the simplest means of disposing of the wasted power."

"I get you—but say, how about disposing of it when we get the thing in a ship out in space? We picked up pretty heavy charges in the *Skylark*—so heavy that I had to hold up several times in the ionized layer of an atmosphere while they faded—and this outfit will burn up tons of copper where the old ones used ounces."

"In the projected space-vessel we shall install converters to utilize all the energy, so that there will be no loss whatever. Since such converters must be designed and built especially for each installation, and since they require a high degree of precision, it is not worth while to construct them for a purely temporary mechanism, such as this one."

The walls of the laboratory were opened, ventilating blowers were built, and refrigerating coils were set up everywhere, even in the tubular structure and behind the visiplates. After assuring themselves that everything combustible had been removed, the two scientists put on under their helmets, goggles whose protecting lenses could be built up to any desired thickness. Rovol then threw a switch, and a hemisphere of flaming golden radiance surrounded the laboratory and extended for miles upon all sides.

"I get most of the stuff you've pulled so far, but why such a light?" asked Seaton.

"As a warning. This entire area will be filled with dangerous frequencies, and that light is a warning for all uninsulated persons to give our theater of operations a wide berth."

"I see. What next?"

"All that remains to be done is to take our lens-material and go," replied Rovol, as he took from a cupboard the largest faidon that Seaton had ever seen.

"Oh, that's what you're going to use! You know, I've been wondering about that stuff. I took one back with me to the Earth to experiment on. I gave it everything I could think of and couldn't touch it. I couldn't even make it change its temperature. What is it, anyway?"

"It is not matter at all, in the ordinary sense of the word. It is almost pure crystallized energy. You have, of course, noticed that it looks transparent, but that it is not. You cannot see into its substance a millionth of a micron—the illusion of transparency being purely a surface phenomenon, and peculiar to this one form of substance. I have told you that the ether is a fourth-order substance—this also is a fourth-order substance, but it is crystalline, whereas the ether is probably fluid and amorphous. You might call this faidon crystallized ether without being far wrong."

"But it should weigh tons, and it is hardly heavier than air—or no, wait a minute. Gravitation is also a fourth-order phenomenon, so it might not weigh anything at all—but it would have terrific mass—or would it, not having protons? Crystallized ether would displace fluid ether, so it might—I'll give up! It's too deep for me!" said Seaton.

"Its theory is abstruse, and I cannot explain it to you any more fully than I have, until after we have given you a knowledge of the fourth and fifth orders. Pure fourth-order material would be without weight and without mass; but these crystals as they are found are not absolutely pure. In crystallizing from the magma, they entrapped sufficient numbers of particles of the higher orders to give them the characteristics which you have observed. The impurities, however, are not sufficient in quantity to offer a point of attack to any ordinary reagent."

"But how could such material possibly be formed?"

"It could be formed only in some such gigantic cosmic body as this, our green system, formed incalculable ages ago, when all the mass comprising it existed as one colossal sun. Picture for yourself the condition in the center of that sun. It has attained the theoretical maximum of temperature—some seventy million of your centigrade degrees—the electrons have been stripped from the protons until the entire central core is one solid ball of neutronium and can be compressed no more without destruction of the protons themselves. Still the pressure increases. The temperature, already at the theoretical maximum, can no longer increase. What happens?"

"Disruption."

"Precisely. And just at the instant of disruption, during the very instant of generation of the frightful forces that are to hurl suns, planets and satellites millions of miles out into space—in that instant of time, as a result of those unimaginable temperatures and pressures, the faidon comes into being. It can be formed only by the absolute maximum of temperature and at a pressure which can exist only momentarily, even in the largest conceivable masses."

"Then how can you make a lens of it? It must be impossible to work it in any way."

"It cannot be worked in any ordinary way, but we shall take this crystal into the depths of that white dwarf star, into a region in which obtain pressures and temperatures only less than those giving it birth. There we shall play forces upon it which, under those conditions, will be able to work it quite readily."

"Hm—m—m. I want to see that! Let's go!"

They seated themselves at the panels, and Rovol began to manipulate keys, levers and dials. Instantly a complex structure of visible force—rods, beams and flat areas of flaming scarlet energy—appeared at the end of the tubular, telescope-like network.

"Why red?"

"Merely to render them visible. One cannot work well with invisible tools, hence I have imposed a colored light frequency upon the invisible frequencies of the forces. We will have an assortment of colors if you prefer," and as he spoke each ray assumed a different color, so that the end of the projector was almost lost beneath a riot of color.

Looking into the visiplate, he was out in space in person, hurtling through space at a pace, beside which the best effort of the Skylark seemed the veriest crawl.

The structure of force, which Seaton knew was the secondary projector, swung around as if sentient, and a lurid green ray extended itself, picked up the faidon, and lengthened out, hurling the jewel a thousand yards out through the open side of the laboratory. Rovol moved more controls and the structure again righted itself, swinging back into perfect alignment with the tube and carrying the faidon upon its extremity, a thousand yards beyond the roof of the laboratory.

"We are now ready to start our projection. Be sure your suit and goggles are perfectly tight. We must see what we are doing, so the light-rays must be heterodyned upon our carrier wave. Therefore the laboratory and all its neighborhood will be flooded with dangerous frequencies from the sun we are to visit, as well as with those from our own generators."

"O. K., chief! All tight here. You say it's ten light-years to that star. How long's it going to take us to get there?"

"About ten minutes. We could travel that far in less than ten seconds but for the fact that we must take the faidon with us. Slight as is its mass, it will require much energy in its acceleration. Our projections, of course, have no mass, and will require only the energy of propagation."

Rovol flicked a finger, a massive pair of plunger switches shot into their sockets, and Seaton, seated at his board and staring into his visiplate, was astounded to find that he apparently possessed a dual personality. He *knew* that he was seated motionless in the operator's chair in the base of the rigidly anchored primary projector, and by taking his eyes away from the visiplate before him, he could see that nothing in the laboratory had changed, except that the pyrotechnic display from the power-bar was of unusual intensity. Yet, looking into the visiplate, he was out in space *in person*, hurtling through space at a pace beside which the best effort of the *Skylark* seemed the veriest crawl. Swinging his controls to look backward, he gasped as he saw, so stupendous was their velocity, that the green system was only barely discernible as a faint green star!

Again looking forward, it seemed as though a fierce white star had separated from the immovable firmament and was now so close to the structure of force in which he was riding that it was already showing a disk perceptible to the unaided eye. A few moments more and the violet-white splendor became so intense that the watchers began to build up, layer by layer, the protective goggles before their eyes. As they approached still closer, falling with their unthinkable velocity into that incandescent inferno, a sight was revealed to their eyes such as man had never before been privileged to gaze upon. They were falling into a white dwarf star, could see everything visible during such an unheard-of journey, and would live to remember what they had seen! They saw the magnificent spectacle of solar prominences shooting hundreds of thousands of miles into space, and directly in their path they saw an immense sunspot, a combined volcanic eruption and cyclonic storm in a gaseous-liquid medium of blinding incandescence.

"Better dodge that spot, hadn't we, ace? Mightn't it be generating interfering fourth-order frequencies?" cried Seaton.

"It is undoubtedly generating fourth-order rays, but nothing can interfere with us, since we are controlling every component of our beam from Norlamin."

Seaton gripped his hand-rail violently and involuntarily drew himself together into the smallest possible compass as, with their awful speed unchecked, they plunged through that flaming, incandescent photosphere and on, straight down, into the unexplored, unimaginable interior of that frightful and searing orb. Through the protecting goggles, now a full four inches of that peculiar, golden, shielding metal, Seaton could see the structure of force in which he was, and could also see the faidon—in outline, as transparent diamonds are visible in equally transparent water. Their apparent motion slowed rapidly and the material about them thickened and became more and more opaque. The faidon drew back toward them until it was actually touching the projector, and eddy currents and striae became visible in the mass about them as their progress grew slower and slower.

"'Smatter? Something gone screwy?" demanded Seaton.

"Not at all, everything is working perfectly. The substance is now so dense that it is becoming opaque to rays of the fourth order, so that we are now partially displacing the medium instead of moving through it without friction. At the point where we can barely see to work; that is, when the fourth-order rays will be so retarded that they can no longer carry the heterodyned light waves without complete distortion, we shall stop automatically, as the material at that depth will have the required density to refract the fifth-order rays to the correct degree."

"How can our foundations stand it?" asked Seaton. "This stuff must be a hundred times as dense as platinum already, and we must he pushing a horrible load in going through it."

"We are exerting no force whatever upon our foundations nor upon Norlamin. The force is transmitted without loss from the power-plant in our laboratory to this secondary projector here inside the star, where it is liberated in the correct band to pull us through the mass, using all the mass ahead of us as anchorage. When we wish to return, we shall simply change the pull into a push. Ah! we are now at a standstill—now comes the most important moment of the entire project!"

All apparent motion had ceased, and Seaton could see only dimly the outlines of the faidon, now directly before his eyes. The structure of force slowly warped around until its front portion held the faidon as in a vise. Rovol pressed a lever and behind them, in the laboratory, four enormous plunger switches drove home. A plane of pure energy, flaming radiantly even in the indescribable incandescence of the core of that seething star, bisected the faidon neatly, and ten gigantic beams, five upon each half of the jewel, rapidly molded two sections of a geometrically-perfect hollow lens. The two sections were then brought together by the closing of the jaws of the mighty vise, their edges in exact alignment. Instantly the plane and the beams of energy became transformed into two terrific opposing tubes of force—vibrant, glowing tubes, whose edges in contact coincided with the almost invisible seam between the two halves of the lens.

Like a welding arc raised to the *nth* power these two immeasurable and irresistible forces met exactly in opposition—a meeting of such incredible violence that seismic disturbances occurred throughout the entire mass of that dense, violet-white star. Sunspots of unprecedented size appeared, prominences erupted to hundreds of times their normal distances, and although the two scientists deep in the core of the tormented star were unaware of what was happening upon its surface, convulsion after Titanic convulsion wracked the mighty globe, and enormous masses of molten and gaseous material were riven from it and hurled far out into space—masses which would in time become planets of that youthful and turbulent luminary.

Seaton felt his air-supply grow hot. Suddenly it became icy cold, and knowing that Rovol had energized the refrigerator system, Seaton turned away from the fascinating welding operation for a quick look around the laboratory. As he did so, he realized Rovol's vast knowledge and understood the reason for the new system of relief-points and ground-rods, as well as the necessity for the all-embracing scheme of refrigeration.

Even through the practically opaque goggles he could see that the laboratory was one mass of genuine lightning. Not only from the relief-points, but from every metallic corner and protuberance the pent-up losses from the disintegrating bar were hurling themselves upon the flaring, blue-white, rapidly-volatilizing ground-rods; and the very air of the room, renewed second by second though it was by the powerful blowers, was beginning to take on the pearly luster of the highly-ionized corona. The bar was plainly visible, a scintillating demon of pure violet radiance, and a momentary spasm of fear seized him as he saw how rapidly that great mass of copper was shrinking—fear that their power would be exhausted with their task still uncompleted.

But the calculations of the aged physicist had been accurate. The lens was completed with some hundreds of pounds of copper to spare, and that geometrical form, with its precious content of semi-neutronium, was following the secondary projector back toward the green system. Rovol left his seat, discarded his armor, and signaled Seaton to do the same.

"I've got to hand it to you, ace—you sure are a blinding flash and a deafening report!" Seaton exclaimed, writhing out of his insulating suit. "I feel as though I'd been pulled half-way through a knot-hole and riveted over on both ends! How big a lens did you make, anyway? Looked as though it would hold a couple of liters; maybe three."

"Its contents are almost exactly three liters."

"Hm—m—m. Seven and a half million kilograms—say eight thousand tons. *Some* mass, I'd say, to put into a gallon jug. Of course, being inside the faidon, it won't have any weight, but it'll have all its full quota of inertia. That's why you're taking so long to bring it in, of course."

"Yes. The projector will now bring it here into the laboratory without any further attention from us. The period of labor is about to end, and tomorrow we shall find the lens awaiting us when we arrive to begin work."

"How about cooling it off? It had a temperature of something like forty million degree centigrade before you started working on it; and when you got done with it, it was hot."

"You're forgetting again, son. Remember that the hot, dense material is entirely enclosed in an envelope impervious to all vibrations longer than those of the fifth order. You could put your hand upon it now, without receiving any sensation either of heat, or of cold."

"Yeah, that's right, too. I noticed that I could take a faidon right out of an electric arc and it wouldn't even be warm. I couldn't explain why it was, but I see now. So that stuff inside that lens will always stay as hot as it is right now! Zowie! Here's hoping she never explodes! Well, there's the bell—for once in my life, I'm all ready to quit when the whistle blows," and arm in arm the young Terrestrial chemist and the aged Norlaminian physicist strolled out to their waiting airboat.

CHAPTER XII

Flying Visits—Via Projection

"Well, what to do?" asked Seaton as he and Rovol entered the laboratory, "Tear down this fourth-order projector and tackle the big job? I see the lens is here, on schedule, so we can hop right into it."

"We shall have further use for this mechanism. We shall need at least one more lens of this dense material, and other scientists also may have need of one or two. Then, too, the new projector must be so large that it cannot be erected in this room."

As he spoke, Rovol seated himself at his control-desk and ran his fingers lightly over the keys. The entire wall of the laboratory disappeared, hundreds of beams of force darted here and there, seizing and working raw materials, and in the portal there grew up, to Seaton's amazement, a keyboard and panel installation such as the Earth-man, in his wildest moments, had never imagined. Bank upon bank of typewriter-like keys; row upon row of keys, pedals, and stops resembling somewhat those of the console of a gigantic pipe-organ; panel upon panel of meters, switches, and dials—all arranged about two deeply-cushioned chairs and within reach of their occupants.

"Whew! That looks like the combined mince-pie nightmares of a whole flock of linotype operators, pipe-organists, and hard-boiled radio hams!" exclaimed Seaton when the installation was complete. "Now that you've got it, what are you going to do with it?"

"There is not a control system in Norlamin adequate for the task we face, since the problem of the projection of rays of the fifth order has heretofore been of only academic interest. Therefore it becomes necessary to construct such a control. This mechanism will, I am confident, have a sufficiently wide range of application to perform any operation we shall require of it."

"It sure looks as though it could do almost anything, provided the man behind it knows how to play a tune on it—but if that rumble seat is for me, you'd better count me out right now. I followed you for about fifteen seconds, then lost you completely; and now I'm sunk without a trace," said Seaton.

"That is, of course, true, and is a point I was careless enough to overlook." Rovol thought for a moment, then got up, crossed the room to his control desk, and continued, "We shall dismantle the machine and rebuild it at once."

"Oh no—too much work!" protested Seaton, "You've got it about done, haven't you?"

"It is hardly started. Two hundred thousand bands of force must be linked to it, each in its proper place, and it is necessary that you should understand thoroughly every detail of this entire projector," Rovol answered.

"Why? I'm not ashamed to admit that I haven't got brains enough to understand a thing like that."

"You have sufficient brain capacity; it is merely undeveloped. There are two reasons why you must be as familiar with the operation of this mechanism as you are with the operation of one of your Earthly automobiles. The first is that a similar control is to be installed in your new space-vessel, since by its use you can attain a perfection of handling impossible by any other system. The second, and more important reason, is that neither I nor any other man of Norlamin could compel himself, by any force of will, to direct a ray that would take away the life of any fellow-man."

While Rovol was speaking, he reversed his rays, and soon the component parts of the new control had been disassembled and piled in orderly array about the room.

"Hm—m—m. Never thought of that. It's right too," mused Seaton. "How're you going to get it into my thick skull—with an educator?"

"Exactly," and Rovol sent a beam of force after his highly developed educational mechanism. Dials and electrodes were adjusted, connections were established, and the beams and pencils of force began to reconstruct the great central controlling device. But this time, instead of being merely a bewildered spectator, Seaton was an active participant in the work. As each key and meter was wrought and mounted, there were indelibly impressed upon his brain the exact reason for and function of the part, and later, when the control itself was finished and the seemingly interminable task of connecting it up to the output force-bands of the transformers had begun, he had a complete understanding of everything with which he was working, and understood all the means by which the ends he had so long desired were to be attained. For to the ancient scientist the tasks he was then performing were the merest routine, to be performed in reflex fashion, and he devoted most of his attention to transferring from his own brain to that of his young assistant as much of his stupendous knowledge as the smaller brain of the Terrestrial was capable of absorbing. More and more rapidly as the work progressed the mighty flood of knowledge poured into Seaton's mind. After an hour or so, when enough connections had been made so that automatic forces could be so directed as to finish the job, Rovol and Seaton left the laboratory and went into the living room. As they walked, the educator accompanied them, borne upon its beam of force.

"Your brain is behaving very nicely indeed," said Rovol, "much better than I would have thought possible from its size. In fact, it may be possible for me to transfer to you all the knowledge I have which might be of use to you. That is why I took you away from the laboratory. What do you think of the idea?"

"Our psychologists have always maintained that none of us ever uses more than a minute fraction of the actual capacity of his brain," Seaton replied after a moment's thought. "If you think you can give me even a percentage of your knowledge without killing me, go to it—I'm for it, strong!"

"Knowing that you would be, I have already requested Drasnik, the First of Psychology, to come here, and he has just arrived," answered Rovol. And as he spoke, that personage entered the room.

When the facts had been set before him, the psychologist nodded his head

"That is quite possible," he said with enthusiasm, "and I will be only too glad to assist in such an operation."

"But listen!" protested Seaton, "You'll probably change my whole personality! Rovol's brain is three times the size of mine."

"Tut-tut—nothing of the kind," Drasnik reproved him. "As you have said, you are using only a minute portion of the active mass of your brain. The same thing is true with us—many millions of cycles would have to pass before we would be able to fill the brains we now have."

"Then why are your brains so large?"

"Merely a provision of Nature that no possible accession of knowledge shall find her storehouse too small," replied Drasnik, positively. "Ready?"

All three donned the headsets and a wave of mental force swept into Seaton's mind, a wave of such power that the Terrestrial's every sense wilted under the impact. He did not faint, he did not lose consciousness—he simply lost all control of every nerve and fiber as his entire brain passed into the control of the immense mentality of the First of Psychology and became a purely receptive, plastic medium upon which to impress the knowledge of the aged physicist.

Hour after hour the transfer continued, Seaton lying limp as though lifeless, the two Norlaminians tense and rigid, every faculty concentrated upon the ignorant, virgin brain exposed to their gaze. Finally the operation was complete and Seaton, released from the weird, hypnotic grip of that stupendous mind, gasped, shook himself, and writhed to his feet.

"Great Cat!" he exclaimed, his eyes wide with astonishment. "I wouldn't have believed there was as much to know in the entire Universe as I know right now, and I know it as well as I ever knew elementary algebra. Thanks, fellows, a million times—but say, did you leave any open spaces for more? In one way, I seem to know less than I did before, there's so much more to find out. Can I learn anything more, or did you fill me up to capacity?"

The psychologist, who had been listening to the exuberant youth with undisguised pleasure, spoke calmly.

"The mere fact that you appreciate your comparative ignorance shows that you are still capable of learning. Your capacity to learn is greater than it ever was before, even though the waste space has been reduced. Much to our surprise, Rovol and I gave you all of his knowledge that would be of any use to you, and some of my own, and still theoretically you can add to it more than nine times the total of your present knowledge."

The psychologist departed, and Rovol and Seaton returned to the laboratory, where the forces were still merrily at work. There was nothing that could be done to hasten the connecting, and it was late in the following period of labor before they could begin the actual construction of the projector. Once started, however, it progressed with amazing rapidity. Now understanding the system, it did not seem strange to Seaton that he should merely actuate a certain combination of forces when he desired a certain operation performed; nor did it seem unusual or worthy of comment that one flick of his finger over that switchboard would send a force a distance of hundreds of miles to a factory where other forces were busily at work, to seize a hundred angle-bars of transparent purple metal that were to form the backbone of the fifth-order projector. Nor did it seem peculiar that the same force, with no further instruction, should bring these hundred bars back to him, in a high loop through the atmosphere; should deposit them gently in a convenient space near the site of operations; and then should disappear as though it had never existed! With such tools as that, it was a matter of only a few hours before the projector was done—a task that would have required years of planning and building upon Earth.

Two hundred and fifty feet it towered above their heads, a tubular network of braced and latticed bars of purple metal, fifty feet in diameter at the base and tapering smoothly to a diameter of about ten feet at the top. Built of a metal thousands of times as strong and hard as steel, it was not cumbersome in appearance, and yet was strong enough to be absolutely rigid. Ten enormous supporting forces held the lens of neutronium immovable in the exact center of the upper end; at intervals down the shaft similar forces held variously-shaped lenses and prisms formed from zones of force; in the center of the bottom or floor of the towering structure was the double controlling system, with a universal visiplate facing each operator.

"Well, Rovol, that's that," remarked Seaton as the last connection was made. "What say we hop in and give the baby a ride over to the Area of Experiment? Caslor must have the mounting done, and we've got time enough left in this period to try her out."

"In a moment. I am setting the fourth-order projector to go out to the dwarf star after an additional supply of neutronium."

Seaton, knowing from the data of their first journey, that the controls could be so set as to duplicate their feat in every particular without supervision, stepped into his seat in the new controller, pressed a key, and spoke.

"Hi, Dottie, what's on your mind?"

"Nothing much," Dorothy's clear voice answered. "Got it done and can I see it?"

"Sure—sit tight and I'll send a boat after you."

As he spoke, Rovol's flier darted into the air and away; and in two minutes it returned, slowing abruptly as it landed. Dorothy stepped out, radiant, and returned Seaton's enthusiastic caresses with equal fervor before she spoke.

"Lover, I'm afraid you violated all known speed laws getting me over here. Aren't you afraid of getting pinched?"

"Nope—not here. Besides, I didn't want to keep Rovol waiting—we're all ready to go. Hop in here with me, this left-hand control's mine."

Rovol entered the tube, took his place, and waved his hand. Seaton's hands swept over the keys and the whole gigantic structure wafted into the air. Still upright, it was borne upon immense rods of force toward the Area of Experiment, which was soon reached. Covered as the Area was with fantastic equipment, there was no doubt as to their destination, for in plain sight, dominating all the lesser instruments, there rose a stupendous telescopic mounting, with an enormous hollow tube of metallic lattice-work which could be intended for nothing else than their projector. Approaching it carefully, Seaton deftly guided the projector lengthwise into that hollow receptacle and anchored it in the exact optical axis. Flashing beams of force made short work of welding the two tubes together immovably with angles and lattices of the same purple metal, the terminals of the variable-speed motors were attached to the controllers, and everything was in readiness for the first trial.

"What special instructions do we need to run it, if any?" Seaton asked of the First of Mechanism, who had lifted himself up into the projector.

"Very little. This motor governs the hour motion, that one the right ascension. The potentiometers regulate the degree of vernier action—any ratio is possible, from direct drive up to more than a hundred million complete revolutions of that graduated dial to give you one second of arc."

"Plenty fine, I'd say. Thanks a lot, ace. Whither away, Rovol—any choice?"

"Anywhere you please, son, since this is merely a try-out."

"O. K. We'll hop over and tell Dunark hello."

The tube swung around into line with that distant planet and Seaton stepped down hard, upon a pedal. Instantly they seemed infinite myriads of miles out in space, the green system barely visible as a faint green star behind them.

"Wow, that ray's fast!" exclaimed the pilot, ruefully. "I overshot about a thousand light years. We'll try again, with considerably less power," and he rearranged and reset the dials and meters before him. Adjustment after adjustment and many reductions in power had to be made before the projection ceased leaping millions of miles at a touch, but finally the operators became familiar with the new technique and the ray became manageable. Soon they were hovering above what had been Mardonal, and saw that all signs of warfare had disappeared. Slowly turning the controls, Seaton flashed the projection over the girdling Osnomian sea and guided it through the impregnable metal walls of the palace into the throne room of Roban, where they saw the Emperor, Tarnan the Karbix, and Dunark in close conference.

"Well, here we are," remarked Seaton. "Now we'll put on a little visibility and give the natives a treat."

"Sh-sh," whispered Dorothy, "they'll hear you, Dick—we're intruding shamefully."

"No, they won't hear us, because I haven't heterodyned the audio in on the wave yet. And as for intruding, that's exactly what we came over here for."

He imposed the audio system upon the inconceivably high frequency of their carrier wave and spoke in the Osnomian tongue.

"Greetings, Roban, Dunark, and Tarnan, from Seaton." All three jumped to their feet, amazed, staring about the empty room as Seaton went on, "I am not here in person. I am simply sending you my projection. Just a moment and I will put on a little visibility."

He brought more forces into play, and solid images of force appeared in the great hall; images of the three occupants of the controller. Introductions and greetings over, Seaton spoke briefly and to the point.

"We've got everything we came after—much more than I had any idea we could get. You need have no more fear of the Fenachrone—we have found a science superior to theirs. But much remains to be done, and we have none too much time; therefore I have come to you with certain requests."

"The Overlord has but to command," replied Roban.

"Not command, since we are all working together for a common cause. In the name of that cause, Dunark, I ask you to come to me at once, accompanied by Tarnan and any others you may select. You will be piloted by a ray which we shall set upon your controls. Upon your way here you will visit the First City of Dasor, another planet, where you will pick up Sacner Carfon, who will be awaiting you there."

"As you direct, so it shall be," and Seaton flashed the projector to the neighboring planet of Urvania. There he found that the gigantic space-cruiser he had ordered had been completed, and requested Urvan and his commander-in-chief to tow it to Norlamin, piloted by a ray. He then jumped to Dasor, there interviewing Carfon and being assured of the full co-operation of the porpoise-men.

"Well, that's that, folks," said Seaton as he shut off the power. "We can't do much more for a few days, until the gang gets here for the council of war. How'd it be, Rovol, for me to practice with this outfit while you are finishing up the odds and ends you want to clean up? You might suggest to Orlon, too, that it'd be a good deed for him to pilot those folks over here."

As Rovol wafted himself to the ground from their lofty station, Crane and Margaret appeared and were lifted up to the place formerly occupied by the physicist.

"How's tricks, Mart? I hear you're quite an astronomer?" said Seaton.

"Yes, thanks to Orlon and the First of Psychology. He seemed quite interested in increasing our Earthly knowledge. I certainly know much more than I had ever hoped to know of anything."

"Yeah, you can pilot us to the Fenachrone system now without any trouble. You also absorbed some ethnology and kindred sciences. What d'you think—with Dunark and Urvan, do we know enough to go ahead or should we take a chance on holding things up while we get acquainted with some of the other peoples of these planets of the green system?"

"Delay is dangerous, as our time is already short," Crane replied after a time. "We know enough, I believe; and furthermore, any additional assistance is problematical; in fact, it is more than doubtful. The Norlaminians have surveyed the system rather thoroughly, and no other planet seems to have inhabitants who have even approached the development attained here."

"Right—that's the way I dope it, exactly. We'll wait until the gang assembles, then go over the top. In the meantime, I called you over to take a ride in this projector—it's a darb. I'd like to shoot for the Fenachrone system first, but I don't quite dare to."

"Don't *dare* to? You?" scoffed Margaret. "How come?"

"Cancel the 'dare'—change it to 'prefer not to.' Why? Because while they can't work through a zone of force, some of their real scientists—and they have lots of them, not like the bull-headed soldier we captured—may well be able to detect a fifth-order ray—even if they can't work with them intelligently—and if they detected our ray, it'd put them on guard."

"You are exactly right, Dick," agreed Crane. "And there speaks the Norlaminian physicist, and not my old and reckless playmate Richard Seaton."

"Oh, I don't know—I told you I was getting timid as a mouse. But let's not sit here twiddling our thumbs—let's go places and do things. Whither away? I want a destination a good ways off, not something in our own back yard."

"Go back home, of course, stupe," put in Dorothy, "do you have to be told every little thing?"

"Sure—never thought of that," and Seaton, after a moment's rapid mental arithmetic, swung the great tube around, rapidly adjusted a few dials, and stepped down upon a pedal. There was a fleeting instant of unthinkable velocity; then they found themselves poised somewhere in space.

"Well, wonder how far I missed it on my first shot?" Seaton's crisp voice broke the stunned silence. "Guess that's our sun, over to the left, ain't it, Mart?"

"Yes. You were about right for distance, and within a few tenths of a light-year laterally. That is fairly close, I should have said."

"Rotten, for these controls. Except for the effect of relative proper motions, which I can't calculate yet for lack of data. I should be able to hit a gnat right in the left eye at this range—and the difference in proper motions couldn't have thrown me off more than a few hundred feet. Nope, I was too anxious—hurried too much on the settings of the slow verniers. I'll snap back and try it again."

He adjusted the verniers very carefully, and again threw on the power. Again there was the sensation of the barest perceptible moment of unimaginable speed, and they were in the air some fifty feet above the ground of Crane Field, almost above the testing shed. Seaton rapidly adjusted the variable-speed motors until they were perfectly stationary, relative to the surface of the earth.

"You are improving," commended Crane.

"Yeah—that's more like it. Guess maybe I can learn in time to shoot this gun. Well, let's go down."

They dropped through the roof into the laboratory where Maxwell, now in charge of the place, was watching a reaction and occasionally taking notes.

"Hi, Max! Seaton speaking, on a television. Got your range?"

"Exactly, Chief, apparently. I can hear you perfectly, but can't see anything," Maxwell stared about the empty laboratory.

"You will in a minute. I knew I had you, but didn't want to scare you out of a year's growth," and Seaton thickened the image until they were plainly visible.

"Please call Mr. Vaneman on the phone and tell him you're in touch with us," directed Seaton as soon as greetings had been exchanged. "Better yet, after you've broken it to them gently, Dot can talk to them, then we'll go over and see 'em."

The connection established, Dorothy's image floated up to the telephone and apparently spoke.

"Mother? This is the weirdest thing you ever imagined. We're not really here at all you know—we're actually here in Norlamin—no, I mean Dick's just sending a kind of a talking picture of us to see you on earth here.... Oh, no, I don't know anything about it—it's like a talkie sent by radio, only worse, because I am saying this myself right now, without any rehearsal or anything ... we didn't want to burst in on you without warning, because you'd be sure to think you were seeing actual ghosts, and we're not dead the least bit ... we're having the most perfectly gorgeous time you ever imagined.... Oh, I'm so excited I can't explain anything, even if I knew anything about it to explain. We'll all four of us be over there in about a second and tell you all about it. 'Bye!"

Indeed, it was even less than a second—Mrs. Vaneman was still in the act of hanging up the receiver when the image materialized in the living room of Dorothy's girlhood home.

"Hello, mother and dad," Seaton's voice was cheerful but matter-of-fact. "I'll thicken this up so you can see us better in a minute. But don't think that we are flesh and blood. You'll see simply three-dimensional talking pictures of ourselves, transmitted by radio."

For a long time Mr. and Mrs. Vaneman chatted with the four visitors from so far away in space, while Seaton gloried in the working of that marvelous projector.

"Well, our time's about up," Seaton finally ended the visit. "The quitting-whistle's going to blow in five minutes, and they don't like overtime work here where we are. We'll drop in and see you again maybe, sometime before we come back."

"Do you know yet when you are coming back?" asked Mrs. Vaneman.

"Not an idea in the world, mother, any more than we had when we started. But we're getting along fine, having the time of our lives, and are learning a lot besides. So-long!" and Seaton clicked off the power.

As they descended from the projector and walked toward the waiting airboat, Seaton fell in beside Rovol.

"You know they've got our new cruiser built of dagal, and are bringing it over here. Dagal's good stuff, but it isn't as good as your purple metal, inoson, which is the theoretical ultimate in strength possible for any material possessing molecular structure. Why wouldn't it be a sound idea to flash it into inoson when it gets here?"

"That would be an excellent idea, and we shall do so. It also has occurred to me that Caslor of Mechanism, Astron of Energy, Satrazon of Chemistry, myself, and one of two others, should collaborate in installing a very complete fifth-order projector in the new *Skylark*, as well as any other equipment which may seem desirable. The security of the Universe may depend upon the abilities and qualities of you Terrestrials and your vessel, and therefore *nothing* should be left undone which it is possible for us to do."

"You chirped something then, old scout—thanks. You might do that, while I attend to such preliminaries as wiping out the Fenachrone fleet."

In due time the reinforcements from the other planets arrived, and the mammoth space-cruiser attracted attention even before it landed, so enormous was she in comparison with the tiny vessels having her in tow. Resting upon the ground, it seemed absurd that such a structure could possibly move under her own power. For two miles that enormous mass of metal extended over the country-side, and while it was very narrow for its length, still its fifteen hundred feet of diameter dwarfed everything near by. But Rovol and his aged co-workers smiled happily as they saw it, erected their keyboards, and set to work with a will.

Meanwhile a group had gathered about a conference table—a group such as had never before been seen together upon any world. There was Fodan, the ancient Chief of the Five of Norlamin, huge-headed, with his leonine mane and flowing beard of white. There were Dunark and Tarnan of Osnome and Urvan of Urvania—smooth-faced and keen, utterly implacable and ruthless in war. There was Sacner Carfon Twenty Three Forty Six, the immense, porpoise-like, hairless Dasorian. There were Seaton and Crane, representatives of our own Earthly civilization.

Seaton opened the meeting by handing each man a headset and running a reel showing the plans of the Fenachrone; not only as he had secured them from the captain of the marauding vessel, but also everything the First of Psychology had deduced from his own study of that inhuman brain. He then removed the reel and gave them the tentative plans of battle. Headsets removed, he threw the meeting open for discussion—and discussion there was in plenty. Each man had ideas, which were thrown upon the table and studied, for the most part calmly and dispassionately. The conference continued until only one point was left, upon which argument waxed so hot that everyone seemed shouting at once.

"Order!" commanded Seaton, banging his fist upon the table. "Osnome and Urvania wish to strike without warning, Norlamin and Dasor insist upon a formal declaration of war. Earth has the deciding vote. Mart, how do we vote on this?"

"I vote for formal warning, for two reasons, one of which I believe will convince even Dunark. First, because it is the fair thing to do—which reason is, of course, the one actuating the Norlaminians, but which would not be considered by Osnome, nor even remotely understood by the Fenachrone. Second, I am certain that the Fenachrone will merely be enraged by the warning and will defy us. Then what will they do? You have already said that you have been able to locate only a few of their exploring warships. As soon as we declare war upon them they will almost certainly send out torpedoes to every one of their ships of war. We can then follow the torpedoes with our rays, and thus will be enabled to find and to destroy their vessels."

"That settles that," declared the chairman as a shout of agreement arose. "We shall now adjourn to the projector and send the warning. I have a ray upon the torpedo, announcing the destruction by us of their vessel, and that torpedo will arrive at its destination in less than an hour. It seems to me that we should make our announcement immediately after their ruler has received the news of their first defeat."

In the projector, where they were joined by Rovol, Orlon, and several others of the various "Firsts" of Norlamin, they flashed out to the flying torpedo, and Seaton grinned at Crane as their fifth-order carrier beam went through the far-flung detector screens of the Fenachrone without setting up the slightest reaction. In the wake of that speeding messenger they flew through a warm, foggy, dense atmosphere, through a receiving trap in the wall of a gigantic conical structure, and on into the telegraph room. They saw the operator remove spools of tape from the torpedo and attach them to a magnetic sender—heard him speak.

"Pardon, your majesty—we have just received a first-degree emergency torpedo from flagship Y427W of fleet 42. In readiness."

"Put it on, here in the council chamber," a deep voice snapped.

"If he's broadcasting it, we're in for a spell of hunting," Seaton remarked. "Nope, he's putting it on a tight beam—that's fine, we can chase it up," and with a narrow detector beam he traced the invisible transmission beam into the council room.

"'Sfunny. This place seems awfully familiar—I'd swear I'd seen it before, lots of times—seems like I've been in it, more than once," Seaton remarked, puzzled, as he looked around the somber room, with its dull, paneled metal walls covered with charts, maps, screens, and speakers; and with its low, massive furniture. "Oh, sure, I'm familiar with it from studying the brain of that Fenachrone captain. Well, while His Nibs is absorbing the bad news, we'll go over this once more. You, Carfon, having the biggest voice of any of us ever heard uttering intelligible language, are to give the speech. You know about what to say. When I say 'go ahead' do your stuff. Now, everybody else, listen. While he's talking I've got to have audio waves heterodyned both ways in the circuit, and they'll be able to hear any noise any of us make—so all of us except Carfon want to keep absolutely quiet, no matter what happens or what we see. As soon as he's done I'll cut off the audio sending and say something to let you all know we're off the air. Got it?"

"One point has occurred to me about handling the warning," boomed Carfon. "If it should be delivered from apparently empty air, directly at those we wish to address, it would give the enemy an insight into our methods, which might be undesirable."

"H—m—m. Never thought of that ... it sure would, and it would be undesirable," agreed Seaton. "Let's see ... we can get away from that by broadcasting it. They have a very complete system of speakers, but no matter how many private-band speakers a man may have, he always has one on the general wave, which is used for very important announcements of wide interest. I'll broadcast you on that wave, so that every general-wave speaker on the planet will be energized. That way, it'll look as if we're shooting from a distance. You might talk accordingly."

"If we have a minute more, there's something I would like to ask," Dunark broke the ensuing silence. "Here we are, seeing everything that is happening there. Walls, planets, even suns, do not bar our vision, because of the fifth-order carrier wave. I understand that, partially. But how can we see anything there? I always thought that I knew something about rays, but I see that I do not. The light-rays must be released, or deheterodyned, close to the object viewed, with nothing opaque to light intervening. They must then be reflected from the object seen, must be gathered together, again heterodyned upon the fifth-order carrier, and retransmitted back to us. And there is neither receiver nor transmitter at the other end. How can you do all that from our end?"

"We don't," Seaton assured him. "At the other end there are all the things you mentioned, and a lot more besides. Our secondary projector out there is composed of forces, visible or invisible, as we please. Part of those forces comprise the receiving, viewing, and sending instruments. They are not material, it is true, but they are nevertheless fully as actual, and far more efficient, than any other system of radio, television, or telephone in existence anywhere else. It is force, you know, that makes radio or television work—the actual copper, insulation, and other matter serve only to guide and to control the various forces employed. The Norlaminian scientists have found out how to direct and control pure forces without using the cumbersome and hindering material substance...."

He broke off as the record from the torpedo stopped suddenly and the operator's voice came through a speaker.

"General Fenimol! Scoutship K3296, patrolling the detector zone, wishes to give you an urgent emergency report. I told them that you were in council with the Emperor, and they instructed me to interrupt it, no matter how important the council may be. They have on board a survivor of the Y427W, and have captured and killed two men of the same race as those who destroyed our vessel. They say that you will want their report without an instant's delay."

"We do!" barked the general, at a sign from his ruler. "Put it on here. Run the rest of the torpedo report immediately afterward."

In the projector, Seaton stared at Crane a moment, then a light of understanding spread over his features.

"DuQuesne, of course—I'll bet a hat no other Terrestrial is this far from home. I can't help feeling sorry for the poor devil—he's a darn good man gone wrong—but we'd have had to kill him ourselves before we got done with him; so it's probably as well they got him. Pin your ears back, everybody, and watch close—we want to get this, all of it."

CHAPTER XIII

The Declaration of War

The capital city of the Fenachrone lay in a jungle plain surrounded by towering hills. A perfect circle of immense diameter, its buildings of uniform height, of identical design, and constructed of the same dull gray, translucent metal, were arranged in concentric circles, like the annular rings seen upon the stump of a tree. Between each ring of buildings and the one next inside it there were lagoons, lawns and groves—lagoons of tepid, sullenly-steaming water; lawns which were veritable carpets of lush, rank rushes and of dank mosses; groves of palms, gigantic ferns, bamboos, and numerous tropical growths unknown to Earthly botany. At the very edge of the city began jungle unrelieved and primeval; the impenetrable, unconquerable jungle, possible only to such meteorological conditions as obtained there. Wind there was none, nor sunshine. Only occasionally was the sun of that reeking world visible through the omnipresent fog, a pale, wan disk; always the atmosphere was one of oppressive, hot, humid vapor. In the exact center of the city rose an immense structure, a terraced cone of buildings, as though immense disks of smaller and smaller diameter had been piled one upon the other. In these apartments dwelt the nobility and the high officials of the Fenachrone. In the highest disk of all, invisible always from the surface of the planet because of the all-enshrouding mist, were the apartments of the Emperor of that monstrous race.

Seated upon low, heavily-built metal stools about the great table in the council-room were Fenor, Emperor of the Fenachrone; Fenimol, his General-in-Command, and the full Council of Eleven of the planet. Being projected in the air before them was a three-dimensional moving, talking picture—the report of the sole survivor of the warship that had attacked the *Skylark II.* In exact accordance with the facts as the engineer knew them, the details of the battle and complete information concerning the conquerors were shown. As vividly as though the scene were being re-enacted before their eyes they saw the captive revive in the *Violet*, and heard the conversation between the engineer, DuQuesne, and Loring.

In the *Violet* they sped for days and weeks, with ever-mounting velocity, toward the system of the Fenachrone. Finally, power reversed, they approached it, saw the planet looming large, and passed within the detector screen.

DuQuesne tightened the controls of the attractors, which had never been entirely released from their prisoner, thus again pinning the Fenachrone helplessly against the wall.

"Just to be sure you don't try to start something," he explained coldly. "You have done well so far, but I'll run things myself from now on, so that you can't steer us into a trap. Now tell me exactly how to go about getting one of your vessels. After we get it, I'll see about letting you go."

"Fools, you are too late! You would have been too late, even had you killed me out there in space and had fled at your utmost acceleration. Did you but know it, you are as dead, even now—our patrol is upon you!"

DuQuesne whirled, snarling, and his automatic and that of Loring were leaping out when an awful acceleration threw them flat upon the floor, a magnetic force snatched away their weapons, and a heat-ray reduced them to two small piles of gray ash. Immediately thereafter a beam of force from the patrolling cruiser neutralized the retractors bearing upon the captive, and he was transferred to the rescuing vessel.

The emergency report ended, and with a brief "Torpedo message from flagship Y427W resumed at point of interruption," the report from the ill-fated vessel continued the story of its own destruction, but added little in the already complete knowledge of the disaster.

Fenor of the Fenachrone leaped up from the table, his terrible, flame-shot eyes glaring venomously—teetering in Berserk rage upon his block-like legs—but he did not for one second take his full attention from the report until it had been completed. Then he seized the nearest object, which happened to be his chair, and with all his enormous strength hurled it across the floor, where it lay, a tattered, twisted, shapeless mass of metal.

"Thus shall we treat the entire race of the accursed beings who have done this!" he stormed, his heavy voice reverberating throughout the room. "Torture, dismemberment and annihilation to every...."

"Fenor of the Fenachrone!" a tremendous voice, a full octave lower than Fenor's own terrific bass, and of ear-shattering volume and timbre in that dense atmosphere boomed from the general-wave speaker, its deafening roar drowning out Fenor's raging voice and every other lesser sound.

"Fenor of the Fenachrone! I know that you hear, for every general-wave speaker upon your reeking planet is voicing my words. Listen well, for this warning shall not be repeated. I am speaking by and with the authority of the Overlord of the Green System, which you know as the Central System of this, our Galaxy. Upon some of our many planets there are those who wished to destroy you without warning and out of hand, but the Overlord has ruled that you may continue to live provided you heed these, his commands, which he has instructed me to lay upon you.

"You must forthwith abandon forever your vainglorious and senseless scheme of universal conquest. You must immediately withdraw your every vessel to within the boundaries of your solar system, and you must keep them there henceforth.

"You are allowed five minutes to decide whether or not you will obey these commands. If no answer has been received at the end of the calculated time the Overlord will know that you have defied him, and your entire race shall perish utterly. Well he knows that your very existence is an affront to all real civilization, but he holds that even such vileness incarnate, as are the Fenachrone, may perchance have some obscure place in the Great Scheme of Things, and he will not destroy you if you are content to remain in your proper place, upon your own dank and steaming world. Through me, the two thousand three hundred and forty-sixth Sacner Carfon of Dasor, the Overlord has given you your first, last and only warning. Heed its every word, or consider it the formal declaration of a war of utter and complete extinction!"

The awful voice ceased and pandemonium reigned in the council hall. Obeying a common impulse, each Fenachrone leaped to his feet, raised his huge arms aloft, and roared out rage and defiance. Fenor snapped a command, and the others fell silent as he began howling out orders.

"Operator! Send recall torpedoes instantly to every outlying vessel!" He scuttled over to one of the private-band speakers. "X-794-PW! Radio general call for all vessels above E blank E to concentrate on battle stations! Throw out full-power defensive screens, and send the full series of detector screens out to the limit! Guards and patrols on invasion plan XB-218!"

"The immediate steps are taken, gentlemen!" He turned to the Council, his rage unabated. "Never before have we supermen of the Fenachrone been so insulted and so belittled! That upstart Overlord will regret that warning to the instant of his death, which shall be exquisitely postponed. All you of the Council know your duties in such a time as this—you are excused to perform them. General Fenimol, you will stay with me—we shall consider together such other details as require attention."

After the others had left the room Fenor turned to the general.

"Have you any immediate suggestions?"

"I would suggest sending at once for Ravindau, the Chief of the Laboratories of Science. He certainly heard the warning, and may be able to cast some light upon how it could have been sent, and from what point it came."

The Emperor spoke into another sender, and soon the scientist entered, carrying in his hand a small instrument upon which a blue light blazed.

"Do not talk here, there is grave danger of being overheard by that self-styled Overlord," he directed tersely, and led the way into a ray-proof compartment of his private laboratory, several floors below.

"It may interest you to know that you have sealed the doom of our planet and of all the Fenachrone upon it," Ravindau spoke savagely.

"Dare you speak thus to me, your sovereign?" roared Fenor.

"I dare so," replied the other, coldly. "When all the civilization of a planet has been given to destruction by the unreasoning stupidity and insatiable rapacity of its royalty, allegiance to such royalty is at an end. SIT DOWN!" he thundered as Fenor sprang to his feet. "You are no longer in your throne-room, surrounded by servile guards and by automatic rays. You are in MY laboratory, and by a movement of my finger I can hurl you into eternity!"

The general, aware now that the warning was of much more serious import than he had suspected, broke into the acrimonious debate.

"Never mind questions of royalty!" he snapped. "The safety of the race is paramount. Am I to understand that the situation is really grave?"

"It is worse than grave—it is desperate. The only hope for even ultimate triumph is for as many of us as possible to flee instantly clear out of the Galaxy, in the hope that we may escape the certain destruction to be dealt out to us by the Overlord of the Green System."

"You speak folly, surely," returned Fenimol. "Our science is—must be—superior to any other in the Universe?"

"So thought I until this warning came in and I had an opportunity to study it. Then I knew that we are opposed by a science immeasurably higher than our own."

"Such vermin as those two whom one of our smallest scouts captured without a battle, vessel and all? In what respects is their science even comparable to ours?"

"Not those vermin, no. The one who calls himself the Overlord. That one is our master. He can penetrate the impenetrable shield of force and can operate mechanisms of pure force behind it; he can heterodyne, transmit, and use the infra-rays, of whose very existence we were in doubt until recently! While that warning was being delivered he was, in all probability, watching you and listening to you, face to face. You in your ignorance supposed his warning borne by the ether, and thought therefore he must be close to this system. He is very probably at home in the Central System, and is at this moment preparing the forces he intends to hurl against us."

The Emperor fell back into his seat, all his pomposity gone, but the general stiffened eagerly and went straight to the point.

"How do you know these things?"

"Largely by deduction. We of the school of science have cautioned you repeatedly to postpone the Day of Conquest until we should have mastered the secrets of sub-rays and of infra-rays. Unheeding, you of war have gone ahead with your plans, while we of science have continued to study. We know a little of the sub-rays, which we use every day, and practically nothing of the infra-rays. Some time ago I developed a detector for infra-rays, which come to us from outer space in small quantities and which are also liberated by our power-plants. It has been regarded as a scientific curiosity only, but this day it proved of real value. This instrument in my hand is such a detector. At normal impacts of infra-rays its light is blue, as you see it now. Some time before the warning sounded it turned a brilliant red, indicating that an intense source of infra-rays was operating in the neighborhood. By plotting lines of force I located the source as being in the air of the council hall, almost directly above the table of state. Therefore the carrier wave must have come through our whole system of screens without so much as giving an alarm. That fact alone proves it to have been an infra-ray. Furthermore, it carried through those screens and released in the council room a system of forces of great complexity, as is shown by their ability to broadcast from those pure forces without material aid a modulated wave in the exact frequency required to energize our general speakers.

"As soon as I perceived these facts I threw about the council room a screen of force entirely impervious to anything longer than ultra-rays. The warning continued, and I then knew that our fears were only too well grounded—that there is in this Galaxy somewhere a race vastly superior to ours in science and that our destruction is a matter of hours, perhaps of minutes."

"Are these ultra-rays, then, of such a dangerous character?" asked the general. "I had supposed them to be of such infinitely high frequency that they could be of no practical use whatever,"

"I have been trying for years to learn something of their nature, but beyond working out a method for their detection and a method of possible analysis that may or may not succeed I can do nothing with them. It is perfectly evident, however, that they lie below the level of the ether, and therefore have a velocity of propagation infinitely greater than that of light. You may see for yourself, then, that to a science able to guide and control them, to make them act as carrier waves for any other desired frequency—to do all of which the Overlord has this day shown himself capable—they should theoretically afford weapons before which our every defense would be precisely as efficacious as so much vacuum. Think a moment! You know that we know nothing fundamental concerning even our servants, the sub-rays. If we really knew them we could utilize them in thousands of ways as yet unknown to us. We work with the merest handful of forces, empirically, while it is practically certain that the enemy has at his command the entire spectrum, visible and invisible, embracing untold thousands of bands of unknown but terrific potentiality."

"But he spoke of a calculated time necessary before our answer could be received. They must, then, be using vibrations in the ether."

"Not necessarily—not even probably. Would we ourselves reveal unnecessarily to an enemy the possession of such rays? Do not be childish. No, Fenimol, and you, Fenor of the Fenachrone, instant and headlong flight is our only hope of present salvation and of ultimate triumph—flight to a far distant Galaxy, since upon no point in this one shall we be safe from the infra-beams of that self-styled Overlord."

"You snivelling coward! You pusillanimous bookworm!" Fenor had regained his customary spirit as the scientist explained upon what grounds his fears were based. "Upon such a tenuous fabric of evidence would you have such a people as ours turn tail like beaten hounds? Because, forsooth, you detect a peculiar vibration in the air, will you have it that we are to be invaded and destroyed forthwith by a race of supernatural ability? Bah! Your calamity-howling clan has delayed the Day of Conquest from year to year—I more than half believe that you yourself or some other treacherous poltroon of your ignominious breed prepared and sent that warning, in a weak and rat-brained attempt to frighten us into again postponing the Day of Conquest! Know now, spineless weakling, that the time is ripe, and that the Fenachrone in their might are about to strike. But you, foul traducer of your emperor, shall die the death of the cur you are!" The hand within his tunic moved and a vibrator burst into operation.

"Coward I may be, and pusillanimous, and other things as well," the scientist replied stonily, "but, unlike you, I am not a fool. These walls, this very atmosphere, are fields of force that will transmit no rays directed by you. You weak-minded scion of a depraved and obscene house—arrogant, overbearing, rapacious, ignorant—your brain is too feeble to realize that you are clutching at the Universe hundreds of years before the time has come. You by your overweening pride and folly have doomed our beloved planet—the most perfect planet in the Galaxy in its grateful warmth and wonderful dampness and fogginess—and our entire race to certain destruction. Therefore you, fool and dolt that you are, shall die—for too long already have you ruled." He flicked a finger and the body of the monarch shuddered as though an intolerable current of electricity had traversed it, collapsed and lay still.

"It was necessary to destroy this that was our ruler," Ravindau explained to the general. "I have long known that you are not in favor of such precipitate action in the Conquest: hence all this talking upon my part. You know that I hold the honor of Fenachrone dear, and that all my plans are for the ultimate triumph of our race?"

"Yes, and I begin to suspect that those plans have not been made since the warning was received."

"My plans have been made for many years; and ever since an immediate Conquest was decided upon I have been assembling and organizing the means to put them into effect. I would have left this planet in any event shortly after the departure of the grand fleet upon its final expedition—Fenor's senseless defiance of the Overlord has only made it necessary for me to expedite my leave-taking."

"What do you intend to do?"

"I have a vessel twice as large as the largest warship Fenor boasted; completely provisioned, armed, and powered for a cruise of one hundred years at high acceleration. It is hidden in a remote fastness of the jungle. I am placing in that vessel a group of the finest, brainiest, most highly advanced and intelligent of our men and women, with their children. We shall journey at our highest speed to a certain distant Galaxy, where we shall seek out a planet similar in atmosphere, temperature, and mass to the one upon which we now dwell. There we shall multiply and continue our studies; and from that planet, in that day when we shall have attained sufficient knowledge, there shall descend upon the Central System of this Galaxy the vengeance of the Fenachrone. That vengeance will be all the sweeter for the fact that it shall have been delayed."

"But how about libraries, apparatus and equipment? Suppose that we do not live long enough to perfect that knowledge? And with only one vessel and a handful of men we could not cope with that accursed Overlord and his navies of the void."

"Libraries are aboard, so are much apparatus and equipment. What we cannot take with us we can build. As for the knowledge I mentioned, it may not be attained in your lifetime nor in mine. But the racial memory of the Fenachrone is long, as you know; and even if the necessary problems are not solved until our descendants are sufficiently numerous to populate an entire planet, yet will those descendants wreak the vengeance of the Fenachrone upon the races of that hated one, the Overlord, before they go on with the Conquest of the Universe. Many questions will arise, of course; but they shall be solved. Enough! Time passes rapidly, and all too long have I talked. I am using this time upon you because in my organization there is no soldier, and the Fenachrone of the future will need your great knowledge of warfare. Are you going with us?"

"Yes."

"Very well." Ravindau led the general through a door and into an airboat lying upon the terrace outside the laboratory. "Drive us at speed to your home, where we shall pick up your family."

Fenimol took the controls and laid a ray to his home—a ray serving a double purpose. It held the vessel upon its predetermined course through that thick and sticky fog and also rendered collision impossible, since any two of these controller rays repelled each other to such a degree that no two vessels could take paths which would bring them together. Some such provision had been found necessary ages ago, for all Fenachrone craft were provided with the same space-annihilating drive, to which any comprehensible distance was but a journey of a few moments, and at that frightful velocity collision meant annihilation.

"I understand that you could not take any one of the military into your confidence until you were ready to put your plans into effect," the general conceded. "How long will it take you to get ready to leave? You have said that haste is imperative, and I therefore assume that you have already warned the other members of the expedition."

"I flashed the emergency signal before I joined you and Fenor in the council room. Each man of the organization has received that signal, wherever he may have been, and by this time most of them, with their families, are on the way to the hidden cruiser. We shall leave this planet in fifteen minutes from now at most—I dare not stay an instant longer than is absolutely necessary."

The members of the general's family were bundled, amazed, into the airboat, which immediately flew along a ray laid by Ravindau to the secret rendezvous.

In a remote and desolate part of the planet, concealed in the depths of the towering jungle growth, a mammoth space-cruiser was receiving her complement of passengers. Airboats, flying at their terrific velocity through the heavy, steaming fog as closely-spaced as their controller rays would permit, flashed signals along their guiding beams, dove into the apparently impenetrable jungle, and added their passengers to the throng pouring into the great vessel.

As the minute of departure drew near, the feeling of tension aboard the cruiser increased and vigilance was raised to the maximum. None of the passengers had been allowed senders of any description, and now even the hair-line beams guiding the airboats were cut off, and received only when the proper code signal was heard. The doors were shut, no one was allowed outside, and everything was held in readiness for instant flight at the least alarm. Finally a scientist and his family arrived from the opposite side of the planet—the last members of the organization—and, twenty-seven minutes after Ravindau had flashed his signal, the prow of that mighty space-ship reared toward the perpendicular, poising its massive length at the predetermined angle. There it halted momentarily, then disappeared utterly, only a vast column of tortured and shattered vegetation, torn from the ground and carried for miles upward into the air by the vacuum of its wake, remaining to indicate the path taken by the flying projectile.

Hour after hour the Fenachrone vessel bored on, with its frightful and ever-increasing velocity, through the ever-thinning stars, but it was not until the last star had been passed, until everything before them was entirely devoid of light, and until the Galaxy behind them began to take on a well-defined lenticular aspect, that Ravindau would consent to leave the controls and to seek his hard-earned rest.

Day after day and week after week went by, and the Fenachrone vessel still held the rate of motion with which she had started out. Ravindau and Fenimol sat in the control cabin, staring out through the visiplates, abstracted. There was no need of staring, and they were not really looking, for there was nothing at which to look. Outside the transparent metal hull of that monster of the trackless void, there was nothing visible. The Galaxy of which our Earth is an infinitesimal mote, the Galaxy which former astronomers considered the Universe, was so far behind that its immeasurable diameter was too small to affect the vision of the unaided eye. Other Galaxies lay at even greater distances away on either side. The Galaxy toward which they were making their stupendous flight was as yet untold millions of light-years distant. Nothing was visible—before their gaze stretched an infinity of emptiness. No stars, no nebulæ, no meteoric matter, nor even the smallest particle of cosmic dust—absolutely empty space. Absolute vacuum and absolute zero. Absolute nothingness—a concept intrinsically impossible for the most highly trained human mind to grasp.

Conscienceless and heartless monstrosities though they both were, by heredity and training, the immensity of the appalling lack of anything tangible oppressed them. Ravindau was stern and serious, Fenimol moody. Finally the latter spoke.

"It would be endurable if we knew what had happened, or if we ever could know definitely, one way or the other, whether all this was necessary."

"We shall know, general, definitely. I am certain in my own mind, but after a time, when we have settled upon our new home and when the Overlord shall have relaxed his vigilance, you shall come back to the solar system of the Fenachrone in this vessel or a similar one. I know what you shall find—but the trip shall be made, and you shall yourself see what was once our home planet, a seething sun, second only in brilliance to the parent sun about which she shall still be revolving."

"Are we safe, even now—what of possible pursuit?" asked Fenimol, and the monstrous, flame-shot wells of black that were Ravindau's eyes almost emitted tangible fires as he made reply:

"We are far from safe, but we grow stronger minute by minute. Fifty of the greatest minds our world has ever known have been working from the moment of our departure upon a line of investigation suggested to me by certain things my instruments recorded during the visit of the self-styled Overlord. I cannot say anything yet: even to you—except that the Day of Conquest may not be so far in the future as we have supposed."

CHAPTER XIV

Interstellar Extermination

"I hate to leave this meeting—it's great stuff" remarked Seaton as he flashed down to the torpedo room at Fenor's command to send recall messages to all outlying vessels, "but this machine isn't designed to let me be in more than two places at once. Wish it were—maybe after this fracas is over we'll be able to incorporate something like that into it."

The chief operator touched a lever and the chair upon which he sat, with all its control panels, slid rapidly across the floor toward an apparently blank wall. As he reached it, a port opened a metal scroll appeared, containing the numbers and last reported positions of all Fenachrone vessels outside the detector zone, and a vast magazine of torpedoes came up through the floor, with an automatic loader to place a torpedo under the operator's hand the instant its predecessor had been launched.

"Get Peg here quick, Mart—we need a stenographer. Till she gets here, see what you can do in getting those first numbers before they roll off the end of the scroll. No, hold it—as you were! I've got controls enough to put the whole thing on a recorder, so we can study it at our leisure."

Haste was indeed necessary for the operator worked with uncanny quickness of hand. One fleeting glance at the scroll, a lightning adjustment of dials in the torpedo, a touch upon a tiny button, and a messenger was upon its way. But quick as he was, Seaton's flying fingers kept up with him, and before each torpedo disappeared through the ether gate there was fastened upon it a fifth-order tracer ray that would never leave it until the force had been disconnected at the gigantic control board of the Norlaminian projector. One flying minute passed during which seventy torpedoes had been launched, before Seaton spoke.

"Wonder how many ships they've got out, anyway? Didn't get any idea from the brain-record. Anyway, Rovol, it might be a sound idea for you to install me some more tracer rays on this board, I've got only a couple of hundred, and that may not be enough—and I've got both hands full."

Rovol seated himself beside the younger man, like one organist joining another at the console of a tremendous organ. Seaton's nimble fingers would flash here and there, depressing keys and manipulating controls until he had exactly the required combination of forces centered upon the torpedo next to issue. He then would press a tiny switch and upon a panel full of red-topped, numbered plungers; the one next in series would drive home, transferring to itself the assembled beam and releasing the keys for the assembly of other forces. Rovol's fingers were also flying, but the forces he directed were seizing and shaping material, as well as other forces. The Norlaminian physicist, set up one integral, stepped upon a pedal, and a new red-topped stop precisely like the others and numbered in order, appeared as though by magic upon the panel at Seaton's left hand. Rovol then leaned back in his seat—but the red-topped stops continued to appear, at the rate of exactly seventy per minute, upon the panel, which increased in width sufficiently to accommodate another row as soon as a row was completed.

Rovol bent a quizzical glance upon the younger scientist, who blushed a fiery red, rapidly set up another integral, then also leaned back in his place, while his face burned deeper than before.

"That is better, son. Never forget that it is a waste of energy to do the same thing twice with your hands and that if you know precisely what is to be done, you need not do it with your hands at all. Forces are tireless, and they neither slip nor make mistakes."

"Thanks, Rovol—I'll bet this lesson will make it stick in my mind, too."

"You are not thoroughly accustomed to using all your knowledge as yet. That will come with practice, however, and in a few weeks you will be as thoroughly at home with forces as I am."

"Hope so, Chief, but it looks like a tall order to me."

Finally the last torpedo was dispatched, the tube closed, and Seaton moved the projection back up into the council chamber, finding it empty.

"Well, the conference is over—besides, we've got more important fish to fry. War has been declared, on both sides, and we've got to get busy. They've got nine hundred and six vessels out, and every one of them has got to go to Davy Jones' locker before we can sleep sound of nights. My first job'll have to be untangling those nine oh six forces, getting lines on each one of them, and seeing if I can project straight enough to find the ships before the torpedoes overtake them. Mart, you and Orlon, the astronomer, had better dope out the last reported positions of each of those vessels, so we'll know about where to hunt for them. Rovol, you might send out a detector screen a few light years in diameter, to be sure none of them slips a fast one over on us. By starting it right here and expanding it gradually, you can be sure that no Fenachrone is inside it. Then we'll find a hunk of copper on that planet somewhere, plate it with some of their own 'X' metal, and blow them into Kingdom Come."

"May I venture a suggestion?" asked Drasnik, the First of Psychology.

"Absolutely—nothing you've said so far has been idle chatter."

"You know, of course, that there are real scientists among the Fenachrone; and you yourself have suggested that while they cannot penetrate the zone of force nor use fifth-order rays, yet they might know about them in theory, might even be able to know when they were being used—detect them, in other words. Let us assume that such a scientist did detect your rays while you were there a short time ago. What would he do?"

"Search me.... I bite, what would he do?"

"He might do any one of several things, but if I read their nature aright, such a one would gather up a few men and women—as many as he could—and migrate to another planet. For he would of course grasp instantly the fact that you had used fifth-order rays as carrier waves, and would be able to deduce your ability to destroy. He would also realize that in the brief time allowed him, he could not hope to learn to control those unknown forces; and with his terribly savage and vengeful nature and intense pride of race, he would take every possible step both to perpetuate his race and to obtain revenge. Am I right?"

Seaton swung to his controls savagely, and manipulated dials and keys rapidly.

"Right as rain, Drasnik. There—I've thrown around them a fifth-order detector screen, that they can't possibly neutralize. Anything that goes out through it will have a tracer slapped onto it. But say, it's been half an hour since war was declared—suppose we're too late? Maybe some of them have got away already, and if one couple of 'em has beat us to it, we'll have the whole thing to do over again a thousand years or so from now. You've got the massive intellect, Drasnik. What can we do about it? We can't throw a detector screen all over the Galaxy."

"I would suggest that since you have now guarded against further exodus, it is necessary to destroy the planet for a time. Rovol and his co-workers have the other projector nearly done. Let them project me to the world of the Fenachrone, where I shall conduct a thorough mental investigation. By the time you have taken care of the raiding vessels, I believe that I shall have been able to learn everything we need to know."

"Fine—hop to it, and may there be lots of bubbles in your think-tank. Anybody else know of any other loop-holes I've left open?"

No other suggestions were made, and each man bent to his particular task. Crane at the star-chart of the Galaxy and Orlon at the Fenachrone operator's dispatching scroll rapidly worked out the approximate positions of the Fenachrone vessels, and marked them with tiny green lights in a vast model of the Galaxy which they had already caused forces to erect in the air of the projector's base. It was soon learned that a few of the ships were exploring quite close to their home system; so close that the torpedoes, with their unthinkable acceleration, would reach them within a few hours. Ascertaining the stop-number of the tracer ray upon the torpedo which should first reach its destination, Seaton followed it from the stop upon his panel out to the flying messenger. Now moving with a velocity many times that of light, it was, of course, invisible to direct vision; but to the light waves heterodyned upon the fifth-order projector rays, it was as plainly visible as though it were stationary. Lining up the path of the projectile accurately, he then projected himself forward in that exact line, with a flat detector-screen thrown out for half a light year upon each side of him. Setting the controls, he flashed ahead, the detector stopping him the instant that the invisible barrier encountered the power-plant of the exploring raider. An oscillator sounded a shrill and rising note, and Seaton slowly shifted his controls until he stood in the control room of the enemy vessel.

The Fenachrone ship, a thousand feet long and more than a hundred feet in diameter, was tearing through space toward a brilliant blue-white star. Her crew were at battle stations, her navigating officers peering intently into the operating visiplates, all oblivious to the fact that a stranger stood in their very midst.

"Well, here's the first one, gang," said Seaton, "I hate like sin to do this—it's altogether too much like pushing baby chickens into a creek to suit me, but it's a dirty job that's got to be done."

As one man, Orlon and the other remaining Norlaminians leaped out of the projector and floated to the ground below.

"I expected that," remarked Seaton. "They can't even think of a thing like this without getting the blue willies—I don't blame them much, at that. How about you, Carfon? You can be excused if you like."

"I want to watch those forces at work. I do not enjoy destruction, but like you, I can make myself endure it."

Dunark, the fierce and bloodthirsty Osnomian prince, leaped to his feet, his eyes flashing.

"That's one thing I never could get about you, Dick!" he exclaimed in English. "How a man with your brains can be so soft—so sloppily sentimental, gets clear past me. You remind me of a bowl of mush—you wade around in slush clear to your ears. Faugh! It's their lives or ours! Tell me what button to push and I'll be only too glad to push it. I wanted to blow up Urvania and you wouldn't let me; I haven't killed an enemy for ages, and that's my trade. Cut out the sob-sister act and for Cat's sake, let's get busy!"

"'At-a-boy, Dunark! That's tellin' 'im! But it's all right with me—I'll be glad to let you do it. When I say 'shoot' throw in that plunger there—number sixty-three."

Seaton manipulated controls until two electrodes of force were clamped in place, one at either end of the huge power-bar of the enemy vessel; adjusted rheostats and forces to send a disintegrating current through that massive copper cylinder, and gave the word. Dunark threw in the switch with a vicious thrust, as though it were an actual sword which he was thrusting through the vitals of one of the awesome crew, and the very Universe exploded around them—exploded into one mad, searing coruscation of blinding, dazzling light as the gigantic cylinder of copper resolved itself instantaneously into the pure energy from which its metal originally had come into being.

Seaton and Dunark staggered back from the visiplates, blinded by the intolerable glare of light, and even Crane, working at his model of the galaxy, blinked at the intensity of the radiation. Many minutes passed before the two men could see through their tortured eyes.

"Zowie! That was fierce!" exclaimed Seaton, when a slowly-returning perception of things other than dizzy spirals and balls of flame assured him that his eyesight was not permanently gone. "It's nothing but my own fool carelessness, too. I should have known that with all the light frequencies in heterodyne for visibility, enough of that same stuff would leak through to make strong medicine on these visiplates—for I knew that that bar weighed a hundred tons and would liberate energy enough to volatilize our Earth and blow the by-products clear to Arcturus. How're you coming, Dunark? See anything yet?"

"Coming along O. K. now, I guess—but I thought for a few minutes I'd been bloody well jobbed."

"I'll do better next time. I'll cut out the visible spectrum before the flash, and convert and reconvert the infra-red. That'll let us see what happens, without the direct effect of the glare—won't burn our eyes out. What's my force number on the next nearest one, Mart?"

"Twenty-nine."

Seaton fastened a detector ray upon stop twenty-nine of the tracer-ray panel and followed its beam of force out to the torpedo hastening upon its way toward the next doomed cruiser. Flashing ahead in its line as he had done before, he located the vessel and clamped the electrodes of force upon the prodigious driving bar. Again, as Dunark drove home the detonating switch, there was a frightful explosion and a wild glare of frenzied incandescence far out in that desolate region of interstellar space; but this time the eyes behind the visiplates were not torn by the high frequencies, everything that happened was plainly visible. One instant, there was an immense space-cruiser boring on through the void upon its horrid mission, with its full complement of the hellish Fenachrone performing their routine tasks. The next instant there was a flash of light extending for thousands upon untold thousands of miles in every direction. That flare of light vanished as rapidly as it had appeared—instantaneously—and throughout the entire neighborhood of the place where the Fenachrone cruiser had been, there was nothing. Not a plate nor a girder, not a fragment, not the most minute particle nor droplet of disrupted metal nor of condensed vapor. So terrific, so incredibly and incomprehensibly vast were the forces liberated by that mass of copper in its instantaneous decomposition, that every atom of substance in that great vessel had gone with the power-bar—had been resolved into radiations which would at some distant time and in some far-off solitude unite with other radiations, again to form matter, and thus obey Nature's immutable cyclic law.

Thus vessel after vessel was destroyed of that haughty fleet which until now had never suffered a reverse and a little green light in the galactic model winked out and flashed back in rosy pink as each menace was removed. In a few hours the space surrounding the system of the Fenachrone was clear; then progress slackened as it became harder and harder to locate each vessel as the distance between it and its torpedo increased. Time after time Seaton would stab forward with his detector screen extended to its utmost possible spread, upon the most carefully plotted prolongation of the line of the torpedo's flight, only to have the projection flash far beyond the vessel's furthest possible position without a reaction from the far-flung screen. Then he would go back to the torpedo, make a minute alteration in his line, and again flash forward, only to miss it again. Finally, after thirty fruitless attempts to bring his detector screen into contact with the nearest Fenachrone ship, he gave up the attempt, rammed his battered, reeking briar full of the rank blend that was his favorite smoke, and strode up and down the floor of the projector base—his eyes unseeing, his hands jammed deep into his pockets, his jaw thrust forward, clamped upon the stem of his pipe, emitting dense, blue clouds of strangling vapor.

"The maestro is thinking, I perceive," remarked Dorothy, sweetly, entering the projector from an airboat. "You must all be blind, I guess—you no hear the bell blow, what? I've come after you—it's time to eat!"

"'At-a-girl, Dot—never miss the eats! Thanks," and Seaton put his problem away, with perceptible effort.

"This is going to be a job, Mart," he went back to it as soon as they were seated in the airboat, flying toward "home." "I can nail them, with an increasing shift in azimuth, up to about thirty thousand light-years, but after that it gets awfully hard to get the right shift, and up around a hundred thousand it seems to be darn near impossible—gets to be pure guesswork. It can't be the controls, because they can hold a point rigidly at five hundred thousand. Of course, we've got a pretty short back-line to sight on, but the shift is more than a hundred times as great as the possible error in backsight could account for, and there's apparently nothing either regular or systematic about it that I can figure out. But.... I don't know.... Space is curved in the fourth dimension, of course.... I wonder if ... hm—m—m." He fell silent and Crane made a rapid signal to Dorothy, who was opening her mouth to say something. She shut it, feeling ridiculous, and nothing was said until they had disembarked at their destination.

"Did you solve the puzzle, Dickie?"

"Don't think so—got myself in deeper than ever, I'm afraid," he answered, then went on, thinking aloud rather than addressing any one in particular:

"Space is curved in the fourth dimension, and fifth-order rays, with their velocity, may not follow the same path in that dimension that light does—in fact, they do not. If that path is to be plotted it requires the solution of five simultaneous equations, each complete and general, and each of the fifth degree, and also an exponential series with the unknown in the final exponent, before the fourth-dimensional concept can be derived ... hm—m—m. No use—we've struck something that not even Norlaminian theory can handle."

"You surprise me." Crane said. "I supposed that they had everything worked out."

"Not on fifth-order stuff—it's new, you know. It begins to look as though we'd have to stick around until every one of those torpedoes gets somewhere near its mother-ship. Hate to do it, too—it'll take six months, at least, to reach the vessels clear across the Galaxy. I'll put it up to the gang at dinner—guess they'll let me talk business a couple of minutes overtime, especially after they find out what I've got to say."

He explained the phenomenon to an interested group of white-bearded scientists as they ate. Rovol, to Seaton's surprise, was elated and enthusiastic.

"Wonderful, my boy!" he breathed. "Marvelous! A perfect subject for years after year of deepest study and the most profound thought. Perfect!"

"But what can we *do* about it?" asked Seaton, exasperated. "We don't want to hang around here twiddling our thumbs for a year waiting for those torpedoes to get to wherever they're going!"

"We can do nothing but wait and study. That problem is one of splendid difficulty, as you yourself realize. Its solution may well be a matter of lifetimes instead of years. But what is a year, more or less? You can destroy the Fenachrone eventually, so be content."

"But content is just exactly what I'm *not*!" declared Seaton, emphatically. "I want to do it, and do it *now*!"

"Perhaps I might volunteer a suggestion," said Caslor, diffidently; and as both Rovol and Seaton looked at him in surprise he went on: "Do not misunderstand me. I do not mean concerning the mathematical problem in discussion, about which I am entirely ignorant. But has it occurred to you that those torpedoes are not intelligent entities, acting upon their own volition and steering themselves as a result of their own ordered mental processes? No, they are mechanisms, in my own province, and I venture to say with the utmost confidence that they are guided to their destinations by streamers of force of some nature, emanating from the vessels upon whose tracks they are."

"'Nobody Holme' is right!" exclaimed Seaton, tapping his temple with an admonitory forefinger. "'Sright, ace—I thought maybe I'd quit using my head for nothing but a hatrack now, but I guess that's all it's good for, yet. Thanks a lot for the idea—that gives me something I can get my teeth into, and now that Rovol's got a problem to work on for the next century or so, everybody's happy."

"How does that help matters?" asked Crane in wonder. "Of course it is not surprising that no lines of force were visible, but I thought that your detectors screens would have found them if any such guiding beams had been present."

"The ordinary bands, if of sufficient power, yes. But there are many possible tracer rays not reactive to a screen such as I was using. It was very light and weak, designed for terrific velocity and for instantaneous automatic arrest when in contact with the enormous forces of a power bar. It wouldn't react at all to the minute energy of the kind of beams they'd be most likely to use for that work. Caslor's certainly right. They're steering their torpedoes with tracer rays of almost infinitesimal power, amplified in the torpedoes themselves—that's the way I'd do it myself. It may take a little while to rig up the apparatus, but we'll get it—and then we'll run those birds ragged—so fast that their ankles'll catch fire—and won't need the fourth-dimensional correction after all."

When the bell announced the beginning of the following period of labor, Seaton and his co-workers were in the Area of Experiment waiting, and the work was soon under way.

"How are you going about this, Dick?" asked Crane.

"Going to examine the nose of one of those torpedoes first, and see what it actually works on. Then build me a tracer detector that'll pick it up at high velocity. Beats the band, doesn't it, that neither Rovol nor I, who should have thought of it first, ever did see anything as plain as that? That those things are following a ray?"

"That is easily explained, and is no more than natural. Both of you were not only devoting all your thoughts to the curvature of space, but were also too close to the problem—like the man in the woods, who cannot see the forest because of the trees."

"Yeah, may be something in that, too. Plain enough, when Caslor showed it to us," said Seaton.

While he was talking, Seaton had projected himself into the torpedo he had lined up so many times the previous day. With the automatic motions set to hold him stationary in the tiny instrument compartment of the craft, now traveling at a velocity many times that of light, he set to work. A glance located the detector mechanism, a set of short-wave coils and amplifiers, and a brief study made plain to him the principles underlying the directional loop finders and the controls which guided the flying shell along the path of the tracer ray. He then built a detector structure of pure force immediately in front of the torpedo, and varied the frequency of his own apparatus until a meter upon one of the panels before his eyes informed him that his detector was in perfect resonance with the frequency of the tracer ray. He then moved ahead of the torpedo, along the guiding ray.

"Guiding it, eh?" Dunark congratulated him.

"Kinda. My directors out there aren't quite so hot, though. I'm a trifle shy on control somewhere, so much so that if I put on anywhere near full velocity, I lose the ray. Think I can clear that up with a little experimenting, though."

He fingered controls lightly, depressed a few more keys, and set one vernier, already at a ratio of a million to one, down to ten million. He then stepped up his velocity, and found that the guides worked well up to a speed much greater than any ever reached by Fenachrone vessels or torpedoes, but failed utterly to hold the ray at anything approaching the full velocity possible to his fifth-order projector. After hours and days of work and study—in the course of which hundreds of the Fenachrone vessels were destroyed—after employing all the resources of his mind, now stored with the knowledge of rays accumulated by hundreds of generations of highly-trained research specialists in rays, he became convinced that it was an inherent impossibility to trace any ether wave with the velocity he desired.

"Can't be done, I guess, Mart," he confessed, ruefully. "You see, it works fine up to a certain point; but beyond that, nothing doing. I've just found out why—and in so doing, I think I've made a contribution to science. At velocities well below that of light, light-waves are shifted a minute amount, you know. At the velocity of light, and up to a velocity not even approached by the Fenachrone vessels on their longest trips, the distortion is still not serious—no matter how fast we want to travel in the *Skylark*, I think I can guarantee that we will still be able to see things. That is to be expected from the generally-accepted idea that the apparent velocity of any ether vibration is independent of the velocity of either source or receiver. However, that relationship fails at velocities far below that of fifth-order rays. At only a very small fraction of that speed the tracers I am following are so badly distorted that they disappear altogether, and I have to distort them backwards. That wouldn't be too bad, but when I get up to about one per cent of the velocity I want to use, I can't calculate a force that will operate to distort them back into recognizable wave-forms. That's another problem for Rovol to chew on, for another hundred years."

"That will, of course, slow up the work of clearing the Galaxy of the Fenachrone, but at the same time I see nothing about which to be alarmed," Crane replied. "You are working very much faster than you could have done by waiting for the torpedoes to arrive. The present condition is very satisfactory, I should say," and he waved his hand at the galactic model, in nearly three-fourths of whose volume the green lights had been replaced by pink ones.

"Yeah, pretty fair as far as that goes—we'll clean up in ten days or so—but I hate to be licked. Well, I might as well quit sobbing and get busy!"

In due time the nine hundred and sixth Fenachrone vessel was checked off on the model, and the two Terrestrials went in search of Drasnik, whom they found in his study, summing up and analyzing a mass of data, facts, and ideas which were being projected in the air around him.

"Well, our first job's done," Seaton stated. "What do you know that you feel like passing around?"

"My investigation is practically complete," replied the First of Psychology, gravely. "I have explored many Fenachrone minds, and without exception I have found them chambers of horror of a kind unimaginable to one of us. However, you are not interested in their psychology, but in facts bearing upon your problem. While such facts were scarce, I did discover a few interesting items. I spied upon them in public and in their most private haunts. I analyzed them individually and collectively, and from the few known facts and from the great deal of guesswork and conjecture there available to me, I have formulated a theory. I shall first give you the known facts. Their scientists cannot direct nor control any ray not propagated through ether, but they can detect one such frequency or band of frequencies which they call 'infra-rays' and which are probably the fifth-order rays, since they lie in the first level below the ether. The detector proper is a type of lamp, which gives a blue light at the ordinary intensity of such rays as would come from space or from an ordinary power plant, but gives a red light under strong excitation."

"Uh-huh, I get that O. K.," said Seaton. "Rovol's great-great-great-grandfather had 'em—I know all about 'em," Seaton encouraged Drasnik, who had paused, with a questioning glance. "I know exactly how and why such a detector works. We gave 'em an alarm, all right. Even though we were working on a tight beam from here to there, our secondary projector there was radiating enough to affect every such detector within a thousand miles."

Drasnik continued: "Another significant fact is that a great many persons—I learned of some five hundred, and there were probably many more—have disappeared without explanation and without leaving a trace; and it seems that they disappeared very shortly after our communication was delivered. One of these was Fenor, the Emperor. His family remain, however, and his son is not only ruling in his stead, but is carrying out his father's policies. The other disappearances are all alike and are peculiar in certain respects. First, every man who vanished belonged to the Party of Postponement—the minority party of the Fenachrone, who believe that the time for the Conquest has not yet come. Second, every one of them was a leader in thought in some field of usefulness, and every such field is represented by at least one disappearance—even the army, as General Fenimol, the Commander-in-Chief, and his whole family, are among the absentees. Third, and most remarkable, each such disappearance included an entire family, clear down to children and grand-children, however young. Another fact is that the Fenachrone Department of Navigation keeps a very close check upon all vessels, particularly vessels capable of navigating outer space. Every vessel built must be registered, and its location is always known from its individual tracer ray. No Fenachrone vessel is missing."

"I also sifted a mass of gossip and conjecture, some of which may bear upon the subject. One belief is that all the persons were put to death by Fenor's secret service, and that the Emperor was assassinated in revenge. The most widespread belief, however, is that they have fled. Some hold that they are in hiding in some remote shelter in the jungle, arguing that the rigid registration of all vessels renders a journey of any great length impossible and that the detector screens would have given warning of any vessel leaving the planet. Others think that persons as powerful as Fenimol and Ravindau could have built any vessel they chose with neither the knowledge nor consent of the Department of Navigation, or that they could have stolen a Navy vessel, destroying its records; and that Ravindau certainly could have so neutralized the screens that they would have given no alarm. These believe that the absent ones have migrated to some other solar system or to some other planet of the same sun. One old general loudly gave it as his opinion that the cowardly traitors had probably fled clear out of the Galaxy, and that it would be a good thing to send the rest of the Party of Postponement after them. There, in brief, are the salient points of my investigation in so far as it concerns your immediate problem."

"A good many straws pointing this way and that," commented Seaton. "However, we know that the 'postponers' are just as rabid on the idea of conquering the Universe as the others are—only they are a lot more cautious and won't take even a gambler's chance of a defeat. But you've formed a theory—what is it, Drasnik?"

"From my analysis of these facts and conjectures, in conjunction with certain purely psychological indices which we need not take time to go into now, I am certain that they have left their solar system, probably in an immense vessel built a long time ago and held in readiness for just such an emergency. I am not certain of their destination, but it is my opinion that they have left this Galaxy, and are planning upon starting anew upon some suitable planet in some other Galaxy, from which, at some future date, the Conquest of the Universe shall proceed as it was originally planned."

"Great balls of fire!" blurted Seaton. "They couldn't—not in a million years!" He thought a moment, then continued more slowly: "But they could—and, with their dispositions, they probably would. You're one hundred per cent. right, Drasnik. We've got a real job of hunting on our hands now. So-long, and thanks a lot."

Back in the projector Seaton prowled about in brown abstraction, his villainous pipe poisoning the circumambient air, while Crane sat, quiet and self-possessed as always, waiting for the nimble brain of his friend to find a way over, around, or through the obstacle confronting them.

"Got it, Mart!" Seaton yelled, darting to the board and setting up one integral after another. "If they did leave the planet in a ship, we'll be able to watch them go—and we'll see what they did, anyway, no matter what it was!"

"How? They've been gone almost a month already," protested Crane.

"We know within half an hour the exact time of their departure. We'll simply go out the distance light has traveled since that time, gather in the rays given off, amplify them a few billion times, and take a look at whatever went on."

"But we have no idea of what region of the planet to study, or whether it was night or day at the point of departure when they left."

"We'll get the council room, and trace events from there. Day or night makes no difference—we'll have to use infra-red anyway, because of the fog, and that's almost as good at night as in the daytime. There is no such thing as absolute darkness upon any planet, anyway, and we've got power enough to make anything visible that happened there, night or day. Mart, I've got power enough here to see and to photograph the actual construction of the pyramids of Egypt in that same way—and they were built thousands of years ago!"

"Heavens, what astounding possibilities!" breathed Crane. "Why, you could...."

"Yeah, I could do a lot of things," Seaton interrupted him rudely, "but right now we've got other fish to fry. I've just got the city we visited, at about the time we were there. General Fenimol, who disappeared, must be in the council room down here right now. I'll retard our projection, so that time will apparently pass more quickly, and we'll duck down there and see what actually did happen. I can heterodyne, combine, and recombine just as though we were watching the actual scene—it's more complicated, of course, since I have to follow it and amplify it too, but it works out all right."

"This is unbelievable, Dick. Think of actually seeing something that really happened in the past!"

"Yeah, it's kinda strong, all right. As Dot would say, it's just too perfectly darn outrageous. But we're doing it, ain't we? I know just how, and why. When we get some time I'll shoot the method into your brain. Well, here we are!"

Peering into the visiplates, the two men were poised above the immense central cone of the capital city of the Fenachrone. Viewing with infra-red light as they were, the fog presented no obstacle and the indescribable beauty of the city of concentric rings and the wonderfully luxuriant jungle growth were clearly visible. They plunged down into the council chamber, and saw Fenor, Ravindau, and Fenimol deep in conversation.

"With all the other feats of skill and sorcery you have accomplished, why don't you reconstruct their speech, also?" asked Crane, with a challenging glance.

"Well, old Doubting Thomas, it might not be absolutely impossible, at that. It would mean two projectors, however, due to the difference in speed of sound-waves and light-waves. Theoretically, sound-waves also extend to an infinite distance, but I don't believe that any possible detector and amplifier could reconstruct a voice more than an hour or so after it had spoken. It might, though—we'll have to try it some time, and see. You're fairly good at lip-reading, as I remember it. Get as much of it as you can, will you?"

As though they were watching the scene itself as it happened—which, in a sense, they were—they saw everything that had occurred. They saw Fenor die, saw the general's family board the airboat, saw the orderly embarkation of Ravindau's organization. Finally they saw the stupendous take-off of the first inter-galactic cruiser, and with that take-off, Seaton went into action. Faster and faster he drove that fifth-order beam along the track of the fugitive, until a speed was attained beyond which his detecting converters could not hold the ether-rays they were following. For many minutes Seaton stared intently into the visiplate, plotting lines and calculating forces, then he swung around to Crane.

"Well, Mart, noble old bean, solving the disappearances was easier than I thought it would be; but the situation as regards wiping out the last of the Fenachrone is getting no better, fast."

"I glean from the instruments that they are heading straight out into space away from the Galaxy, and I assume that they are using their utmost acceleration?"

"I'll say they're traveling! They're out in absolute space, you know, with nothing in the way and with no intention of reversing their power or slowing down—they must've had absolute top acceleration on every minute since they left. Anyway, they're so far out already that I couldn't hold even a detector on them, let alone a force that I can control. Well, let's snap into it, fellow—on our way!"

"Just a minute, Dick. Take it easy, what are your plans?"

"Plans! Why worry about plans? Blow up that planet before any more of 'em get away, and then chase that boat clear to Andromeda, if necessary. Let's go!"

"Calm down and be reasonable—you are getting hysterical again. They have a maximum acceleration of five times the velocity of light. So have we, exactly, since we adopted their own drive. Now if our acceleration is the same as theirs, and they have a month's start, how long will it take us to catch them?"

"Right again. Mart—I sure was going off half-cocked again," Seaton conceded ruefully, after a moment's thought. "They'd always be going a million or so times as fast as we would be, and getting further ahead of us in geometrical ratio. What's your idea?"

"I agree with you that the time has come to destroy the planet of Fenachrone. As for pursuing that vessel through intergalactic space, that is your problem. You must figure out some method of increasing our acceleration. Highly efficient as is this system of propulsion, it seems to me that the knowledge of the Norlaminians should be able to improve it in some detail. Even a slight increase in acceleration would enable us to overtake them eventually."

"Hm—m—m." Seaton, no longer impetuous, was thinking deeply. "How far are we apt to have to go?"

"Until we get close enough to them to use your rays—say half a million light-years."

"But surely they'll stop, some time?"

"Of course, but not necessarily for many years. They are powered and provisioned for a hundred years, you remember, and are going to 'a distant galaxy.' Such a one as Ravindau would not have specified a *distant* Galaxy idly, and the very closest Galaxies are so far away that even the Fenachrone astronomers, with their reflecting mirrors five miles in diameter, could form only the very roughest approximations of the true distances."

"Our astronomers are all wet in their guesses, then?"

"Their estimates are, without exception, far below the true values. They are not even of the correct order of magnitude.'"

"Well, then, let's mop up on that planet. Then we'll go places and do things."

Seaton had already located the magazines in which the power bars of the Fenachrone war-vessels were stored, and it was a short task to erect a secondary projector of force in the Fenachrone atmosphere. Working out of that projector, beams of force seized one of the immense cylinders of plated copper and at Seaton's direction transported it rapidly to one of the poles of the planet, where electrodes of force were clamped upon it. In a similar fashion seventeen more of the frightful bombs were placed, equidistant over the surface of the world of the Fenachrone, so that when they were simultaneously exploded, the downward forces would be certain to meet sufficient resistance to assure complete demolition of the entire globe. Everything in readiness, Seaton's hand went to the plunger switch and closed upon it. Then, his face white and wet, he dropped his hand.

"No use, Mart—I can't do it. It pulls my cork. I know darn well you can't either—I'll yell for help."

"Have you got it on the infra-red?" asked Dunark calmly, as he shot up into the projector in reply to Seaton's call. "I want to see this, all of it."

"It's on—you're welcome to it," and, as the Terrestrials turned away, the whole projector base was illuminated by a flare of intense, though subdued light. For several minutes Dunark stared into the visiplate, savage satisfaction in every line of his fierce green face as he surveyed the havoc wrought by those eighteen enormous charges of incredible explosive.

"A nice job of clean-up, Dick," the Osnomian prince reported, turning away from the visiplate. "It made a sun of it—the original sun is now quite a splendid double star. Everything was volatized, clear out, far beyond their outermost screen."

"It had to be done, of course—it was either them or else all the rest of the Universe," Season said, jerkily. "However, even that fact doesn't make it go down easy. Well, we're done with this projector. From now on it's strictly up to us and *Skylark Three*. Let's beat it over there and see if they've got her done yet—they were due to finish up today, you know."

It was a silent group who embarked in the little airboat. Half way to their destination, however, Seaton came out of his blue mood with a yell.

"Mart, I've got it! We can give the *Lark* a lot more acceleration than they are getting—and won't need the assistance of all the minds of Norlamin, either."

"How?"

"By using one of the very heavy metals for fuel. The intensity of the power liberated is a function of atomic weight, or atomic number, and density; but the fact of liberation depends upon atomic configuration—a fact which you and I figured out long ago. However, our figuring didn't go far enough—it couldn't: we didn't know anything then. Copper happens to be the most efficient of the few metals which can be decomposed at all under ordinary excitation—that is, by using an ordinary coil, such as we and the Fenachrone both use. But by using special exciters, sending out all the orders of rays necessary to initiate the disruptive processes, we can use any metal we want to. Osnome has unlimited quantities of the heaviest metals, including radium and uranium. Of course we can't use radium and live—but we can and will use uranium, and that will give us something like four times the acceleration possible with copper. Dunark, what say you snap over there and smelt us a cubic mile of uranium? No—hold it—I'll put a flock of forces on the job. They'll do it quicker, and I'll make 'em deliver the goods. They'll deliver 'em fast, too, believe us—we'll see to that with a ten-ton bar. The uranium bars'll be ready to load tomorrow, and we'll have enough power to chase those birds all the rest of our lives!"

Returning to the projector, Seaton actuated the complex system of forces required for the smelting and transportation of the enormous amount of metal necessary, and as the three men again boarded their aerial conveyance, the power-bar in the projector behind them flared into violet incandescence under the load already put upon it by the new uranium mine in distant Osnome.

The *Skylark* lay stretched out over two miles of country, exactly as they had last seen her, but now, instead of being water-white, the ten-thousand-foot cruiser of the void was one jointless, seamless structure of sparkling, transparent, purple inoson. Entering one of the open doors, they stepped into an elevator and were whisked upward into the control room, in which a dozen of the aged, white-bearded students of Norlamin were grouped about a banked and tiered mass of keyboards, which Seaton knew must be the operating mechanism of the extraordinarily complete fifth-order projector he had been promised.

"Ah, youngsters, you are just in time. Everything is complete and we are just about to begin loading."

"Sorry, Rovol, but we'll have to make a couple of changes—have to rebuild the exciter or build another one," and Seaton rapidly related what they had learned, and what they had decided to do.

"Of course, uranium is a much more efficient source of power," agreed Rovol, "and you are to be congratulated for thinking of it. It perhaps would not have occurred to one of us, since the heavy metals of that highly efficient group are very rare here. Building a new exciter for uranium is a simple task, and the converters for the corona-loss will, of course, require no change, since their action depends only upon the frequency of the emitted losses, not upon their magnitude."

"Hadn't you suspected that some of the Fenachrone might be going to lead us a life-long chase?" asked Dunark curiously.

"We have not given the matter a thought, my son," the Chief of the Five made answer. "As your years increase, you will learn not to anticipate trouble and worry. Had we thought and worried over the matter before the time had arrived, you will note that it would have been pain wasted, for our young friend Seaton has avoided that difficulty in a truly scholarly fashion."

"All set, then, Rovol?" asked Seaton, when the forces flying from the projector had built the compound exciter which would make possible the disruption of the atoms of uranium. "The metal, enough of it to fill all the spare space in the hull, will be here tomorrow. You might give Crane and me the method of operating this projector, which I see is vastly more complex even than the one in the Area of Experiment."

"It is the most complete thing ever seen upon Norlamin," replied Rovol with a smile. "Each of us installed everything in it that he could conceive of ever being of the slightest use, and since our combined knowledge covers a large field, the projector is accordingly quite comprehensive."

Multiple headsets were donned, and from each of the Norlaminian brains there poured into the minds of the two Terrestrials a complete and minute knowledge of every possible application of the stupendous force-control banked in all its massed intricacy before them.

"Well, that's some outfit!" exulted Seaton in pleased astonishment as the instructions were concluded. "It can do anything but lay an egg—and I'm not a darn bit sure that we couldn't make it do that! Well, let's call the girls and show them around this thing that's going to be their home for quite a while."

While they were waiting, Dunark led Seaton aside.

"Dick, will you need me on this trip?" he asked. "Of course I knew there was something on your mind when you didn't send me home when you let Urvan, Carfon and the others go back."

"No, we're going it alone—unless you want to come along. I did want you to stick around until I got to a good chance to talk to you alone—now will be a good a time as any. You and I have traded brains, and besides, we've been through quite a lot of grief together, here and there—I want to apologize to you for not passing along to you all this stuff I've been getting here. In fact, I really wish I didn't have to have it myself. Get me?"

"Got you? I'm 'way ahead of you! Don't want it, not any part of it—that's why I've stayed away from any chance of learning any of it, and the one reason why I am going back home instead of going with you. I have just brains enough to realize that neither I nor any other man of my race should have it. By the time we grow up to it naturally we shall be able to handle it, but not until then."

The two brain brothers grasped hands strongly, and Dunark continued in a lighter vein: "It takes all kinds of people to make a world, you know—and all kinds of races, except the Fenachrone, to make a Universe. With Mardonale gone, the evolution of Osnome shall progress rapidly, and while we may not reach the Ultimate Goal, I have learned enough from you already to speed up our progress considerably."

"Well, that's that. Had to get it off my chest, although I knew you'd get the idea all right. Here are the girls—Sitar too. We'll show 'em around."

Seaton's first thought was for the very brain of the ship—the precious lens of neutronium in its thin envelope of the eternal jewel—without which the beam of fifth-order rays could not be directed. He found it a quarter of a mile back from the needle-sharp prow, exactly in the longitudinal axis of the hull, protected from any possible damage by bulkhead after massive bulkhead of impregnable inoson. Satisfied upon that point, he went in search of the others, who were exploring their vast new space-ship.

Huge as she was, there was no waste space—her design was as compact as that of a fine radio set. The living quarters were grouped closely about the central compartment, which housed the power plants, the many ray generators and projectors, and the myriads of controls of the marvelous mechanism for the projection and direction of fifth-order rays. Several large compartments were devoted to the machinery which automatically serviced the vessel—refrigerators, heaters, generators and purifiers for water and air, and the numberless other mechanisms which would make the cruiser a comfortable and secure home, as well as an invincible battleship, in the heatless, lightless, airless, matterless waste of illimitable, inter-galactic space. Many compartments were for the storage of food-supplies, and these were even then being filled by forces under the able direction of the first of Chemistry.

"All the comforts of home, even to the labels," Seaton grinned, as he read "Dole No. 1" upon cans of pineapple which had never been within thousands of light-years of the Hawaiian Islands, and saw quarter after quarter of fresh meat going into the freezer room from a planet upon which no animal other than man had existed for many thousands of years. Nearly all of the remaining millions of cubic feet of space were for the storage of uranium for power, a few rooms already having been filled with ingot inoson for repairs. Between the many bulkheads that divided the ship into numberless airtight sections, and between the many concentric skins of purple metal that rendered the vessel space-worthy and sound, even though slabs many feet thick were to be shown off in any direction—in every nook and cranny could be stored the metal to keep those voracious generators full-fed, no matter how long or how severe the demand for power. Every room was connected through a series of tubular tunnels, along which force-propelled cars or elevators slid smoothly—tubes whose walls fell together into air-tight seals at any point, in case of a rupture.

As they made their way back to the great control-room room of the vessel, they saw something that because of its small size and clear transparency they had not previously seen. Below that room, not too near the outer skin, in a specially-built spherical launching space, there was *Skylark Two*, completely equipped and ready for an interstellar journey on her own account!

"Why, hello, little stranger!" Margaret called. "Rovol, that was a kind thought on your part. Home wouldn't quite be home without our old *Skylark*, would it, Martin?"

"A practical thought, as well as a kind one," Crane responded. "We undoubtedly will have occasion to visit places altogether too small for the really enormous bulk of this vessel."

"Yes, and whoever heard of a sea-going ship without a small boat?" put in irrepressible Dorothy. "She's just too perfectly kippy for words, sitting up there, isn't she?"

CHAPTER XV

The Extra-Galactic Duel

Loaded until her outer skin almost bulged with tightly packed bars of uranium and equipped to meet any emergency of which the combined efforts of the mightiest intellects of Norlamin could foresee even the slightest possibility, *Skylark Three* lay quiescent. Quiescent, but surcharged with power, she seemed to Seaton's tense mind to share his own eagerness to be off; seemed to be motionlessly straining at her neutral controls in a futile endeavor to leave that unnatural and unpleasant environment of atmosphere and of material substance, to soar outward into absolute zero of temperature and pressure, into the pure and undefiled ether which was her natural and familiar medium.

The five human beings were grouped near an open door of their cruiser; before them were the ancient scientists, who for so many days had been laboring with them in their attempt to crush the monstrous race which was threatening the Universe. With the elders were the Terrestrials' many friends from the Country of Youth, and surrounding the immense vessel in a throng covering an area to be measured only in square miles were massed myriads of Norlaminians. From their tasks everywhere had come the mental laborers; the Country of Youth had been left depopulated; even those who, their lifework done, had betaken themselves to the placid Nirvana of the Country of Age, returned briefly to the Country of Study to speed upon its way that stupendous Ship of Peace.

The majestic Fodan, Chief of the Five, was concluding his address:

"And may the Unknowable Force direct your minor forces to a successful conclusion of your task. If, upon the other hand, it should by some unforeseen chance be graven upon the Sphere that you are to pass in this supreme venture, you may pass in all tranquillity, for the massed intellect of our entire race is here supporting me in my solemn affirmation that the Fenachrone shall not be allowed to prevail. In the name of all Norlamin, I bid you farewell."

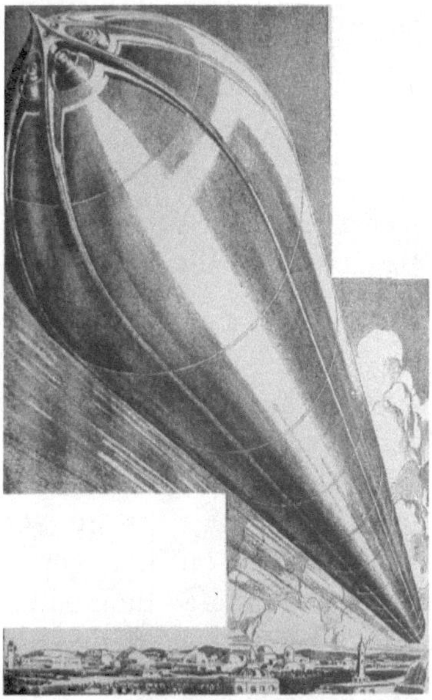

Very slowly at first, the unimaginable mass of the vessel floated lightly upward.

Crane spoke briefly in reply and the little group of Earthly wanderers stepped into the elevator. As they sped upward toward the control room, door after door shot into place behind them, establishing a manifold seal. Seaton's hand played over the controls and the great cruiser of the void tilted slowly upward until its narrow prow pointed almost directly into the zenith. Then, very slowly at first, the unimaginable mass of the vessel floated lightly upward, with a slowly increasing velocity. Faster and faster she flew—out beyond measurable atmosphere, out beyond the outermost limits of the green system. Finally, in interstellar space, Seaton threw out super-powered detector and repelling screens, anchored himself at the driving console with a force, set the power control at "molecular" so that the propulsive force affected alike every molecule of the vessel and its contents, and, all sense of weight and acceleration lost, he threw in the plunger switch which released every iota of the theoretically possible power of the driving mass of uranium.

Staring intently into the visiplate, he corrected their course from time to time by minute fractions of a second of arc; then, satisfied at last, he set the automatic forces which would guide them, temporarily out of their course, around any obstacles, such as the uncounted thousands of solar systems lying in or near their path. He then removed the restraining forces from his body and legs, and with a small pencil of force wafted himself over to Crane and the two women.

"Well, bunch," he stated, matter-of-fact, "we're on our way. We'll be this way for some time, so we might as well get used to it. Any little thing you want to talk over?"

"How long will it take us to catch 'em?" asked Dorothy "Traveling this way isn't half as much fun as it is when you let us have some weight to hold us down."

"Hard to tell exactly, Dottie. If we had precisely four times their acceleration and had started from the same place, we would of course overtake them in just the number of days they had the start of us, since the distance covered at any constant positive acceleration is proportional to the square of the time elapsed. However, there are several complicating factors in the actual situation. We started out not only twenty-nine days behind them, but also a matter of five hundred thousand light-years of distance. It will take us quite a while to get to their starting-point. I can't tell even that very close, as we will probably have to reduce this acceleration before we get out of the Galaxy, in order to give detectors and repellers time to act on stars and other loose impediments. Powerful as those screens are and fast as they work, there is a limit to the velocity we can use here in this crowded Galaxy. Outside it, in free space, of course we can open her up again. Then, too, our acceleration is not exactly four times theirs, only three point nine one eight six. On the other hand, we don't have to catch them to go to work on them. We can operate very nicely at five thousand light-centuries. So there you are—it'll probably be somewhere between thirty-nine and forty-one days, but it may be a day or so more or less."

"How do you know they are using copper?" asked Margaret. "Maybe their scientists stored up some uranium and know how to use it."

"Nope, that's out like a light. First, Mart and I saw only copper bars in their ship. Second, copper is the most efficient metal found in quantity upon their planet. Third, even if they had uranium or any metal of its class, they couldn't use it without a complete knowledge of, and ability to handle, the fourth and fifth orders of rays."

"It is your opinion, then, that destroying this last Fenachrone vessel is to prove as simple a matter as did the destruction of the others?" Crane queried, pointedly.

"Hm-m-m. Never thought about it from that angle at all, Mart.... You're still the ground-and-lofty thinker of the outfit, ain't you? Now that you mention it, though, we may find that the Last of the Mohicans ain't entirely toothless, at that. But say, Mart, how come I'm as wild and cock-eyed as I ever was? Rovol's a slow and thoughtful old codger, and with his accumulation of knowledge it looks like I'd be the same way."

"Far from it," Crane replied. "Your nature and mine remain unchanged. Temperament is a basic trait of heredity, and is neither affected nor acquired by increase of knowledge. You acquired knowledge from Rovol, Drasnik, and others, as did I—but you are still the flashing genius and I am still your balance wheel. As for Fenachrone toothlessness: now that you have considered it, what is your opinion?"

"Hard to say. They didn't know how to control the fifth order rays, or they wouldn't have run. They've got real brains, though, and they'll have something like seventy days to work on the problem. While it doesn't stand to reason that they could find out much in seventy days, still they may have had a set-up of instruments on their detectors that would have enabled them to analyze our fields and thus compute the structure of the secondary projector we used there. If so, it wouldn't take them long to find out enough to give us plenty of grief—but I don't really believe that they knew enough. I don't quite know what to think. They may be easy and they may not; but, easy or hard to get, we're loaded for bear and I'm plenty sure that we'll pull their corks."

"So am I, really, but we must consider every contingency. We know that they had at least a detector of fifth-order rays...."

"And if they did have an analytical detector," Seaton interrupted, "they'll probably slap a ray on us as soon as we stick our nose out of the Galaxy!"

"They may—and even though I do not believe that there is any probability of them actually doing it, it will be well to be armed against the possibility."

"Right, old top—we'll do that little thing!"

Uneventful days passed, and true to Seaton's calculations, the awful acceleration with which they had started out could not be maintained. A few days before the edge of the Galaxy was reached, it became necessary to cut off the molecular drive, and to proceed with an acceleration equal only to that of gravitation at the surface of the Earth. Tired of weightlessness and its attendant discomforts to everyday life, the travelers enjoyed the interlude immensely, but it was all too short—too soon the stars thinned out ahead of "*Three's*" needle prow. As soon as the way ahead of them was clear, Seaton again put on the maximum power of his terrific bars and, held securely at the console, set up a long and involved integral. Ready to transfer the blended and assembled forces to a plunger, he stayed his hand, thought a moment, and turned to Crane.

"Want some advice, Mart. I'd thought of setting up three or four courses of five-ply screen on the board—a detector screen on the outside of each course, next to it a repeller, then a full-coverage ether-ray screen, then a zone of force, and a full-coverage fifth-order ray-screen as a liner. Then, with them all set up on the board, but not out, throw out a wide detector. That detector would react upon the board at impact with anything hostile, and automatically throw out the courses it found necessary."

"That sounds like ample protection, but I am not enough of a ray-specialist to pass an opinion. Upon what point are you doubtful?"

"About leaving them on the board. The only trouble is that the reaction isn't absolutely instantaneous. Even fifth-order rays would require a millionth of a second or so to set the courses. Now if they were using ether waves, that would be lots of time to block them, but if they *should* happen to have fifth-order stuff it'd get here the same time our own detector-impulse would, and it's just barely conceivable that they might give us a nasty jolt before the defenses went out. Nope, I'm developing a cautious streak myself now, when I take time to do it. We've got lots of uranium, and I'm going to put one course out."

"You cannot put everything out, can you?"

"Not quite, but pretty nearly, I'll leave a hole in the ether screen to pass visible light—no, I won't either. You folks can see just as well, even on the direct-vision wall plates, with light heterodyned on the fifth, so we'll close all ether bands, absolutely. All we'll have to leave open will be the one extremely narrow band upon which our projector is operating, and I'll protect that with a detector screen. Also, I'm going to send out all four courses, instead of only one—then I'll *know* we're all right."

"Suppose they find our one band, narrow as it is? Of course, if that were shut off automatically by the detector, we'd be safe; but would we not be out of control?"

"Not necessarily—I see you didn't get quite all this stuff over the educator. The other projector worked that way, on one fixed band out of the nine thousand odd possible. But this one is an ultra-projector, an improvement invented at the last minute. Its carrier wave can be shifted at will from one band of the fifth order to any other one; and I'll bet a hat that's *one* thing the Fenachrone haven't got! Any other suggestions?... all right, let's get busy!"

A single light, quick-acting detector was sent out ahead of four courses of five-ply screen, then Seaton's fingers again played over the keys, fabricating a detector screen so tenuous that it would react to nothing weaker than a copper power bar in full operation and with so nearly absolute zero resistance that it could be driven at the full velocity of his ultra-projector. Then, while Crane watched the instruments closely and while Dorothy and Margaret watched the faces of their husbands with only mild interest, Seaton drove home the plunger that sent that prodigious and ever-widening fan ahead of them with a velocity unthinkable millions of times that of light. For five minutes, until that far-flung screen had gone as far as it could be thrown by the utmost power of the uranium bar, the two men stared at the unresponsive instruments, then Seaton shrugged his shoulders.

"I had a hunch," he remarked with a grin. "They didn't wait for us a second. 'I don't care for some,' says they, 'I've already had any.' They're running in a straight line, with full power on, and don't intend to stop or slow down."

"How do you know?" asked Dorothy. "By the distance? How far away are they?"

"I know, Red-Top, by what I didn't find out with that screen I just put out. It didn't reach them, and it went so far that the distance is absolutely meaningless, even expressed in parsecs. Well, a stern chase is proverbially a long chase, and I guess this one isn't going to be any exception."

Every eight hours Seaton launched his all-embracing ultra-detector, but day after day passed and the instruments remained motionless after each cast of that gigantic net. For several days the Galaxy behind them had been dwindling from a mass of stars down to a huge bright lens; down to a small, faint lens; down to a faintly luminous patch. At the previous cast of the detector it had still been visible as a barely-perceptible point of light in the highest telescopic power of the visiplate. Now, as Dorothy and Seaton, alone in the control room, stared into that visiplate, everything was blank and black; sheer, indescribable blackness; the utter and absolute absence of everything visible or tangible.

"This is awful, Dick.... It's just too darn horrible. It simply scares me pea-green!" she shuddered as she drew herself to him, and he swept both his mighty arms around her in a soul-satisfying embrace.

"'Sall right, darling. That stuff out there'd scare anybody—I'm scared purple myself. It isn't in any finite mind to understand anything infinite or absolute. There's one redeeming feature, though, cuddle-pup—we're together."

"You chirped it, lover!" Dorothy returned his caresses with all her old-time fervor and enthusiasm. "I feel lots better now. If it gets to you that way, too, I know it's perfectly normal—I was beginning to think maybe I was yellow or something ... but maybe you're kidding me?" she held him off at arm's length, looking deep into his eyes: then, reassured, went back-into his arms. "Nope, you feel it, too," and her glorious auburn head found its natural resting-place in the curve of his mighty shoulder.

"Yellow!... You?" Seaton pressed his wife closer still! and laughed aloud. "Maybe—but so is picric acid; so is nitroglycerin; and so is pure gold."

"Flatterer!" Her low, entrancing chuckle bubbled over. "But you know I just revel in it. I'll kiss you for that!"

"It *is* awfully lonesome out here, without even a star to look at," she went on, after a time, then laughed again. "If the Cranes and Shiro weren't along, we'd be really 'alone at last,' wouldn't we?"

"I'll say we would! But that reminds me of something. According to my figures, we might have been able to detect the Fenachrone on the last test, but we didn't. Think I'll try 'em again before we turn in."

Once more he flung out that tenuous net of force, and as it reached the extreme limit of its travel, the needle of the micro-ammeter flickered slightly, barely moving off its zero mark.

"Whee! Whoopee!" he yelled. "Mart, we're on 'em!"

"Close?" demanded Crane, hurrying into the control room upon his beam.

"Anything but. Barely touched 'em—current something less than a thousandth of a micro-ampere on a million to one step-up. However, it proves our ideas are O. K."

The next day—*Skylark III* was running on Eastern Standard Time, of the Terrestrial United States of America—the two mathematicians covered sheet after sheet of paper with computations and curves. After checking and rechecking the figures, Seaton shut off the power, released the molecular drive, and applied acceleration of twenty-nine point six oh two feet per second; and five human beings breathed as one a profound sigh of relief as an almost-normal force of gravitation was restored to them.

"Why the let-up?" asked Dorothy. "They're an awful long ways off yet, aren't they? Why not hurry up and catch them?"

"Because we're going infinitely faster than they are now. If we kept up full acceleration, we'd pass them so fast that we couldn't fight them at all. This way, we'll still be going a lot faster than they are when we get close to them, but not enough faster to keep us from maneuvering relatively to their vessel, if things should go that far. Guess I'll take another reading on 'em."

"I do not believe that I should," Crane suggested, thoughtfully. "After all, they may have perfected their instruments, and yet may not have detected that extremely light touch of our ray last night. If so, why put them on guard?"

"They're probably on guard, all right, without having to be put there—but it's a sound idea, anyway. Along the same line I'll release the fifth-order screens, with the fastest possible detector on guard. We're just about within reach of a light copper-driven ray right now, but it's a cinch they can't send anything heavy this far, and if they think we're overconfident, so much the better."

"There," he continued, after a few minutes at the keyboard. "All set. If they put a detector on us, I've got a force set to make a noise like a New York City fire siren. If pressed, I'd reluctantly admit that in my opinion we're carrying caution to a point ten thousand degrees below the absolute zero of sanity. I'll bet my shirt that we don't hear a yip out of them before we touch 'em off. Furthermore...."

The rest of his sentence was lost in a crescendo bellow of sound. Seaton, still at the controls, shut off the noise, studied his meters carefully, and turned around to Crane with a grin.

"You win the shirt, Mart. I'll give it to you next Wednesday, when my other one comes back from the laundry. It's a fifth-order detector ray, coming in beautifully on band forty-seven fifty, right in the middle of the order."

"Aren't you going to put a ray on 'em?" asked Dorothy in surprise.

"Nope—what's the use? I can read theirs as well as I could one of my own. Maybe they know that too—if they don't we'll let 'em think we're coming along, as innocent as Mary's little lamb, so I'll let their ray stay on us. It's too thin to carry anything, and if they thicken it up much I've got an axe set to chop it off." Seaton whistled a merry lilting refrain as his fingers played over the stops and keys.

"Why, Dick, you seem actually pleased about it." Margaret was plainly ill at ease.

"Sure am. I never did like to drown baby kittens, and it kinda goes against the grain to stab a guy in the back, when he ain't even looking, even if he is a Fenachrone. If they can fight back some I'll get mad enough to blow 'em up happy."

"But suppose they fight back too hard?"

"They can't—the worst that can possibly happen is that we can't lick them. They certainly can't lick us, because we can outrun 'em. If we can't get 'em alone, we'll beat it back to Norlamin and bring up re-enforcements."

"I am not so sure," Crane spoke slowly. "There is, I believe, a theoretical possibility that sixth-order rays exist. Would an extension of the methods of detection of fifth-order rays reveal them?"

"*Sixth*? Sweet spirits of niter! Nobody knows anything about them. However, I've had one surprise already, so maybe your suggestion isn't as crazy as it sounds. We've got three or four days yet before either side can send anything except on the sixth, so I'll find out what I can do."

He flew at the task, and for the next three days could hardly be torn from it for rest; but

"O. K., Mart," he finally announced. "They exist, all right, and I can detect 'em. Look here," and he pointed to a tiny receiver, upon which a small lamp flared in brilliant scarlet light.

"Are they sending them?"

"No, fortunately. They're coming from our bar. See, it shines blue when I put a grounded shield between it and the bar, and stays blue when I attach it to their detector ray."

"Can you direct them?"

"Not a chance in the world. That means a lifetime, probably many lifetimes, of research, unless somebody uses a fairly complete pattern of them close enough to this detector so that I can analyze it. 'Sa good deal like calculus in that respect. It took thousands of years to get it in the first place, but it's easy when somebody that already knows it shows you how it goes."

"The Fenachrone learned to direct fifth-order rays so quickly, then, by an analysis of our fifth-order projector there?"

"Our secondary projector, yes. They must have had some neutronium in stock, too—but it would have been funny if they hadn't, at that—they've had intra-atomic power for ages."

Silent and grim, he seated himself at the console, and for an hour he wove an intricate pattern of forces upon the inexhaustible supply of keys afforded by the ultra-projector before he once touched a plunger.

"What are you doing? I followed you for a few hundred steps, but could go no farther."

"Merely a little safety-first stuff. In case they should send any real pattern of sixth-order rays this set-up will analyze it, record the complete analysis, throw out a screen against every frequency of the pattern, throw on the molecular drive, and pull us back toward the galaxy at full acceleration, while switching the frequency of our carrier wave a thousand times a second, to keep them from shooting a hot one through our open band. It'll do it all in about a millionth of a second, too—I want to get us all back alive if possible! Hm—m. They've shut off their ray—they know we've tapped onto it. Well, war's declared now—we'll see what we can see."

Transferring the assembled beam to a plunger, he sent out a secondary projector toward the Fenachrone vessel, as fast as it could be driven, close behind a widespread detector net. He soon found the enemy cruiser, but so immense was the distance that it was impossible to hold the projection anywhere in its neighborhood. They flashed beyond it and through it and upon all sides of it, but the utmost delicacy of the controls would not permit of holding even upon the immense bulk of the vessel, to say nothing of holding upon such a relatively tiny object as the power bar. As they flashed repeatedly through the warship, they saw piecemeal and sketchily her formidable armament and the hundreds of men of her crew, each man at battle station at the controls of some frightful engine of destruction. Suddenly they were cut off as a screen closed behind them—the Earth-men felt an instant of unreasoning terror as it seemed that one-half of their peculiar dual personalities vanished utterly. Seaton laughed.

"That was a funny sensation, wasn't it? It just means that they've climbed a tree and pulled the tree up after them."

"I do not like the odds, Dick," Crane's face was grave. "They have many hundreds of men, all trained; and we are only two. Yes, only one, for I count for nothing at those controls."

"All the better, Mart. This board more than makes up the difference. They've got a lot of stuff, of course, but they haven't got anything like this control system. Their captain's got to issue orders, whereas I've got everything right under my hands. Not so uneven as they think!"

Within battle range at last, Seaton hurled his utmost concentration of direct forces, under the impact of which three courses of Fenachrone defensive screen flared through the ultra-violet and went black. There the massed direct attack was stopped—at what cost the enemy alone knew—and the Fenachrone countered instantly and in a manner totally unexpected. Through the narrow slit in the fifth-order screen through which Seaton was operating, in the bare one-thousandth of a second that it was open, so exactly synchronized and timed that the screens did not even glow as it went through the narrow opening, a gigantic beam of heterodyned force struck full upon the bow of the *Skylark*, near the sharply-pointed prow, and the stubborn metal instantly flared blinding white and exploded outward in puffs of incandescent gas under the awful power of that Titanic thrust.

Through four successive skins of inoson, the theoretical ultimate of possible strength, toughness, and resistance, that frightful beam drove before the automatically-reacting detector closed the slit and the impregnable defensive screens, driven by their mighty uranium bars, flared into incandescent defense. Driven as they were, they held, and the Fenachrone, finding that particular attack useless, shut off their power.

"Wow! They sure have got something!" Seaton exclaimed in unfeigned admiration. "They sure gave us a solid kick that time! We will now take time out for repairs. Also, I'm going to cut our slit down to a width of one kilocycle, if I can possibly figure out a way of working on that narrow a band, and I'm going to step up our shifting speed to a hundred thousand. It's a good thing they built this ship of ours in a lot of layers—if that'd go through the interior we would have been punctured for fair. You might weld up those holes, Mart, while I see what I can do here."

Then Seaton noticed the women, white and trembling, upon a seat.

"'Smatter? Cheer up, kids, you ain't seen nothing yet. That was just a couple of little preliminary love-taps, like two boxers kinda feeling each other out in the first ten seconds of the first round."

"Preliminary love-taps!" repeated Dorothy, looking into Seaton's eyes and being reassured by the serene confidence she read there. "But they hit us, and hurt us badly—why, there's a hole in our *Skylark* as big as a house, and it goes through four or five layers!"

"Yes, but we're not hurt a bit. They're easily fixed, and we've lost nothing but a few tons of inoson and uranium. We've got lots of spare metal. I don't know what I did to him, any more than he knows what he did to us, but I'll bet my other shirt that he knows he's been nudged!"

Repairs completed and the changes made in the method of projection, Seaton actuated the rapidly-shifting slit and peered through it at the enemy vessel. Finding their screens still up, he directed a complete-coverage attack upon them with four bars, while with the entire massed power of the remaining generators concentrated into one frequency, he shifted that frequency up and down the spectrum, probing, probing, ever probing with that gigantic beam of intolerable energy—feeling for some crack, however slight, into which he could insert that searing sheet of concentrated destruction. Although much of the available power of the Fenachrone was perforce devoted to repelling the continuous attack of the Terrestrials, they maintained an equally continuous attack offensive, and in spite of the narrowness of the open slit and the rapidity with which that slit was changing from frequency to frequency, enough of the frightful forces came through to keep the ultra-powered defensive screens radiating far into the violet—and, the utmost power of the refrigerating system proving absolutely useless against the concentrated beams being employed, mass after mass of inoson was literally blown from the outer and secondary skins of the *Skylark* by the comparatively tiny jets of force that leaked through the momentarily open slit from time to time, as exact synchronization was accidentally obtained.

Seaton, grimly watching his instruments, glanced at Crane, who, calm but watchful at his console, was repairing the damage as fast as it was done.

"They're sending more stuff, Mart, and it's getting hotter to handle. That means they're building more projectors. We can play that game, too. They're using up their fuel reserves fast; but we're bigger than they are, carry more metal, and it's more efficient metal, too. Only one way out of it, I guess—what say we put in enough generators to smother them down by brute force, no matter how much power it takes?"

"Why don't you use some of those awful copper shells? Or aren't we close enough yet?" Dorothy's low voice came clearly, so utterly silent was that frightful combat.

"Close! We're still better than two hundred thousand light-years apart! There may have been longer-range battles than this somewhere in the Universe, but I doubt it. And as for copper, even if we could get it to them, it'd be just like so many candy kisses compared to the stuff we're both using. Dear girl, there are fields of force extending for thousands of miles from each of these vessels beside which the exact center of the biggest lightning flash you ever saw would be a dead area!"

He set up a series of integrals and, machine after machine, in a space left vacant by the rapidly-vanishing store of uranium, there appeared inside the fourth skin of the *Skylark* a row of gigantic generators, each one adding its hellish output to the already inconceivable stream of energy being directed at the foe. As that frightful flow increased by leaps and bounds, the intensity of the Fenachrone attack diminished, and finally it ceased altogether as every iota of the enemy's power became necessary for the maintenance of the defenses. Still greater grew the stream of force from the *Skylark*, and, now that the attack had ceased, Seaton opened the slit wider and stopped its shifting, in order still further to increase the efficiency of his terrible weapon. Face set in a fighting mask and eyes hard as gray iron, deeper and deeper he drove his now irresistible forces. His flying fingers were upon the keys of his console; his keen and merciless eyes were in a secondary projector near the now doomed ship of the Fenachrone, directing masterfully his terrible attack. As the output of his generators still increased, Seaton began to compress a searing hollow sphere of seething energy upon the furiously-straining defensive screens of the Fenachrone.

Course after course of the heaviest possible screen was sent out, driven by massed batteries of copper now disintegrating at the rate of tons in every second, only to flare through the ultra-violet and to go down before that dreadful, that irresistible onslaught. Finally, as the inexorable sphere still contracted, the utmost efforts of the defenders could not keep their screens away from their own vessel, and simultaneously the prow and the stern of the Fenachrone cruiser was bared to that awful field of force, in which no possible substance could endure for even the most infinitesimal instant of time.

There was a sudden cessation of all resistance, and those Titanic forces, all directed inward, converged upon a point with a power behind which there was the inconceivable energy of four hundred thousand tons of uranium, being disintegrated at the highest possible rate, short of instant disruption. In that same instant of collapse, the enormous mass of power-copper in the Fenachrone cruiser and the vessel's every atom, alike of structure and contents, also exploded into pure energy at the touch of that unimaginable field of force.

In that awful moment before Seaton could shut off his power it seemed to him that space itself must be obliterated by the very concentration of the unknowable and incalculable forces there unleashed—must be swallowed up and lost in the utterly indescribable brilliance of the field of radiance driven to a distance of millions upon incandescent millions of miles from the place where the last representatives of the monstrous civilization of the Fenachrone had made their last stand against the forces of Universal Peace.

Epilogue

The three-dimensional, moving, talking, almost living picture, being shown simultaneously in all the viewing areas throughout the innumerable planets of the Galaxy, faded out and the image of an aged, white-bearded Norlaminian appeared and spoke in the Galactic language.

"As is customary, the showing of this picture has opened the celebration of our great Galactic holiday, Civilization Day. As you all know, it portrays the events leading up to and making possible the formation of the League of Civilization by a mere handful of planets. The League now embraces all of this, the First Galaxy, and is spreading rapidly throughout the Universe. Varied are the physical forms and varied are the mentalities of our almost innumerable races of beings, but in Civilization we are becoming one, since those backward people who will not co-operate with us are rendered impotent to impede our progress among the more enlightened.

"It is peculiarly fitting that the one who has just been chosen to head the Galactic Council—the first person of a race other than one of those of the Central System to prove himself able to wield justly the vast powers of that office—should be a direct descendant of two of the revered persons whose deeds of olden times we have just witnessed.

"I present to you my successor as Chief of the Galactic Council, Richard Ballinger Seaton, the fourteen hundred sixty-ninth, of Earth."

THE END

www.ingramcontent.com/pod-product-compliance
Lightning Source LLC
LaVergne TN
LVHW090336051026
849518LV00005B/1973